Join favourite author

Louise Allen

as she explores the tangled love-lives of

Those Scandalous Ravenhursts

First, you travelled across war-torn Europe
with
THE DANGEROUS MR RYDER

Then you accompanied Mr Ryder's sister,
THE OUTRAGEOUS LADY FELSHAM,
on her quest for a hero.

Now be scandalised by
THE SHOCKING LORD STANDON

Coming soon

THE DISGRACEFUL MR RAVENHURST

THE NOTORIOUS MR HURST

THE PIRATICAL MISS RAVENHURST

Author Note

Gareth Morant, Earl of Standon, is upright, eligible— and a bachelor who views the chancy business of falling in love with alarm.

Marriage just isn't for him, and certainly not to his wild childhood friend Maude. But Maude is going to be in deep trouble if she doesn't marry the highly respectable Earl, so what is a gentleman to do but create a scandal?

It isn't easy to become a rake overnight, as Gareth and I discovered, but finding a naked governess in a brothel certainly helped and, with the enthusiastic support of his cousins Eva and Sebastian Ravenhurst (THE DANGEROUS MR RYDER) and Bel and Ashe Reynard (THE OUTRAGEOUS LADY FELSHAM), Gareth succeeds in shocking Society.

But by then Gareth has dug himself into a moral, emotional and social hole, and he has to climb out of it, greatly hindered by his own treacherous heart, Maude's appalling acting and the surprising allure of the chaste Miss Gifford, who just wants to get back to teaching the piano and the Italian tongue. Or so she says.

I do hope you enjoy the progress of this reluctant rake as he discovers that falling in love is perhaps the most shocking experience of all.

My exploration of the life and loves of *Those Scandalous Ravenhursts* takes me to France next, where bluestocking spinster Elinor is assisting her scholarly mama amidst ecclesiastical ruins, quite unprepared for the eruption into her orderly life of THE DISGRACEFUL MR RAVENHURST, her black sheep of a cousin Theo. He's the last thing she needs—unfortunately she soon discovers he's the one thing she wants.

THE SHOCKING
LORD STANDON

Louise Allen

MILLS & BOON
Pure reading pleasure™

First published in Great Britain 2008
Harlequin Mills & Boon Limited,
Eton House, 18-24 Paradise Road, Richmond, Surrey TW9 1SR

© Melanie Hilton 2008

ISBN: 978 0 263 86276 8

Set in Times Roman 10½ on 13 pt.
04-0908-84084

Printed and bound in Spain
by Litografia Rosés S.A., Barcelona

Louise Allen has been immersing herself in history, real and fictional, for as long as she can remember, and finds landscapes and places evoke powerful images of the past. Louise lives in Bedfordshire, and works as a property manager, but spends as much time as possible with her husband at the cottage they are renovating on the north Norfolk coast, or travelling abroad. Venice, Burgundy and the Greek islands are favourite atmospheric destinations. Please visit Louise's website— www.louiseallenregency.co.uk—for the latest news!

Recent novels by the same author:

A MODEL DEBUTANTE
THE MARRIAGE DEBT
MOONLIGHT AND MISTLETOE
  (in *Christmas Brides*)
THE VISCOUNT'S BETROTHAL
THE BRIDE'S SEDUCTION
NOT QUITE A LADY
A MOST UNCONVENTIONAL COURTSHIP
NO PLACE FOR A LADY
DESERT RAKE
  (in *Hot Desert Nights*)
VIRGIN SLAVE, BARBARIAN KING
THE DANGEROUS MR RYDER*
THE OUTRAGEOUS LADY FELSHAM*

Those Scandalous Ravenhursts

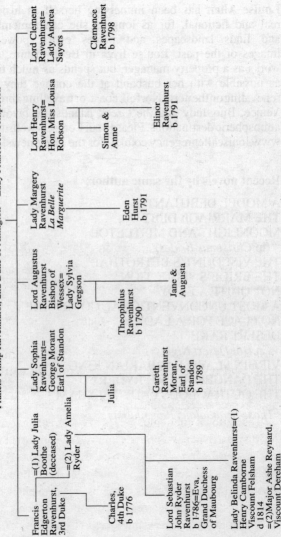

RAVENHURST FAMILY TREE

Francis Philip Ravenhurst, 2nd Duke of Allington = Lady Francesca Templeton

Chapter One

'My lords, your honours, gentlemen! Your attention, please! At midnight, upon the stroke of the hour, Madame Synthia's School of Venus presents our famed Parade of Beauty. Ladies of rich and varied experience! Exotic creatures of every hue! Country-fresh innocents willing and eager to learn their business at the hands of dashing London beaux! Posture girls of amazing flexibility and ingenuity for your delectation! In half an hour, my lords and gentlemen—take your places early and do not be disappointed!'

The ex-town crier employed at considerable expense by Madame Synthia—formerly known as Cynthia Wilkins of Camden Town—shouted himself to a stop and left the platform at the end of the Grand Assembly Lounge. Footmen began to set chairs around the stage and keen patrons jostled to fill the front row, despite there being half an hour to go before the start of the performance.

'Morant, come on.' Gareth Morant, Earl of Standon,

winced as Lord Fellingham nudged him sharply in the ribs. 'Those posture girls are all the go, but you need to be close up to get a proper eyeful.' Fellingham licked his rather full lips. 'They hold up a mirror and there are candles…'

'I doubt they have any feature that any other woman you have had congress with was lacking, Fell.' Gareth set down his almost-full champagne flute and regarded the scrimmage around the stage with bored distaste. 'This place is a vulgar dive, I cannot imagine what we are doing here.'

'You're off your oats, old fellow, in need of a tonic, in my opinion,' Fellingham retorted. 'You're no fun these days, and that's the truth of it. Look at you— you've sat by the fire, toying with one glass the entire time Rotherham's been upstairs with those Chinese twins, and never a word out of you but grunts.'

'Indian twins.' Gareth got to his feet and stretched. 'They are Indian. I'm off to White's, see if I can drum up a decent hand of cards.'

'We can't go without Rotherham,' his friend protested, one eye on the rapidly filling seats before the stage. 'And besides, I want to see this show. I've heard all about it, that's why I wanted to come—remember? Let's go and get old Rothers and watch it and then we'll all go to White's. He must be finished by now, surely. What do you say? Don't be a killjoy.'

'Very well.' Gareth picked up his glass with a suppressed sigh, tossed back the contents and stood up. 'Do you know which room he's in?'

'The Mirrored Chamber. Damn good room that, mirrors all over it, even the ceiling.' Fellingham made for the stairs, pushing his way against the tide of men intent on reaching the stage.

'So I collect. The name gives a slight hint.' Damn it, Fell was right, his temper was short, nothing appealed any more. He wanted—no, *needed*—something, but he had no idea what, although it most definitely was not to be found in this temple to commercial sexual gratification. And the *respectable* novelty being pressed upon him—marriage—held no charms whatsoever either.

His friend snorted, good humoured despite Gareth's tone. 'Jaded, that's what you are, you sarcastic devil. What you need is a good woman. No, make that a thoroughly bad one!' Roaring with laughter at his own feeble wit, Fellingham struck off down a dimly lit corridor. 'Down here somewhere, if I recall.'

'Give me my clothes back!' Jessica Gifford made a wild grab at the bundle of drab garments before the maid tossed them out of the door and slammed it. Outside, the key turned.

'Now then, don't give me trouble or I'll have to get Madame Synthia up here, and you won't like that, believe me.' The maid grinned and went over to the wardrobe with a sway of her hips that indicated that the skimpiness of her gown was more than just an accident in the wash.

'This is all a terrible mistake.' Jessica stood there shivering, stark naked and too bemused and angry to be properly afraid. But at the back of her mind there was a growing awareness that she should be. She should be very frightened indeed, she realised, for it seemed that all the far-fetched tales she had heard about innocent country girls being snatched off the street by evil procurers were nothing less than the truth. But she wasn't some innocent young milkmaid, she was a grown-up, independent, educated woman—this should not be happening to her!

'There has been some error.' She tried a reasonable tone, keeping her breathing light in an attempt to control it. 'I am a governess, here to take up a new position.'

'You'll take up one of those all right.' The maid laughed. 'Lots and lots of new positions. You *are* a virgin, aren't you?' The glance she sent Jessica's shivering, goose-bump-covered body was scornful.

'Of course I am! I said there was some mistake. I asked the woman who greeted me as I got off the coach if she was Lady Hartington's housekeeper and she said *yes* and took me to a carriage and the next thing I know, I am here.'

'Yes, well, Lady H. won't be wanting your services for her precious brats after tonight, especially as Lord H. himself is here and is likely to bid high for you. He'll be getting you to show him the use of the globes, I'll be bound. Or perhaps he'll be slow at his Latin and'll need a good birching. Put these on.' She tossed a handful of flimsy scraps of fabric on to the bed.

'This *is* a brothel?' *As well to have it clear*, the logical, sensible part of Jessica's brain told her, while the rest of it screamed in silent panic.

'Lord love you, of course it is. Best vaulting house in town. Wonder if we ought to do something about your hair.' The maid peered at her. 'Nah. I'll just unpin it, give you that *ready to be tumbled* look. They like that.'

'There has been a mistake,' Jessica repeated, adopting

the tone of clear reason she found effective with some of her more dense pupils. 'I am a governess, I am in the wrong place. If I am kept captive here, that is kidnapping and when I complain to the magistrates someone is going to be in very serious trouble with the law.'

'How're you going to do that, then?' The maid advanced on her with a hairbrush and began to pluck out hairpins. 'You'll stay here until you're properly broken in, then there's nowhere else for you to go because no one respectable will want you. If you want to chat to a magistrate or two, I'm sure there's some here tonight. Very sympathetic they'll be—want to make you feel right at home, I'll be bound.'

Cold fingers of fear slithered down Jessica's spine. She had been earning her own living for three years and she knew just how perilous was the position of an unprotected young woman with the slightest hint of scandal attaching to her name. She knew, all too well, the consequences of that one step off the slippery path of respectability.

If she got out of here and complained, most likely she would be ignored. If she were believed, then she was as good as ruined, whatever happened.

'How can you help them do this to another woman?' She put her hand on the other girl's arm imploringly. In this situation she was not too proud to plead. She would be on her knees begging in a minute. Whatever it took to end this nightmare. 'Don't you want to be out of here yourself?'

The maid stared at her as though she was mad. 'Leave here? I'd be crazy to,' she said shortly. 'Warm room, good food, lots of company, gentlemen giving me

good tips. All I have to do is lie on my back on a clean
comfy bed and do what comes natural. Leave here and
go back to what? A filthy slum in Wapping, that's what.
And there you do it up against the wall for a handful of
coppers and a black eye.' She peered in the mirror and
pinched her own cheeks, bringing some colour into her
pert, sharp-featured face.

'Look, you silly cow,' she said suddenly, with what
Jessica realised was an attempt at kindness, 'it ain't so
bad after the first time. Why make it difficult for
yourself? If you make a scene, Madame will just send
up some of the doormen to break you in, and you won't
like that, believe me.'

Jessica sank down on the end of the huge bed, oblivious to the cold slippery satin under her bare behind.
The choices appeared to be to be deflowered by a group
of bully boys, to be sold to some debauched gentleman
or to throw herself out of the window. Only that was
barred with iron.

Life had been hard, these past three years, but she had
her modest savings, a respectable profession, her self-
respect and she was dependent on no one. Under no circumstances was she going to give that up. Her mind
seemed to move beyond terror into a desperate resolve.

The maid was gathering up her fallen hairpins.
Jessica put her foot carefully on one of them. 'All right,'
she said, having no trouble letting her voice shake.
'What happens now?'

'There, that's better! See how much easier it is if you
stop being so foolish about it? What's your name?'

'Jessica.'

'Well, Jessy, I'm Moll. We get's you into your

costume—that won't take long, there ain't much of it—
then at midnight the show starts. You're the only virgin
on the bill, so the bidding'll be brisk. You'll get a nice
rich gentleman who'll tip you well after, I'll be bound,
seeing you're the real thing.'

'What's the time now?' Jessica reached for the scraps
of muslin the maid held out.

'Twenty to the hour.'

'Well, if there isn't any other option… Isn't there a
costume that's a nicer colour?' she asked, feigning
petulance. 'I don't like lilac. It looks so insipid with
blonde hair.'

Moll did not appear to find the sudden change of tone
suspicious. 'I think there's a green one, that'll be pretty
with your eyes.' She opened the wardrobe doors again.

The maid's shriek was cut off by Jessica bundling her
bodily into the clothes press. One piece of muslin was
around her wrists, the other gagging her mouth before
she could recover her wits. Jessica pulled down more
pieces from the hooks, tying the struggling girl's ankles.

'If you make a noise in the next half-hour, I'll hit you
on the head,' she warned, hoping she sounded convinc-
ingly fierce. 'If you are quiet, nothing will happen.
Understand?'

Wide blue eyes stared at her over the gag, then Molly
nodded energetically. Jessica shut the wardrobe door,
wedged a chair under the handle, retrieved the hairpin
and set about picking the door lock.

In sensation novels, the sort governesses are
supposed never to read and in fact devour by the shelf
full, the beleaguered yet valiant heroine can pick a
dungeon lock in seconds as she escapes from the wicked

duke's evil clutches. Her hands shaking, cold sweat standing out all over her, Jessica could only conclude that either wicked dukes employed inferior locksmiths to brothel keepers or the authors of the Minerva Press were sadly misinformed.

After five minutes she stood up in an attempt to relieve her cramped knees. 'Open, you beastly thing,' she said, almost weeping with frustration, and fetched the lock a thump with her clenched fist. With a click it did just that.

Jessica was out into the corridor before she could think. Opposite her a shadowy figure moved. She gave a yelp of fear and realised that it was her own reflection in a full-length mirror. And she was stark naked.

Behind her the door swung to, the catch snicked closed. She could not go back, that was where they would come for her. *Clothes.* That was the priority. Like this she had no hope, and she was finding it very hard to think clearly. One of these rooms, surely, must contain something she could wear.

She opened the first door that she came to and peered round the edge. Inside was a big bed and on it a welter of naked flesh. Gasping, Jessica made out six legs, two pairs of buttocks, a glimpse of hairy chest… How many people? Doing what? She shut the door, flattening herself instinctively into the recess. The participants in the orgy had appeared totally preoccupied, but even so, she did not think she had the courage to sneak in and steal clothing while *that* was going on.

It was ridiculous to feel even more alarmed and fearful than she was already—how much worse could her predicament possibly get?—but that glimpse into carnal matters beyond her comprehension had shocked her out of any delusion that this was a nightmare. There, for real, was what she risked becoming if she could not escape.

Jessica drew in a deep breath and forced herself to plan. To assume the worst was a self-fulfilling prophecy. Her fate was sealed if she panicked. Steadier, she surveyed the corridor in which she found herself. Opposite was the door she had just escaped through, behind her the room with the orgy in progress. On either side were two more doors and then, in both directions, the passage turned. More cautious now, she applied an ear to each door in turn and from each came the sounds of gasps and sighs, and, from one, the crack of a whip.

Which way to go? Her sense of direction had quite deserted her in the hectic few minutes when she had been bundled out of the carriage and up the stairs. Then, as she hesitated, her arms wrapped around her chilly ribs, the decision was made for her by the sound of a door opening and loud voices from out of sight to her right. Without hesitation Jessica fled around the other corner.

It might have been better, she realised in the second she thudded into a solid wall of male muscle, if she had been looking where she was going and not wildly back over her shoulder.

Her nose was buried in a shirt front, the crisp upper edge of a tailored waistcoat stuck into her chin and her shivering body was pressed against warm superfine and knitted silk. The immovable object stood quite still as the voices behind her grew louder.

Jessica tilted back her head and found she was squinting up past a chin that was already shadowed by an evening beard into amused grey eyes. One dark eyebrow rose. 'Help,' she whispered, her voice fled along with her hope. 'Please help me.'

'This is the room,' a slurred voice from behind the man announced. 'Come on, Morant, in we go.'

'By all means,' a voice as amused as the eyes answered, turning Jessica around and putting one firm hand on her shoulder. 'In we all go.'

Her quivering flesh seemed to steady at the warm touch and the thought came to her that at least, if she was about to be ravished, about to lose her virginity, at least he was not the slavering monster of her imagination; not the gross, sweating horror she had been trying not to think about.

The room was brightly lit, glittering with candles reflected over and over from mirrors all around. It was like being inside a chandelier. Jessica, her eyes hunting frantically around the chamber for some escape, saw three figures entwined on the bed, closed her eyes and stumbled.

The hand on her shoulder tightened, holding her up. 'Come on,' the deep voice said softly in her ear. 'Pay attention, I can't do this all by myself.' He still blocked the door, she realised, as the two golden-skinned women on the bed sat up, a pair of pagan idols, and turned identical faces to watch them. Silken black hair flowed down their backs and, between them, his face mercifully hidden by the thighs of one girl and his loins by those of another, was the prone form of a naked man. A fallen Greek statue.

The man holding her reached out his other hand and lifted an exotic brocade robe off a chair beside the door. 'Put this on.'

With a gasp of relief Jessica struggled into its heavy

silken folds as a plaintive voice said, 'Move, would you, Morant!' She found herself gently turned to one side as the big man stepped into the room and his companion barged in behind him, closing the door.

Jessica pulled the deep collar up to hide the lower half of her face. With clothing came some semblance of inner calm; it was incredible how the very fact of being naked clouded the wits. She found she could look around her and see the whole room, not tiny details of it magnified as though in a nightmare. The two women on the bed became clearly twin mortals; the room was not a crystal palace of light, but simply a tawdry chamber lined with smoke-smudged mirrors; and the naked god sitting up on the rumpled sheets was just a blond young man with an incipient pot belly and a flushed face.

'Hello, Fell, Morant,' he managed before slumping back on to the pillows. 'Brought your own, have you?'

'What?' The man at the back—Fell?—pushed past and stared. 'Where did you get this little ladybird, Morant? We didn't have her with us when we started out, did we?' He reached towards Jessica.

'Hands off,' the big man said easily, pushing his friend towards the bed. 'You go and help Rotherham get his money's worth: he doesn't seem to be up to it, all by himself.'

The two black-haired girls held out their arms in welcome and Fell stumbled forwards, collapsing on to the bed with a hoot of laughter amidst his friend's vehement protests.

The big man reached out and scooped up a pile of clothing from the chair, then propelled Jessica out into

the passageway again. 'Get dressed.' He dropped the
things at her feet. A tall silk hat rolled away, teetered on
its brim for a moment, then fell over.

'These are men's clothes.' Jessica clutched the silk
robe even tighter around her.

'Exactly. Do you think you are going to walk out of
here dressed like that?' He gestured at the robe. Jessica
had a vivid mental picture of her hair, her bare feet, the
naked skin under the lush brocade.

'You are taking me with you, then?'

'Oh, yes.' She could not see properly, but she knew
he was smiling—it was in his voice. 'I am certainly
taking you.' Something inside her, something very complicated indeed, was making it hard to think. He would
take her out of here, yes, but his words meant more
than that—or did they? She shook her head: *deal with
the immediate problem, Jessica.*

'You are right, this is a good idea.' She picked up the
pantaloons and hauled them on under cover of the robe,
rummaged and found the neckcloth and used it to tie
round the waist to hold them up. 'Turn round.' The passageway was barely lit, she could make out the shape
of him, the flash of white teeth as he grinned, the shape
of a closely barbered head.

'I've seen all there is to see already, sweetheart.'

'Well, I don't want you seeing it again,' she retorted
and to her amazement he turned a shoulder with a grunt
of amusement, leant against the panelling and began to
whistle softly while she shucked off the robe, dragged
the shirt over her head and pulled on the greatcoat. It
came down to her feet. Her bare pink toes peeked out.
'Shoes?' she said.

'And hair.' He turned back and looked at her. 'Heaven help us. Here.' His hands on her hair were ruthless. With one hand he gathered up the whole unruly mass, twisted it into a knot and then into the tall hat, which he jammed on her head. It came down to her nose.

He was heeling off his own evening slippers. Balancing on one foot, he dragged off the black silk socks, then repeated the gesture with the other foot before putting the shoes back on. 'Try these. At least your feet won't seem to be bare. If they notice my bare calves, they'll think I was too fuddled to get dressed properly.'

This was insanity, yet now, with this man she could not even see properly, she felt safe. She had no idea how he could rescue her, but somehow she knew that he would. She was going to survive this. But the illusion of safety was just that, an illusion, and she must not forget it.

Feeling like an exceptionally well-dressed scarecrow Jessica stood in front of the looming dark bulk of her rescuer. 'We will never get out of here with all these people still awake.'

He pulled a watch out of his waistcoat pocket and held it up close to his eyes in the gloom. 'Oh, yes, we will, it is two minutes to midnight. Come on.'

What midnight had to do with it Jessica could not imagine, although images of coaches and pumpkins floated into her mind. She obediently padded along in his wake, one hand holding the hat so she could squint under the brim, the other clutching the coat around her.

They reached the head of a broad staircase, not the narrow one she had been so unceremoniously bundled up, struggling and scratching, only an hour before. The heat and the noise rising from the room below were overwhelming. Jessica took a firm hold of the man's coat tails.

'Don't do that,' he said mildly, 'My valet will complain. Here, beside me.' She forced her clenched fist to relax and, stumbling in her trailing greatcoat, went to stand on his left side. She tried to look up, see him now the light was better, but the hat brim defeated her.

'You are drunk,' her rescuer ordered, his deep voice calm and definite. 'You can do that?'

'Yes.' Actually she wanted to scream, have the vapours and faint dead away. Do all the things, in fact, that the well-bred women lucky enough to be in a position to think themselves her superiors would do if they found themselves captives in a brothel. But she owed it to herself, and to this calm capable man, to have courage, even if she was going to have to pay for her rescue by losing her virtue in his bed. She could not imagine any man would remove a naked woman from a brothel and not expect the logical reciprocal gesture. After all, why else would he be here, if not for a woman? That was what he had meant when he had said he would take her.

'Slump against me, then, and, whatever happens, don't panic.' One arm came round her shoulders and clamped her to his side. *He smells nice*, Jessica thought irrelevantly. Spicy citrus and clean linen and leather. 'And whatever happens, hang on to that hat.'

They began to stagger down the stairs, the man keeping up a slurred, grumbling commentary that taught Jessica, in two terrifying minutes, more cant and bad language than she had ever heard in her life.

The noise swelled, overwhelming her; the stink of hot oil, candle wax, alcohol, sweat and excited masculinity enveloped her, driving away the comforting smell of the man beside her. Then their feet hit the level floor of the entranceway and she drew in a deep, sobbing breath. They were down. The door was right in front of them.

'Off already, gentlemen?' It was the false-genteel accents of the woman who had picked her up at the inn, the woman whose face she had glimpsed, hard and merciless, as the bullies had swept her up the stairs into the nightmare of captivity. Madame Synthia.

'Unfort…unfortunately, Madame, Lord Rotherham ish…is overcome. We will have to return another night—see your famed midnight ex'bition.'

Jessica pressed herself against the tall, gently swaying figure as the madam took her rescuer's other arm and tried to urge him into the room. 'He'll be all right, my lord, one of the girls will look after him. Or I'll get the lads to keep an eye on him. Here, Geordie…'

'Hat,' he hissed, sweeping her up and over his shoulder. Jessica made a grab and held it on. 'Too late, Madame, you don't want him throwing up on your nice marble floor.' Then the doors were open and with an exaggerated stagger they were out. Out into the blissful cold of the night, out into the quiet of a side street with only a hackney cab driving past.

'Cab!' The carriage reined in. Jessica tried to catch a glimpse of the man's face in the light from the windows of the brothel, but he bundled her into the musty interior before she could focus.

'Well.' The door slammed shut and he settled down opposite her in the darkness. 'Here we are, then.'

Chapter Two

The dark shape opposite her did not become any clearer, however hard she stared. Dots began to swim in front of her eyes and Jessica gave up. Seeing him clearly was not going to make any difference—she was in those large, capable hands whether she liked it or not.

Count your blessings, she always said to pupils who whined or complained, knowing as she did it just how infuriatingly smug it sounded. But it was the sort of thing expected from teachers. Now she tried to apply her own good advice.

Blessing One: I am not naked, I have clothes on—but they belong to some man who is currently disporting himself in a house of ill repute. Blessing Two: I am not in a brothel about to be ravished by goodness knows who—but I am in the power of a complete stranger who probably has my ravishment high on his agenda. Blessing Three… She appeared to have run out of blessings.

Know your enemy. Another useful dictum. Especially when you did not know how much of an enemy he was.

'My name is Jessica Gifford.' She ignored the impulse

to give a false name. Life was complicated enough without that. 'Miss,' she added with scrupulous care.

'And mine is Gareth Morant.' The deep voice was curiously calming. She had noticed that in the corridor in the brothel, but then, at that point, anyone who had not drooled or sworn at her would have been comforting. Now that her panic had subsided into cold fear she expected to be rather more discriminating—but he still made her feel safe. *Safe-ish*, she corrected scrupulously.

'Mister?'

'Lord.' She could hear he was smiling. 'Earl of Standon.'

'Thank you for rescuing me, my lord.' There was no call to be impolite, even if you were quaking in your silkstockinged feet. *His* silk stockings. That felt almost more indecent than wearing that other man's pantaloons.

An earl. An aristocrat. Oh Lord, she really had jumped from the frying pan into the fire. A nice, respectable baronet might be concerned with rectitude and reputation. A plain gentleman might be law abiding and bound by the conventions of church and received morality.

But everyone knew about the aristocracy. They did what they liked and to hell with anyone else's opinions or values. So long as they paid their gambling debts they disregarded with impunity every standard held dear by lesser mortals. They gambled, they spent with wild extravagance, their sexual morals were a scandal, they duelled and they did not give a fig for the opinion of anyone else outside their own charmed and privileged circle. *Look at Papa,* she thought with an inward sigh. *And look at Mama—which is rather more to the point under the circumstances.*

'So, what am I going to do with you, Miss Gifford?' Lord Standon enquired. The thread of amusement was still there in the deep voice—he knew exactly what he was going to do with her, she supposed.

'Take me to a respectable inn?' she suggested hopefully.

'You have your luggage safely somewhere, then?'

'No. They took it all.'

'But you have some money?'

'No.' Obviously she did not have any money, he must know that perfectly well.

'Some respectable acquaintance in London to whom I could deliver you?'

'No,' she repeated through gritted teeth. He was finding this amusing, the beast.

'Then I think you are coming home with me.'

Where you will expect me to show my suitable gratitude for this rescue, she thought with a sinking heart. The trouble was, it was not sinking quite as much as it ought, given that she was a respectable virgin completely in the power of a rakish aristocrat. There was something about his size that made it very hard not to feel safe with him, and something about the amused kindness in his voice that made her want to talk to him. *And something about the sheer masculine splendour of him that makes me want to put my hands on him. All over him...*

'Are you frightened?' he asked suddenly.

'Yes.' It was the honest truth. Frightened of him, frightened for the future, terrified of her own, purely female, responses to him.

'Sensible of you.' He did not appear insulted by her response. She supposed she should have tried a little feminine fluttering: *I feel so safe with you, my lord...*'In fact you are an admirably sensible female, are you not, Miss Gifford? Strange how one can tell that in a mere twenty minutes' acquaintance.'

'Not sensible enough to avoid being tricked by a brothel keeper,' Jessica said bitterly. She was not flattered to be told she was sensible. She knew she was, it was her chief virtue and stock in trade and, try as she might, she could not sound anything else.

'Well, you will not be caught a second time. If my solution is not to your liking, what would *you* like me to do with you?'

Have your wicked way with me? she thought wildly, then caught herself up with a effort. She was exhausted, frightened and completely out of her depth, but that was no excuse for hysteria.

'Would you lend me some money, my lord? Then I can go to a respectable inn tonight and seek employment from an agency in the morning. I am a governess.'

'Go to an inn dressed like that? I am afraid all the shops are shut and I do not carry ladies' clothing on my person.'

'Oh. No, of course you do not.' He must think her completely buffle-headed.

'However, I do have some available.' He let the sentence hang. 'At my house.'

'You mean your wife will lend me something?' she enquired sweetly. How she knew it Jessica could not say, but this man was quite definitely not married. The clothing in question was doubtless the silks and laces of some past or present mistress.

'I am not married.' She had the impression that she had slightly unsettled him. 'If I were married, I would not be patronising establishments such as the one we have just left.'

'You have no need to explain yourself to me, my lord.' And having a wife at home made no difference to whether a lord kept a mistress or frequented the muslin company.

'No,' he agreed with the calm that appeared to be natural to him. 'I was explaining it to myself. A tawdry place—there is little excuse for its existence.'

'Other than that gentlemen patronise it.' She thought sadly of Moll, grateful to be employed in a brothel because there she had regular food and nobody blacked her eyes. She hoped someone had found her by now and released her from the clothes press.

The hackney cab drew up with a lurch. 'My town house,' Lord Standon said, getting up and opening the door. He held out his hands to help her down and Jessica paused in the doorway, seeing him for the first time in the light of the torchères either side of the wide black front door.

He was big. She already knew that. His hair was dark and she could not make out the exact colour, but what held her was the power of his face. No one would ever call Gareth Morant handsome, but no one would ever be able to call him less than impressive. Someone—she could not imagine who, unless it was a blacksmith with a hammer—had managed to break a large nose that had not been particularly distinguished to start with. His jaw was strong and determined, in contrast to the peaceable tone he seemed to habitually employ. His eyes, which she already knew were grey, were shadowed below dark brows and his mouth, which she could see all too clearly, was wide, sensual with a lurking smile.

He was waiting with patience for her to move and to alight from the hackney. Jessica thought frantically. Had she any option other than to enter this man's house? No, she had not. 'Thank you, my lord,' she said as placidly as she knew how, and allowed him to take her hand as she jumped down to the pavement.

Doubtless she should embrace death rather than dishonour, but that seemed both unpleasant and disproportionate under the circumstances. *Like mother, like daughter*. The thought flickered through her brain and was instantly banished. Mama…Mama had been *different*. And beside any other considerations, Miss Jessica Gifford believed strongly that one honoured one's obligations. Up to now that had sometimes been onerous, but never quite so frightening to contemplate.

She stood and waited while he paid the driver, her stockinged feet cold and damp on the flags, her ridiculous hat pulled down over her face, then allowed him to take her arm and guide her towards the shallow steps. Despite the hour a butler materialised as Lord Standon closed the door behind him.

'Ah, Jordan. Is Mrs Childe still up?'

'No, my lord, she retired an hour ago, as have all the maids. Would you wish me to rouse one of them?' His very lack of interest in the bizarrely clad figure shivering beside his master revealed the superiority of an upper servant, but Jessica would have been grateful for a look of surprise—she was beginning to feel invisible.

'No, there is no need to disturb them. This young lady has had an unpleasant experience and requires a bedchamber, some supper and some suitable clothing. A fire in the room, please, Jordan.'

'Yes, my lord. Would the young lady care to come into the library to eat while her room is prepared? There is a fire there as usual.'

'Yes, that would be best.' The earl turned and regarded Jessica, who stared back from under the brim of her hat. Her feet were beginning to grow numb on the cold marble. 'Clothes first, though. Come along, Miss Gifford, we should find something in the Chinese bedchamber.'

He led the way to the sweep of stone stairs rising from the chequerboard marble. Jessica grabbed her trailing coat and struggled up after him, clutching the elegant wrought-iron handrail with her free hand. The position gave her an unrivalled opportunity to study long well-shaped legs, narrow hips and broad athletic shoulders. Having run into him at speed, she did not make the mistake of imagining that Lord Standon's figure owed anything to his tailor, who must give thanks daily for a customer who did so much credit to his creations.

On the other hand, she thought critically as she reached the landing and he turned to make sure she was following, he definitely was not a handsome man. The good light showed that her impression outside on the pavement had been correct. At least, she corrected herself, as she plodded along in his wake, trying to lift her tired feet up out of the thick carpet, he was not a *classically* handsome man. Neither Lord Byron's romantically tumbled locks, nor Mr Brummell's much-vaunted beauty need fear competition from the Earl of Standon. On the other hand, he was unmistakably a very virile, masculine creature and she knew perfectly well that his size was provoking a thoroughly unwise desire to cast herself upon his broad chest and beg to be looked after.

Jessica reminded herself that she was not a woman who could afford to succumb to romantic notions, but one who lived by her intelligence and common sense, and that what she was striving for in life was respectable, dull, safe security. Men played no part in that ambition and aristocrats who frequented brothels, however kind they seemed, and however much one wanted to wrap one's arms around as much of them as possible, were the shortest way to the primrose path that led inexorably downwards to shame and degradation. *Look at Mama.*

Well, possibly shame and degradation were rather strong words for it in Mama's case, but it had certainly led to her being cut off without a penny, shunned by her family and living the sort of life that Jessica had sworn, at the age of fourteen, that she would never, ever, risk. Mama had thought the world well lost for love; then, when that love itself had gone, she had lived on her wits, her beauty and her charm.

As far as Jessica was concerned, falling in love ranked somewhat below wagering one's entire substance on a lottery ticket as a sensible way of carrying on for a woman.

Sensation novels promised true love would find you if you only waited long enough and the Old Testament was littered with prophets being sustained entirely by faith and passing ravens, but a good education and hard work seemed more positive routes to security, food on the table and a roof over her head to Jessica than prayer and patience.

Lord Standon stopped and Jessica walked into the back of him. 'Sorry. It is this hat.'

'I believe you might safely remove it now, Miss Gifford.' He opened the door and she stepped inside, pulling off the tall-crowned hat as she did so. There was no point in being a ninny about this. She must do what she had to do to get her life back on course. This was an interlude, then she could get back to being Miss Gifford, superior governess—pianoforte, harp, water-colours and the Italian tongue included.

They had entered what was presumably the Chinese bedchamber. Jessica stood inside the door while his lordship touched a taper to the candelabra standing around the room, trying not to be overawed by the fine painted wallpaper, the golden silk hangings or the rich carpet. It was, when all was said and done, merely a room for sleeping in. She swallowed, hoping that whatever happened before the sleep was not going to occur here under the jewelled eyes of dragons. Common sense and resignation were not proving as fortifying to the spirits as she might have hoped.

'There should be night things at least.' He pulled out drawers and turned over fabrics. 'Yes. Help yourself.' A carved panel opened at a touch and revealed hanging rails. 'And there are robes in there as well, and slippers. Will you be able to find your way down again? Jordan will show you where the library is.'

So, it was not going to happen here and now in this room. Jessica placed the tall hat on a chest and nodded, managing her breathing somehow. 'Thank you, my lord. I will not be long.' He smiled and went out, closing the door behind him. Jessica went to look down into the open drawer at the fine lawn and rich Brussels lace, the satin ribbons and the shimmer of silk. It seemed she was going to lose her virtue whilst lavishly dressed—if that were any consolation.

Gareth stood frowning down at the meal his butler was setting out on the side table in the library. 'Jordan, Miss Gifford was kidnapped by bullies from a brothel as she arrived on the stage this evening.'

'Tsk. Shocking. One hears about such things, of course. How fortunate you were able to assist her.' The man shook his head at the wickedness of the world and adjusted the position of the cruet slightly. 'Miss Gifford will doubtless be hungry, my lord. Snatched meals at post inns are not sustaining fare and I presume she has had nothing since. I will bring a slice of fruit pie in addition to the sweetmeats.' He regarded the table, apparently satisfied with its arrangement. 'Will Miss Gifford be staying with us long, my lord?'

'Until I have settled her future, Jordan.' There was a tap and the door opened. 'Ah, that is better.' Gareth regarded the slim figure in the open doorway and found himself fighting back a grin. Top to toe in Julia's luxurious lingerie, Miss Gifford still managed to look like a governess. Her hair was braided down her back, her feet were neatly together and her hands clasped at her waist. She had managed to find the plainest of the robes and, from the lack of frills showing under it, one of the simplest of the nightgowns.

The memory of her naked, her hair in glorious disarray around white shoulders, those small, high, rounded breasts pressed against his shirt front, filled him

with a pleasurable glow that none of the exotic pleasures promised at Madame Synthia's had evoked.
Something must have shown in his eyes, for her chin
came up a fraction and those wide green eyes narrowed
into suspicious slits. However naïve Miss Jessica
Gifford had been in stepping into a brothel-keeper's
carriage, she was not lacking in either courage or per-
ception.

'Come and sit down by the fire and eat, you must be
hungry.' He pulled out a chair for her and waited while she
came and seated herself, managing it neatly and without
glancing down at the chair as he pushed it in. *Used to
dinner parties.* Gareth added the fact to his slim mental
dossier on Miss Gifford. Obviously a superior governess,
and one with much to lose from this night's events.

'Thank you, my lord.' She waited, hands folded in her
lap while Jordan pulled out a chair for him. 'I confess
I am a trifle peckish.'

'Tea, Miss Gifford? Or lemonade, perhaps?' Gareth
saw her glance from the waiting butler to the opened bottle
of white Chablis standing in an ice bucket by his side.

'Wine, if you please.' There was a touch of defiance
about the choice. *Dutch courage*, he thought, wondering just why she was still so tense. There would be a
period of uncertainty while she recovered from the
shock, no doubt, but she would feel better in the
morning. Mrs Childe would find her ready-made clothes
and she could visit some agencies. He had no doubt she
would soon find a suitable appointment; in the
meantime he would have to find her somewhere to stay.
Maude would help.

She was eating elegantly, he noticed, yet with a
single-minded approach that was making inroads into

the cold meats before her. Her lack of the vapours appealed to him and he plied her with food until she sat back with a sigh of repletion. 'Thank you, my lord. I cannot remember when I last ate anything beside the merest snack.'

'You have travelled far to London?' Gareth picked up his wine and stood to pull back her chair. 'Shall we sit by the fire?'

She gave him a long, searching look from under lashes that seemed ridiculously lavish for such a neat, self-contained creature. 'Yes, thank you,' she said at last, picking up her own half-empty glass and moving to the chair he indicated.

'I have come down from Leicestershire,' she explained. In the big, masculine, winged chair she looked more fragile than he had thought before. Despite her poise, she also seemed vulnerable in a way that was different from her panic in the brothel. Her eyes were wide and watchful on him and she seemed braced for something. 'My last position ended when my pupil went to stay with her grandmother in Bath. I have…had…a position with Lady Hartington to teach languages to her two older daughters. I understand that Lord Hartington was at that place tonight.'

'Yes. In any case, you are better off not employed in that household, Miss Gifford. Lady Hartington is a bitter woman and her husband has a poor reputation.'

Jessica shrugged, a slight, unconsciously graceful gesture. 'It is my job to fit in and make the best of what I find. Few households can be said to be ideal.'

'No doubt you are right. Finish your wine now, it is time for us to retire.' He got to his feet and reached for a candle to give her.

There was no mistaking the tension that shot through her at his innocuous words. She stood up, lifted her chin and said with just the merest tremor in her voice, 'Of course my lord. I am quite…ready.'

Ready for what? Then he realised what the tightly clasped hands and the pulse beating visibly at her throat meant. She thought he had brought her home to—*Damn it, does she take me for some libertine?* Gareth leashed his temper with an effort. 'So, you think you have jumped out of the frying pan into the fire, do you, Jessica?'

Her eyes widened at his use of her name, the pupils expanded so their green light became almost black. 'You had gone to that place for a purpose and thanks to me you were not able to accomplish it.' She stood quite still, although he could see the edge of the nightgown moving. She was trembling and suddenly that made him furious.

'Are you a virgin?' he asked, his voice harsh.

She went white. 'Yes. I am.'

'And you think I am in the habit of ravishing virginal young ladies?'

'I am not a lady, I am a governess.' Her lips tightened for a moment. 'From my observations, the aristocracy regards governesses in much the same light as chambermaids.'

'As fair game?' Obviously being an aristocrat weighed heavily against him.

'Yes.' She gave a little huffing breath as though to recover herself after running. 'And I owe you for rescuing me—I pay my debts.'

'Indeed?' Gareth set the candlestick down with a snap, suddenly too angry to analyse why. 'Would it be

worth my while, I wonder? Virgins are no doubt interesting, but then there is the lack of experience…'

'I learn quickly my lord.'

'Do you, Jessica?' He closed the distance between them
and cupped his hands around her shoulders. Under his big
palms her bones felt fragile. 'Let us see just how quickly',
and he bent his head and kissed her full on the mouth.

Chapter Three

Jessica had just enough warning to drag a breath down into her lungs and then her world changed. One moment she had no idea what a man's mouth felt like, what a male body crushed against hers would feel like or how her own body would react to such contact—and the next everything became a sensual blur filled with this man's heat and scent and taste and the pressure of his lips devouring hers.

She was up on tiptoe, held hard to him, his big body forcing hers to curve and mould into his. His mouth moved on hers with purpose that confused her until she realised that he wanted her to open to him. With a little gasp she did so and his tongue filled her, hot and moist and indecently exciting. She could taste the wine they had been drinking and something else that must be simply him. He was possessing her mouth with what she hazily realised was an echo of a far more complete possession and she melted, boneless, shameless, against him.

When Gareth Morant lifted his mouth from hers and set her square on her feet again she had lost the power of speech, of movement and, utterly, the will to resist him. Jessica gripped the powerful forearms as his hands steadied her. She tried not to pant.

'Miss Gifford.' Unfortunately he did not appear to have been reduced to the same state. His breathing was perfectly even, his face calm, his colour normal. 'Miss Gifford, you are a delightful young lady and a pleasure to kiss, but I hope you will believe me when I tell you that I have not the slightest intention of taking you to my bed. I went to that place this evening at the behest of my friends, not to seek a woman, and you may rest assured that even if I had that intention, I am capable of suppressing my animal instincts for one night.'

'Oh.'

'And I am not in the habit of ravishing virgins, nor of extracting a price from someone whose plight should have prompted any gentleman to rescue her.' He paused and the corner of his mouth twitched. 'Or even any aristocrat.'

'Oh.' Jessica struggled to get her brain out of the morass of warm porridge into which it appeared to have fallen and to say something coherent. 'Then I must say that was the most embarrassing mistake I have ever made,' she admitted with painful honesty.

'Kissing me?' His eyebrows shot up. Obviously his lordship was not used to having his caresses dismissed as embarrassing. He was probably offended that, having reduced her to a quivering puddle, she was not begging for more.

'No. I had no choice about that, had I?' Jessica glared at him. 'I mean, assuming that you would expect—you know.'

'Well, I do not.' He picked up the candlestick again

and handed it to her. 'I will ring for Jordan to show you to your room.'

'Why *did* you kiss me, my lord?' She had not meant to say it, she had meant to say *Thank you* in a calm and dignified manner, but the question just escaped.

'Because you made me cross.' He stood watching her and she made herself stand up to the scrutiny without fidgeting until the corner of his mouth quirked into a ghost of a smile. 'And because I wanted to.' He reached for the bell pull. 'You may sleep in peace, Miss Gifford, my curiosity has been satisfied.'

Well, that was a flattening piece of reassurance to be sure! Jessica produced a perfectly correct curtsy and stalked out in the butler's wake. So his lordship's curiosity had been satisfied, had it? And what if it had not been? Would he have persisted? Obviously he was used to far more sophisticated kissing than she could provide.

'Your room, Miss Gifford.'

Her agitation melted away on a sigh. Warm firelight flickered on rose-coloured walls. A bed heaped with white linens sat comfortably in the far corner. Steam curled upwards from the ewer standing on the wash-stand and the curtains were closed tight against the damp London night and all the dangers it held. This was not some rake's love nest. Lord Standon was treating her as a guest and she had cast aspersions on his motives.

'Oh dear.'

She had realised she had spoken aloud. Jordan turned. 'Miss Gifford? Is something wrong?'

'I have just realised that perhaps I expressed my gratitude to Lord Standon insufficiently just now.'

What might have been a fleeting smile passed over

the impassive countenance. 'It is easy, if I might make an observation, miss, to misinterpret things, especially when one is tired and in some distress.'

'Yes. Thank you, Jordan.' The man bowed and left her. Jessica took off the heavy apricot satin robe, pulled the cream silk nightgown over her head and went to pour water into the basin. Her feet were filthy, but her whole being felt contaminated from those desperate hours in the brothel and she stood for long minutes lathering the sweet-scented soap over every inch of her body before she began to feel clean again.

Fresh and dry at last Jessica slipped back into the nightgown, luxuriating in its soft fabric and luxurious detail. Sinful behaviour obviously had its rewards, she decided, climbing between the warm sheets and snuggling down, wishing now that she had chosen one of the more elaborately trimmed garments—she would never have the opportunity to indulge in such opulence again.

It had been an eventful day. She had been inside a brothel, she was sleeping in silk—and she had been kissed by a man. Jessica blew out the remaining candle and lay watching the pattern of firelight on the walls. She should be making plans, but…. As her agitation slowly ebbed away and she relaxed into the warmth and safety of the bedchamber, the sensual memory of that kiss flooded back. She had resigned herself to never being kissed—the path she had set herself precluded any relationship with men beyond that of employee and employer.

Now she knew what it felt like to be held so tightly, and yet want to be held tighter yet. She knew what a man tasted like, how his skin smelt, how her own body yearned to betray every standard and scruple just to experience that glory again. And that was just a kiss. What would it be like to be made love to by Lord Standon? Perhaps, if she willed herself to sleep, she would dream about him.

The rattle of curtain rings woke Jessica from a deep sleep undisturbed by the nightmares of Madam Synthia's or the bliss of Lord Standon's arms.

'Good morning, Miss Gifford.' Jessica sat up and found a neatly clad maid setting a tray down beside her bed. 'I am Mary, miss, and I'm to look after you while you are here. Mr Jordan told us about what had happened—what a dreadful thing, miss!—and Mrs Childe will be going out in a minute to buy you some day clothes. Here's your chocolate, miss, and his lordship says, would you care to join him for breakfast? In your dressing gown's quite all right, miss.' She ran out of breath at last and stood beaming.

'Thank you, Mary.' Jessica took a reviving mouthful of chocolate. *Oh, the luxury!* It seemed to stroke down inside her like warm velvet, soothing and invigorating, both at the same time. 'How will Mrs Childe know what size clothes to get for me?'

'His lordship lined us all up and said Polly was just the right size, miss.' Mary bustled about. 'I'll fetch your hot water, shall I?'

Oh Lord! So he had told them Polly was the right size, had he? Just in case the rest of the household had no idea that their master had had the opportunity to scrutinise her in intimate detail. Jessica had become very familiar with the inner world of households, their miniature social hierarchies, their taboos and their rules. The servants would not be kind about a governess gone astray; she and her kind were usually regarded as being neither gentry nor servants and as a result were an outcast class between the two. Not that Mary appeared hostile.

The maid bustled back with the water and drew the screen round the washstand. 'Here you are, miss, I've brought a fresh nightgown as well.'

Gareth pushed back his chair as the door opened on to the breakfast parlour and Jessica walked in. He saw with relief that she did not appear much affected by her adventures the night before—neither the kidnap nor his insane kiss. He was still kicking himself about that, and he had suffered long sleepless hours reviewing just how unwise it had been to yield to temptation. He was not sure whether it was the ache in his groin or in his conscience that had most disturbed his slumber, but they had both proved damnably uncomfortable.

'Miss Gifford. I trust you slept well?'

'Very well, thank you, my lord. That was a most comfortable room, I could not have been better cared for.' She hesitated, one hand lying with unconscious elegance on the back of a dining chair. 'I leapt to an unforgivable conclusion last night, my lord, and I apologise for it.'

Coals of fire heaped on his tender scruples. 'And I apologise for what followed. I suggest we both forget about it, Miss Gifford. Now, would you like to take a seat and I will fetch you some breakfast from the buffet?'

She inclined her head and Gareth felt a flicker of admiration for her poise. 'Very well, thank you. But I will not forget your kindness. And please, do not let your own meal get cold, I will help myself.'

He sat, watching with a carefully suppressed smile of appreciation as she walked past him to the back of the room where the chafing dishes had been laid out on the sideboard under their silver domes. This morning rich silk ruffles flounced from under the heavy hem of the apricot robe and her hair had been brushed until it shone and then caught up with skilful simplicity. There was far less of the prim governess on show this morning. Julia always said Mary was the most accomplished of the maids.

'Mrs Childe has gone shopping on your behalf,' he began, reaching for the mustard pot.

'So I understand.' There was a muted clang as she turned back a lid and began to fill her plate. 'I understand you could accurately identify Polly as being just my size.' *Ah.* Mary might be skilful as a lady's maid, but she was obviously somewhat lacking in tact. 'Goodness, black pudding, what a treat.' There was another clang. Gareth began to amuse himself following Jessica's progress along the buffet by sound alone. 'Who else is coming to breakfast, my lord?'

'Just us.' He bit into the rare sirloin.

'Indeed? How lavish it is.'

He suspected he was on the receiving end of a very governessy look, to do with extravagance and possibly gluttony. Gareth grinned at his rapidly diminishing steak and contemplated what response would be most calculated to tease her.

'I do not believe in stinting—' He broke off at the sound of raised voices in the hall. Or at least, of one, very familiar, female voice raised in argument and Jordan's even tones attempting to head her off. Impossible, the man should know that by now.

'—his lordship is up!' The door swung open. 'You see, he was in here all the time. Good morning, Gareth darling.'

'Maude.' Gareth got to his feet and submitted to being pecked on the cheek by the black-haired whirl-wind who swept in, thrusting her vast muff into Jordan's hands. 'What on earth do you keep in a muff that size? A small pony? And what are you doing here at this hour of the day and without a chaperon?'

'They are all the crack this size. And as for chape-rons—piffle.' She sat down next to him, tugged off her bonnet and reached for a cup. 'Is that coffee?'

'Yes.' Resigned to the invasion, he sat down again and passed the pot. 'And it is not piffle. Do you want to end up marrying me?'

'Lord, no!' She laughed at him, glossy black curls bouncing, the morning chill colouring her cheeks and lending sparkle to her blue eyes. She really was the most lovely creature and he was strongly tempted to box her ears. 'That's why I am here, this marriage thing is getting serious. Papa has Pronounced. Say what I will, he is fixed upon our union. You are the only man for me, in his opinion—as well as being well bred, healthy, in your right mind and rich, you are also, he tells me, a pillar of rectitude and just what a flibbertigibbet like me requires in a husband.'

'I don't want to marry you,' Gareth said flatly. 'None of this is news, Maude. You don't want to marry me either. Our parents came up with this idiot agreement, it isn't legally binding.'

'I know that! But most of society believes we are be-trothed. Gareth, how am I ever going to find a man to marry if they are all afraid of you?'

'What do you want me to do about it?' Gareth poured them both more coffee. 'I have never confirmed the rumours, I have never given your father any indication that I might do as he wishes.'

'He will not listen. And neither do all the gorgeous men out there who are avoiding me like the plague!' Maude set her elbow on the table, put her pointed chin on the palm of her hand and gazed at him earnestly. 'There is only one thing to do Gareth, you are going to have to embark on a life of sin and debauchery.'

The gasp behind him had Maude swinging round on her seat, her eyes searching the less well-lit end of the room. 'Gareth! You fraud—you've already started.'

The eruption into the room of one of the loveliest young women she had ever seen froze Jessica in front of the buffet. Even in the flat light of a winter morning the intruder seemed to gleam like a highly finished piece of jewellery. Her hair was a glossy mass of black ringlets, her clothes had the dull sheen of silk and merino, her eyes glinted like Ceylon sapphires and her teeth as she laughed at Lord Standon were white and perfect.

Jessica stood quite still, her plate clasped in both hands while this lovely creature, quivering with barely suppressed energy, swept on. Despite her lack of a chaperon, she did not need Lord Standon's words to realise that this was a lady and not, despite her scandalous presence in an unmarried man's breakfast parlour, one of the muslin company. Maude, whoever she was, was quite obviously well bred, wealthy and supremely self-confident.

'…you are going to have to embark on a life of sin and debauchery.'

Jessica gasped, all too aware of the picture she must present. There was no way out of the room unseen.

Maude swung round, her face lighting up into a picture of delighted mischief at the sight of Jessica. 'Gareth! You fraud—you've already started.'

'I—' Jessica put down her plate and walked towards the door. 'Excuse me, you will wish to be alone, Lord Standon.'

'Miss Gifford.' He stood up. 'Please, sit down and have your breakfast. Lady Maude is just going.' He held out a chair for her on the opposite side of the table and waited. Jessica sat while he retrieved her plate, placed it in front of her and poured her coffee. There did not appear to be any choice.

'Thank you, my lord. But—'

'My pleasure. Maude, go home.'

'Certainly not, this is far too interesting.' Lady Maude settled herself squarely to the table and reached for the bread and butter. 'Introduce us properly, Gareth.' She beamed at Jessica. 'That's Julia's robe, I was with her when she bought it. Are you a friend of hers? I was rather hoping that you were an exotic bird of paradise and that Gareth was about to launch himself into a life of scandalous dissipation and save us both. But I can see you are a lady. Which is a disappointment, I must admit.'

Jessica blinked in the face of this torrent and plucked out one name. 'Who is Julia?'

'Lady Blundell, Gareth's sister. Would you pass the honey? Thank you so much.'

So she had completely misjudged him. He had lent her his sister's clothes, not his mistress's, he had no intention of ravishing her—and now she was embarrassing him by being here when this extraordinary young woman descended upon him.

Jessica shot Lord Standon a cautious sideways glance. He had pushed his plate to one side and had buried his face in his hands, which she supposed was a reasonable reaction from anyone attempting to deal with Lady Maude. She looked back at the other woman. Maude gazed back, her lovely face a picture of cheerful curiosity. Jessica succumbed to it, unable to think of a single fabrication that might cover her presence there.

'My name is Jessica Gifford. I am a governess and yesterday I was abducted off the stage by a brothel keeper. Lord Standon rescued me and his housekeeper is buying me clothes so I can go to an employment agency today and secure another position.'

'Goodness. How beautifully concise and organised you are. I shall see if I can match you. I am Maude Templeton, my papa is the Earl of Pangbourne and my entire ambition at the moment is not to end up married to Gareth.'

'Why?' Jessica enquired bluntly. 'His lordship appears eminently eligible to me.' This was greeted by a faint moan from the head of the table. Lady Maude rolled her eyes.

'Gareth, stop it. Miss Gifford is obviously a woman of sense and her breakfast is getting cold. We can all agree that you are completely eligible, utterly gorgeous and I am demented not to want to marry you. Likewise I am lovely, desirable, incredibly well bred and amazingly well dowered. You must be all about in the head not to want me. Let us all finish our breakfast and then we can decide what to do about it.'

'I know exactly what I am going to do.' Lord Standon

lowered his hands and regarded both of them with disfavour. 'I am going to ring for Jordan, who will put you in your carriage and send you home, Maude. Miss Gifford is going to finish her breakfast and then, when Mrs Childe returns with her new clothes, I will send her in the barouche to interview as many employment agencies as she sees fit to visit. You, meanwhile, will stand ready to provide whatever references Miss Gifford requires to cover the period of unemployment she is currently experiencing. In fact, come to think of it, she can stay with you until she finds a new position.'

'Lord Standon, I could not possibly impose upon La—'

'Of course you can. What fun. Do call me Maude, we are going to be great friends, I can see.' Maude smiled at her, then turned a gimlet stare back on Lord Standon. 'Gareth, what about me? I am truly desperate and if you don't—'

The door opened, Jordan positively slid through the gap and closed it behind him, his back to the panels. 'My lord,' he murmured, his voice hushed, 'Lord Pangbourne is here, demanding an interview.'

'Papa?' Maude stood up with a faint shriek.

'Yes, my lady.'

'Shh!' Lord Standon set down his coffee cup. 'Tell him I am not at home Jordan.'

'I attempted so to do, my lord. The earl says he will wait in the hall. He has resisted all my efforts to establish him comfortably in your study—he appears suspicious that you will attempt to evade him.'

'Damn right,' his lordship said grimly.

'Jordan!' The masculine voice from the hall had all

three of them at the table regarding the door warily. The handle rattled. 'Is Standon in there?'

'Just coming, my lord,' the butler called back, then lurched forward as the door partly opened behind him.

'Maude,' Lord Standon hissed, 'get under the table and take your bonnet with you.' As she slid out of view he was on his feet, pulling Jessica to hers.

'What—?'

'I'll make this up to you. Promise.' His fingers were in her hair, dragging out pins, sending her curls tumbling around her shoulders, then he yanked open the satin sash, pushed the robe back off her shoulders and fell back in his chair, Jessica tumbling into his lap. 'Kiss me.'

The door burst open. Her mouth captured by Gareth Morant's, her body held hard against his, all Jessica could do was to fight to keep her senses. The pressure on her mouth eased a little. 'Help me, I can't do this all by myself,' he whispered. The echo of his words to her in the brothel. Jessica stopped struggling. This was how she could repay him.

She snaked her arms around his neck, opened her mouth under his and arched her back. The robe slithered free and the warm air caressed the swell of her breasts revealed by the silken gown. Deep in his throat he made a soft sound, a growl. Something inside Jessica turned to liquid fire. Was this only playacting?

An infuriated voice thundered, 'Damn it, Jordan, get out of my way.' There was silence, broken only by the thunder of her heartbeat. Then, 'Morant, you libertine! What the devil do you think you are doing?'

Chapter Four

Lord Standon shifted Jessica in his arms so that her face was hidden in his shoulder. She clung, quivering with mingled excitement and embarrassment.

'I am attempting to eat my breakfast in my own dining room,' he replied coldly. 'You will forgive me if I do not get up. I believe Jordan did attempt to intimate that I was not receiving.'

'You've been avoiding me, Sir! And neglecting poor Maude—and now I see why.'

'Maude is hardly moping without my presence, Templeton.' Jessica gave a little wriggle as she felt the satin of her nightgown sliding over his knees. Lord Standon closed his hand more firmly over her hip and pressed her to him.

'You are betrothed to Maude, damn it,' the older man snapped. Jessica could imagine him, red faced with bristling eyebrows.

'Forgive me, but we are not betrothed, whatever you and my honoured father cooked up between you. And neither of us wish to be. With respect, sir, you cannot force me to make a declaration to Maude.'

'I can stop her marrying anyone else. What do you say to that, eh?' Jessica, her senses filled with the smell and feel of the man who held her, struggled to focus on what was happening on the far side of the table. Lord Pangbourne appeared to be pacing.

'I would say that I find it hard to believe that you would be such an unfeeling father.'

'Bah! I'll talk to you again, Morant, when you haven't got most of your mind on your doxy. I give you good day!'

The door slammed. Lord Standon exhaled, his breath feathering hot all down her neck. 'You can come out now, Maude.' Jessica wriggled, sitting upright, but he still held her on his lap, apparently forgetting that they were merely playacting. The sensation of a man's legs pressed so close to her derrière was breathtaking. Jessica felt the shift of thigh muscles and sat very still.

Maude popped out from under the table, pushing back her tumbled curls. 'You see? He is quite impossible.' She brushed down her skirt and stood regarding them. 'Gareth, are you still supposed to be cuddling Jessica?'

'What? Lord, I beg your pardon, Jessica, you felt so right there I quite—' He broke off, shaking his head as though surprised at his own words and opened his arms. Jessica slid off his lap and returned to her own place, her cheeks glowing.

'My lord…' She pulled her robe into some sort of order and pushed her hair back over her shoulders. This was a madhouse and she needed to extricate herself from it and go and interview employment agencies before she became any more embroiled.

'Gareth. I think we have gone beyond the use of titles, do you not?'

Gareth. It suited him, a solid, warm name. But she could hardly imagine herself using it, except in her head.

'You see, don't you, Gareth?' Maude continued. 'Papa finds you in the torrid embraces of a scarlet woman, and *still* persists in saying we should marry. What on earth do you have to do to make him realise we are not suited?'

'Perhaps Lord Standon could marry someone else?' Jessica suggested. She suppressed the turmoil the last few minutes had thrown her into and tried to apply some logic to the situation. Someone had to. 'It seems the commonsense solution.'

'So it is, if there was anyone I wished to marry.' Gareth grimaced, pouring more coffee. 'I'd sooner marry Maude than some female I don't like.'

'Then why?' Jessica persisted, determined to make sense of it all. Her food was lukewarm. She pushed the plate to one side and started on the bread and butter and honey. 'Why is Lord Pangbourne so insistent and why, when you obviously both like each other very much, don't you do what he wants?'

Maude and Gareth exchanged looks, then he shrugged and gestured for her to start. 'Once upon a time,' she began, her voice taking on the singsong tone of the storyteller with a much-told tale, 'Gareth's uncle fell in love with my aunt. Our families' lands march together and it was true love and a marvellous romance. He was the son of the duke, she was a great beauty. Everyone was thrilled, but on the eve of the wedding they were killed in a carriage accident. Both families were plunged into deepest mourning and our fathers vowed that when we grew up—I had just been born— we would marry and recreate the legendary love match.'

Jessica's thoughts—that this was a piece of sentimental nonsense—must have shown, despite her careful lack of comment, for Gareth grinned. 'It was not such a foolish piece of romance as you might assume. As we grew up it became obvious that because of her poor mother's continuous ill health Maude was going to remain an only child—and there we were, presenting the perfect alliance to unite two great estates.'

'Our fathers exchanged letters formally agreeing to the betrothal,' Maude picked up the story. 'And here we are.'

'But you are not legally bound?'

'No, this is not the Middle Ages, thank goodness, but Papa controls my money until I am thirty or I marry with his consent. And he has made sure everyone believes us to be betrothed.'

'Then why don't you do as he asks?' Jessica persisted. 'You can hardly object to Lord Standon, surely?'

'Thank you Jessica,' he said gravely.

'I meant,' she said repressively, kicking herself under the table for thinking aloud, 'you are apparently highly eligible and you like each other.'

'They made the mistake of bringing us up like brother and sister—we simply can't think of each other except as that. And I know perfectly well that somewhere, out there, is the man I am going to fall in love with,' Maude said flatly. 'And I do not want to be married to someone else when we meet. Doomed love and broken hearts may be all very well in novels, but I have no intention of subjecting myself to such discomfort.' She attacked an apple with a pearl-handled knife and a fierce expression. 'But I will never get to know any men to fall in love with because no one will do more than make polite conversation because they are all scared of Gareth.'

'He is rather formidable,' Jessica agreed, eyeing his lordship's brooding figure at the head of the table.

'Thank you,' he said again, politely. 'We are agreed that I am eligible and formidable and that Maude cannot be sacrificed upon the altar of matrimony other than to a man she truly loves. You will also have observed that her father is a thick-skinned old termagant who won't take *no* for an answer. You are a young lady whose common sense is her stock in trade—what do you suggest?'

Jessica pondered the problem, her abstracted gaze fixed on the rather attractive whorl of Gareth's left ear where the crisp brown curl of his hair set the defined shape into sharp relief. She knew exactly what the skin there smelled like.

'Um… You could pretend to become betrothed to someone else. Lord Pangbourne would admit defeat then, surely? But that means you need to find a com-placent lady who would not mind such a charade, and you risk finding yourself permanently attached if she proves unscrupulous. Or you could do what Lady Maude suggested and embark upon a course of de-bauchery so public that even Lord Pangbourne will be forced to admit that he cannot marry his daughter to you. After all, he has just surprised you apparently making love amidst the marmalade.'

Maude suppressed an unladylike snort. Jessica con-templated another slice of bread and honey, decided that she was eating merely to keep her mind distracted from Gareth's proximity and sucked the tips of her sticky fingers. Then she realised his gaze was resting on her lips and promptly snatched up her napkin. 'The latter course would be safer—the debauchery, I mean, not the marmalade.' Maude gave way to giggles. 'I imagine that you could hire a professional without risk of finding yourself sued for breach of promise.'

She closed her eyes for a moment, imagining Gareth back in that brothel interviewing candidates for a charade of debauchery. Only, once having paid for them, she assumed it would require a saint not to avail himself of the services thus acquired, so playacting would not be required. *He is a man*, she reminded herself briskly. *That is what men do. And in any case, what is it to me?*

'Excellent. We have a plan.' Maude tossed her napkin on to the table and stood up, ignoring Lord Standon's grimace and shaken head. 'You see, Gareth, Jessica agrees with me.' She smiled across the table. 'Now, I will drive home and then send my carriage back to collect you and take you round the agencies. As soon as that is done you can come and stay with me until you are settled.'

'But Lord Pangbourne has seen me.'

'He saw a wanton female with her hair down, half-dressed in a improper nightgown and from the back. He will not recognise you, Jessica, take my word for it.' Gareth walked across and opened the door. 'Maude's offer of the carriage is a sensible one.'

Gareth strolled through the doors of White's, nodded absently at the porter who relieved him of his outer garments, and climbed the stairs to the library. He needed some peace and quiet to think about Maude's predicament. For himself, although it was tiresome,

Lord Pangbourne's ambitions were merely a nuisance. He could, and would, marry where he chose. One of these days. When he got round to it.

But Maude was a considerable heiress and, if her father truly intended to, he could keep her financially dependent on him until she was thirty. She could choose herself a husband, he supposed, always provided she could find someone prepared to ignore the persistent rumour that she was already betrothed to him, or who was prepared to take a dowerless wife, but that was assuming a case of love at first sight and a determined lover at that.

He could put an advertisement in the paper, denying the rumours, but that would create a scandal—the presumption would be that there was some reason discreditable to her, which was why he did not want to marry Maude. He could carry on denying it whenever it was mentioned—but no one believed him when he did. By common consent, he would be insane to refuse to marry a lovely, high-born, wealthy young woman who would bring the Pangbourne acres to join his own. And everyone knew that Gareth Morant was no fool. He was simply, the gossips concluded, in no hurry to assume the ties of matrimony.

Meanwhile poor Maude was effectively out of bounds to any gentleman who might otherwise court her, unless he took the first step and married.

Gareth picked up a copy of *The Times* and found a secluded corner to read it in. Ten minutes later it was still folded on his knee and he was passing in review each of the young ladies currently on the Marriage Mart and dismissing all of them. There was a new Season about to start in a week or two; that would bring the new crop fluttering on to the scene.

Gareth steepled his fingers and contemplated marriage to a seventeen- or eighteen-year-old. It was not appealing. He liked intelligence, maturity, wit, sophistication…

'Morant, thought I might find you here.'

Hell and damnation and… 'Templeton.' Gareth tossed his newspaper on to a side table and got to his feet. He might feel like strangling Maude's father, but good manners forced him to show respect for the older man.

'Gave me a shock this morning! Ha!' Lord Pangbourne cast himself into the wing chair opposite Gareth and glared around to make sure they were alone. 'Young devil.'

'If I had expected you, my lord—' Gareth began.

'You'd have kept your new doxy upstairs, I'll be bound.'

'And what makes you think she's a new one?' Despite his irritation, Gareth was intrigued.

'No sign of her before. Discreet, that's good. I was a bit out of sorts.'

It was, Gareth realised, an apology of a kind. The best he was likely to receive. He snatched at the sign of reasonableness. 'You know, my lord, that neither Maude nor I wish to marry each other; we have told you time and again.'

'You'll grow out of that nonsense.'

'Sir, I am seven and twenty. Maude is only four years younger. She'll be on the shelf if she has to wait much longer.'

'She's on *your* shelf, that's the thing.' The older man looked smug. 'Snuff?'

'No, thank you.' Gareth scarcely glanced at the proffered box. 'And if I do not marry her?'

'You will, I have every confidence in your good sense. You are perfect for her and she'll bring the Pang-bourne estates with her when I go. Mind you, I'm not going to put up with these vapours of hers much longer. One more Season I'll stand for and then she can go back to the country and wait for you there.'

Frustrated, Gareth tipped back his head and stared up at the chaste plasterwork of the ceiling. Maude would go mad in the country, and no suitor was going to find her stuck in rural solitude. If that was what the old devil intended then he, Gareth, was probably going to have to make the sacrifice and marry someone else.

'Is there anything,' he said between gritted teeth, 'that would convince you that I am not suited for your daughter?'

'Nothing.' Lord Pangbourne beamed at him, his hands folded neatly over his considerable stomach. 'I watched you with some anxiety in your salad years, I have to admit. Never can tell which way you young bucks will go—and I wouldn't have given her to you if you'd been some rakehell, not fair on the girl to have to live with scandal and dissipation.' He grimaced. 'Diseases and all that. But look at you now. Perfect.'

Gareth felt far from flattered. 'This morning you called me a libertine,' he pointed out. 'I was exhibiting behaviour that might well be characterised as both scan-dalous and dissipated,' he added hopefully.

'Mere irritation of nerves on my part—that daughter of mine is enough to try the patience of saint. Keeps telling me that her own true love is out there somewhere and she can't find him with you in the way. True love, my eye! Balderdash! As for your little ladybird—don't expect you to be a monk, my boy, just be a bit discriminating and don't upset Maude while you're about it.'

Lord Pangbourne hauled himself to his feet and nodded abruptly. 'I'll be off. See to it now, Morant—make her a declaration and all will be right and tight.'

Gareth watched the broad shoulders vanishing behind the book stacks with a sense of being caught in a trap. His thoughts churned. *Damn the old... Scandal and dissipation...*Coherent phrases spoken in a clear, dispassionate voice penetrated his anger. *Embark upon a course of debauchery so public that even Lord Pangbourne will be forced to admit that he cannot marry his daughter to you.* That was what the eminently sensible Miss Gifford had counselled.

It had been Maude's idea first, but, fond of her though he was, Gareth was used to Maude's schemes—most of them hare-brained, to put it mildly. Miss Jessica Gifford with her wide green eyes, her clear gaze, her common sense, her sweet, high breasts and innocently generous mouth—*Stop that, damn it!*—her calm governess manner, now she would not suggest something hare-brained.

A business arrangement, that was what was needed. He needed to create a scandal with no repercussions once it was all over, so that Templeton accepted he was too unreliable for his Maude.

Gareth steepled his fingers and tapped the tips absently against his lips. London was filled with highly skilled courtesans with a flair for the dramatic and a love of money. Finding one to misbehave with would be simple. And distasteful. He tried to sort out why. He had taken mistresses in the past, but that had been a straightforward relationship. Something made him recoil from involving a stranger in his business and Maude's feelings.

His errant memory conjured up a cool voice observing that a lady could hardly object to Lord Standon, a pair of warm, innocent lips against his and a slight figure shivering at his side in Rotherham's clothes, terrified yet gamely playing her role. Playing a role…

'Morant, there you are! I've been looking for you everywhere—what have you done with my clothes, you—'

Gareth got to his feet as his friend marched into his sanctuary, his chubby face set in a scowl. 'Rotherham, if you want to pluck a crow with me, you'll have to do it some other time. I'll get my man to pack them up and send them round this afternoon. I'm busy now.' He added something under his breath as he passed Lord Rotherham, giving him an absentminded slap on the shoulder as he went.

The younger man stood staring after him. 'I say, Morant, did you just say you were off to create a scandal?' He received no response. 'Damn funny way to carry on,' he grumbled, picking up Gareth's discarded newspaper and dropping into his chair. 'Damn funny.'

An hour after breakfast, her hair braided into severity, and clad in one of the sombre and respectable gowns and pelisses Mrs Childe had purchased, Jessica began her round of the agencies. She knew them all by experience or reputation, although her previous employment had been as much as a result of answering personal advertisements as through their efforts. She did not expect much trouble in finding something suitable. Her accomplishments were superior, her references excellent and Lady Maude Templeton's address could only, she was certain, add a certain *cachet*.

By four in the afternoon Jessica was hungry, thirsty and dispirited. No one, it seemed, was seeking superior governesses just now. The Climpson Agency could offer her a family of lively small boys—Jessica knew enough to interpret that as *thoroughly out of control*. Another bureau suggested a family in Northumberland who were seeking an *adaptable* governess for a daughter who, as the owner Mrs Lambert explained, was 'Just a little, er…eccentric.' Yes, she confirmed, there was rather a high turnover of governesses for that post.

And, as always, there were any number of middle-class families who were looking for governesses who would also act as general companions. Jessica had heard about those sort of positions; they translated as general dogsbody to the lady of the house.

'It will be the start of the Season soon,' Mr Climpson explained, running an inky finger down his ledgers and shaking his head. 'People have made arrangements already so they can concentrate upon social matters. There are sure to be more opportunities once the summer is upon us; many people make changes then for some reason.'

'I had hoped to find something suitable more quickly than that.' Jessica looked down at the dark blue wool of her skirts. Every stitch she wore was borrowed, she had not a penny piece of her own until she could write to her bank in Leicester. And then she would have to dig into her precious savings, her only and last resource. How on earth was she going to cope otherwise—unless she took one of those posts that no one else wanted?

'Your references and experience are excellent,' Mr Climpson added, obviously intending to be encouraging. She knew they were, and knew without arrogance that they were the result of her own hard work and careful selection of posts. To take anything less would diminish her status, but it did not appear she had much choice.

How long could she possibly impose upon Lady Maude? A week perhaps? 'I will call back in a few days.' She stood up with a bright smile—it would not do to appear desperate. And there were always the newspapers to scan. Lord Pangbourne's household would be sure to be well supplied with those.

The coachman was waiting patiently outside the agency. 'That will be all for today, thank you.' Jessica smiled as the footman flipped down the steps for her and held the door. 'Please can you take me to Lady Maude's house now.' The carriage was such a luxury with its lap rug and heated bricks—it would not do to become used to such things. Jessica sat up straight and gave herself a mental talking to. She was lucky to be here, she knew it. If it had not been for Gareth, she would be living a nightmare of degradation and shame. She had begun from very little when Mama had died—now she had experience and references. Soon she would find employment and, in the meantime, at least she had a safe and comfortable refuge for a few days.

The carriage drew up and she peered out of the window on to the gloomy early evening scene. This must be the Pangbourne's residence. A door opened and a tall liveried footman ran down the steps and opened the carriage door. She half-rose, expecting him to offer her his hand to descend.

'Miss Gifford? I have a note from Lady Maude.'

Jessica unfolded it, confused, tipping the note to read it in the light from the open door. Maude's handwriting was as bold as her personality, the words slashing across the expensive cream paper.

Dear Jessica, Things have got Much Worse—but Gareth has a plan, if only you will help us. Please will you go back to his house? Papa must not see you. Imploring your understanding, your good friend, Maude.

She looked up at the impassive footman. 'Please tell Lady Maude I will do what she requests. Will you ask the driver to return to Lord Standon's residence, please?'

He closed the door and the carriage rumbled off into the light drizzle. Jessica felt her shoulders sagging again, and this time found it an effort to straighten them. Now what was going to become of her?

Chapter Five

'**W**hen did you last eat?' Gareth demanded, his hands fisted on his hips as he looked at her.

It was not what Jessica was expecting and she stared blankly at him while she made herself think. Jordan removed her bonnet and pelisse from her unresisting hands. 'Breakfast?' she hazarded.

'I thought so, you look ready to drop. Jordan! Food for Miss Gifford, in the library as soon as possible.'

'At once, my lord.'

'I thought you were the sensible one in all this—what were you thinking of, to starve yourself?' Gareth was positively scolding as he guided her into the book-lined room and sat her firmly down in one of the big wing chairs in front of the fire.

'There were so many agencies to get round,' Jessica protested, stretching out her feet to the hearth and letting her tired back rest against the soft old leather. It was seductively easy to allow him to take charge and organise her. It gave her an entirely false sense that all would be well and she knew she could not succumb to that: she was in charge of her own destiny and no one could help her but herself.

'This is not a race—you know I will find you somewhere to stay for as long as you need.' Gareth dropped into the chair opposite and crossed his legs, the silver tassels on his Hessian boots swinging. A pair of those boots would keep her for months. It was a timely reminder of just how far apart their worlds were.

'It seems the residence you suggested for me is not so suitable after all.' Jessica held out the note. Gareth took it, scanned it and grimaced. 'And I am afraid I was unable to find anything in the way of employment today. I will have to look at the newspapers and try the agencies again in a day or two.'

'Nothing suitable? Please, Jessica, don't let it worry you.' He read the note again. 'Maude has such a taste for the dramatic it is a pity a career on the stage is so ineligible.' Gareth screwed it up and tossed it on to the fire. 'It is true that if you agree to our plan it will be impossible for you to stay with her, but did you think we were going to cast you out?'

'I am having trouble thinking clearly at all,' she confessed. 'I am so disorientated, so much out of my depth. I fear I must ask you for a loan of money until I can get funds from my bank in Leicester.'

'You have funds?' He was regarding her steadily, his face thoughtful. It was like being interviewed for a post.

'My savings.' *My precious savings.*

'Well, you will not want to dip into those.' She found herself nodding agreement and forced herself to sit still. It was dangerous to agree with anything he said. 'Jessica, I have to say I am selfishly glad that you have not secured employment yet. I have a proposition for you. Maude may be dramatic, but she is right, things have deteriorated.'

'Yes?'

He smiled at her wary tone, and she wondered why she had not thought him handsome before. *And Maude does not want him? She must be about in her head...*

'You are right to sound so cool, my sensible Miss Gifford. Ah, here is something for you to eat. We will talk when you are a little revived.'

It took considerable self-control to sit quietly and eat the savoury omelette, the soft white roll and butter and the dish of lemon posset that the footman set out on the little table before her. Jessica sipped the glass of red wine Gareth poured and schooled her tongue and her patience.

When she had finished she waited while he lifted the table to the side and then folded her hands in her lap with as much composure as she could muster. 'You say you have a proposition for me, my lord?'

'Gareth.' He waited until she repeated his name. 'You made an eminently sensible suggestion at breakfast, Jessica.'

'That you should appear to follow a path of dissipation with a mistress and scandalise Lord Pangbourne so that he will consider you unsuitable for Lady Maude?'

'Indeed. He called upon me at my club this morning and made it very clear that he means what he says—but he also betrayed the fact that openly scandalous behaviour would not be tolerated. I think it is the only solution if I am to free Maude from this situation.'

'And yourself?' she asked, curious about his own

position. He must be of an age where he was looking to marry, set up his nursery, ensure the succession to the title.

'I have no desire to marry yet and, when I do, I foresee no problem. In this case it is, as so often, the woman who is weakest.'

Jessica nodded, surprised at his understanding. It seemed Gareth Morant could comprehend the difficulties of women more generally than just those applying to his friend Maude.

'Then in what way can I assist you?' The only possibility she could think of was that Lady Maude might require a companion to support her in this masquerade if Lord Pangbourne became even more difficult. It might even help to have another virtuous female voice echoing Maude's assumed shock and outrage.

'I would like you to be my mistress.'

The empty wine glass fell from her fingers and rolled away on the Oriental rug unregarded until it clinked against the table leg.

'*What?* Outrageous! What do you take me for?' Jessica sprang to her feet and took three strides away from the fireside before she swung round to face him, more words of righteous indignation trembling on her lips. And then it hit her—the memory of his mouth over hers, the heat and the smell and the feel of him. The long, hard body—

Furious and horrified at herself, Jessica shut her mouth with a snap as Gareth got slowly to his feet. 'A masquerade, Jessica. I am asking you to *pretend* to be my mistress.' His voice was steady, but there was a trace of colour across his cheekbones. 'I would not insult you by proposing anything else.'

'I… You… No, you would not. You made that clear last night. I beg your pardon; I seem to be more tired and less rational than I thought.' Jessica walked back to her chair and sat, her legs suddenly stiff and awkward. She knew why she had reacted with such vehemence: Mama, of course. But mostly it was because of her own guilty desires. Self-knowledge, an admirable trait she had always thought, did nothing to improve her mood.

'You must be tired.' Gareth sat again too, making the silver boot tassels swing as he crossed his long legs. Jessica found herself staring at them and dragged her eyes up to meet his somewhat rueful gaze. 'It is the shock of yesterday's experiences; you should not underestimate the effect such trauma has on the body and mind. And then you have spent the day without proper refreshment or rest. Not very sensible of you, Miss Gifford.'

'Then let us be sensible at all costs,' she retorted, taking a grip on her emotions. 'What, exactly, are you proposing, my…Gareth?'

He steepled his fingers and bent his head to touch the tips to his mouth as if collecting his thoughts, then he raised his head and looked at her steadily. *How changeable his eyes are. From the light grey of a cloudy sky to hard steel from moment to moment.*

'I believe the course of shocking Lord Pangbourne is the only way to reach a speedy resolution of this problem. But I am reluctant to involve a professional— actress or Cyprian—in our personal affairs. One places too much trust in their discretion and too much power in their hands should they choose to make mischief later: I cannot risk that with Maude. Nor, I find, can I contemplate some vulgar piece of play-acting.'

Gareth paused, marshalling his thoughts. 'I believe this wants more than simply my apparent misbehaviour with one of the *demi-monde*. A man of Pangbourne's generation considers that almost routine. The scenario I believe would be most effective is a flagrant dalliance with a lady on the thin edge between scandal and respectability. To have the maximum impact my liaison must be conducted under the noses of the *ton*, not merely observed at the theatre or in the park.'

'But who, then, do you want me to be?'

'A wicked widow.' Gareth smiled suddenly, and she found her own lips curving in response. She caught herself and pressed them tight together. 'A lady returned from abroad where her husband died. A lady on the fringes of respectability, yet with an entrée into London society as she searches for her next protector. And I am going to fall head over heels in my blatant pursuit of her favours.'

'I can see that that would, indeed, cause talk and scandalise Lord Pangbourne, especially if you insultingly ignored Lady Maude in the process,' Jessica agreed. 'But firstly you will need to secure an entrée for this impostor and secondly—look at me! Do I look like a glamorous and dangerous adventuress?'

As she spoke she gestured at the overmantel mirror that reflected the upper parts of their bodies as they sat before the fire. Her blonde hair was still neatly in its governess's braids and bands, its colour pretty, but, in its tight confinement, quite ordinary. Her gown was high at the neck, shrouding her figure that, while brisk walks and healthy eating might have kept neat, was by no means the voluptuous form she assumed such a siren as Gareth was describing would possess. And her deportment was that of a respectable professional woman—contained, controlled, immaculate, designed to be the very opposite of obvious.

'Not at the moment, I must agree.' That smile again, turning a well-looking man into one of dangerous appeal. 'You look charming and eminently respectable. But you forget, I know exactly what you look like without that drab gown and those neat braids.' He ignored her inarticulate sound of protest and her reddening cheeks and added, 'And you *could* look spectacular, Jessica. No, do not shake your head at me—it will take two things, the transformation of your wardrobe and your coiffure and for you to think like an adventuress, a woman on the edge, a dangerous, predatory, beautiful huntress.'

Despite everything Jessica's sense of humour got the better of her. She laughed at him, 'You think the church mouse can turn into the hunting cat, Gareth?'

'No, I think the fireside tabby can arch her back and flex her claws and become a tigress.'

She shook her head, unconvinced. There was no need to panic over his scandalous scheme—it would fall at the first hurdle, her inability to be the woman he was describing. She would humour him a little.

'And who are you going to prevail upon to let this dangerous female loose in a respectable setting?'

'My cousin Bel, who has recently remarried. She and Maude are both deeply involved in a charity to secure employment for soldiers returning from the wars. One of Maude's schemes to raise money for this cause is to hold a subscription ball, but as she is an unmarried girl the hostess issuing the invitations will be Bel, now Lady Dereham. Everyone who is anyone will be there, for they plan to make it one of the grand opening events of the Season—and that will include Lord Pangbourne.'

'And how, exactly, am I going to prevail upon the respectable Lady Dereham to invite me?'

'She would do it as a favour to me, but for the public explanation of the acquaintance we depend upon another cousin of mine, Bel's brother, Lord Sebastian Ravenhurst. He is married to Eva, the Grand Duchess of Maubourg.'

'But I read about that in the newspapers—it was a most romantic affair by all accounts!' The dashing Lord Sebastian had snatched the Grand Duchess from the claws of French agents and had smuggled her across France to arrive in Brussels on the day of the Battle of Waterloo. The Grand Duchess had been reunited with her son in London and returned to Maubourg with the young Grand Duke and the man she had fallen in love with on their perilous journey.

'It was, and there was considerably more romance to it than you would guess, even reading between the lines. However, for now I think we can agree that your late husband was employed in some manner by the Duchy. As an economic adviser perhaps? I will ask Eva's advice.'

'She is in England?' A few days ago Jessica had been attempting to instil the basics of Italian conversation and Mozart sonatas into the daughter of a baronet. Since then she had been kidnapped, flung herself naked into the arms of a man, escaped from a brothel and been kissed for the first time. Now, it appeared, she was to be thrust into proximity with minor royalty.

'She and Sebastian divide their time between his estates here—where she is Lady Sebastian Ravenhurst, a private citizen—and Maubourg where she is the Grand Duchess and Sebastian seems to have taken over as Minister for Agriculture, although I am not sure I entirely believe that. Fréderic, her son, is at school at Eton. Eva has decided she would like to do the London Season for a change, so they arrived last week and the Duke of Allington, Sebastian's brother, has loaned them the town house.'

And now dukes, Jessica thought faintly, then pulled herself together. She was never going to be the sultry temptress Gareth was deluded enough to imagine, but at least she could continue to apply common sense to this madcap scheme.

'And where am I going to live whilst I am scandalising London?'

'In Bel's house in Half Moon Street, which is currently empty while she decides whether to sell it, keep it or lease it out. You will appear to have purchased it.'

'Or perhaps the Grand Duchess has done so in recognition of my late husband's contribution to the Duchy?' She had meant to be faintly sarcastic, but Gareth nodded.

'Good idea.'

Jessica sat and regarded him, trying to convince herself she was not dreaming. Although whether this was a dream or a nightmare was debatable. 'I arrive, transformed by some miracle into a *femme fatale*. We conduct a very public, flagrant liaison, Lady Maude goes into a shocked decline, Lord Pangbourne cuts your acquaintance—and then what?'

'We keep it up for the Season.' *Three months of flirting—or worse—with Gareth? Oh, my God...*'And then you vanish off to Maubourg, seduced by one of Eva's court, perhaps, and I am left a sadder and wiser man. One who is, most obviously, unworthy of Templeton's ewe lamb.'

'And I return to seeking work as a governess, with no doubt some good explanation of what I have been doing for three months?'

Gareth dropped his hands and clasped them together, his eyes on her, searching, it seemed, for some insight into her thoughts. Jessica felt they should be more than obvious.

'Do you enjoy being a governess? No, let me rephrase that—do you have a dedication to education?' She shrugged. 'Why then do you seek employment in that way?'

'Because I wish to eat! And I find I am a good teacher.'

'You have no relatives?' he asked, frowning at her snappish tone.

'Yes—an aunt, cousins.' Jessica began to see the drift of his questions and produced her usual prevarication—it was not so very far from the truth in some ways. 'You wonder why I do not live with them? I do not chose to be beholden to anyone and dwindle into an unpaid companion, dependent on family charity for my very existence. I wish to be independent and to provide for my old age. I have no aptitude as a milliner or a dressmaker. There is very little money or security as a paid companion. But I do have skills that I can teach and I have chosen my employers with great care to enhance my references and my reputation.'

Gareth nodded as though she was confirming his own thoughts. 'So your long-term aim is for financial security and respectable independence?'

'Exactly.' It seemed she was getting through to him at last. 'And I can think of few things more damaging to that ambition than flaunting myself in London society as your mistress!'

'Certainly if you wish for further employment, I can quite see that.' He appeared unconscious of Jessica's frowning regard. 'Would I be accurate if I said that you would hope to reach the point one day where you could afford a small house in a charming village or market town with adequate funds to employ a small staff and perhaps own a gig? To be in the position where you had no need to work, but might, if you wished, take the occasional pupil for individual tuition in an instrument or a language?'

'You have painted a picture of my exact ambition.' The image of roses round the door, a cheerful maidservant bringing in a tea tray, an earnest child happily learning the piano, flickered before Jessica's gaze. 'And to achieve the half of that I need to work. Work hard for years,' she added.

'I am offering you work.' Gareth stood up and walked round the chair to lean his folded arms on its padded back while he watched her. 'I am asking you to take on an onerous acting job for three months and then I will give you the house and an annuity that will allow you to do just as you please.'

'But—'

'You think I am offering too high a price? I can assure you—'

'I think you are offering a very fair price for such an outrageous request,' she retorted robustly. 'Gareth— look at me. Do I look like a seductress? Do I seem to you to have any wiles, any aptitude for casting out lures? I have never flirted in my life, not even mildly. How do you expect me to learn?'

'I will teach you,' he said and the smile he sent her was pure, wicked, promise. 'I will teach you so well, Miss Gifford, that half the men in London will be at your feet and every lady in society will wish to scratch your eyes out.'

'No…I could not.' She had to be strong. It was impossible, she could never do this.

Gareth walked round and picked up her hand as it clasped the arm of her chair. His fingers were warm and his thumb brushed gently against the soft mound of flesh at the base of her thumb.

'What colour are the roses round the door in your dream house?' he asked her, his eyes intent and dark on her face.

'Red,' she murmured. And was lost.

Chapter Six

'How do you intend teaching me these arts of fascination?' Jessica rescued her hand from Gareth's grip and tried to make her voice as businesslike and brisk as possible. He sank back in his chair, recognising her capitulation and, she could only hope, not seeing the churning mix of terror and anticipation behind her question.

'It will be easier for you once you have your new hairstyle and your new clothes, I imagine. I will send a note around to my cousin Bel and ask her to call tomorrow and take you under her wing.'

'Will she agree?' Jessica wondered. 'It is a scandalous deception. She might well disapprove.' He had not answered her question, she noted. One faculty life as a governess taught you was to recognise evasion when you saw it. Lord Standon might not be a naughty eight-year-old with a toad in his pocket, but in her opinion all males of whatever age were that boy under the skin.

'Bel? I suspect not. She was first married to Lord Felsham, who was generally accounted to be the most boring man in the *ton*. When she was barely out of mourning she encountered Ashe Reynard, Viscount Dereham, who was just back from Waterloo. By all accounts it was a lively courtship. I have no idea of the details, but our highly respectable bluestocking of a cousin Miss Elinor Ravenhurst, who is a great friend of Bel's, blushes whenever she mentions Reynard.'

'It would be a relief if she does help us, because I do not feel we should involve Lady Maude in this.' Jessica waited, trying her best stare to see if Gareth was going to answer her question about her lessons in flirtation.

'I agree. Tell me, Jessica, why are you regarding me as though I have not finished my Latin exercises?'

'I am waiting for an answer to my question about how you intend to teach me—and I fear you may be evading one.'

'Very well. This is not something I have attempted before, believe me, but I will try. May I be frank?'

'Ye…s,' she responded, suspicious. His lordship was studying her closely. She felt uncomfortable meeting his gaze, but it was equally unnerving trying to find something innocuous to look at. Her immediate field of view seemed very full of large, disturbing, male. She settled upon his neckcloth and attempted to regard it tranquilly.

'You are a very contained person, are you not?' Startled, she nodded, the neckcloth and its intricate folds forgotten. 'You sit very still, you occupy your own space and do not intrude into that of other people. You communicate with your voice and with the force of your argument, not with touch, or teasing or cajoling.'

'Yes. That is appropriate to my role in life.' That stillness and self-control had been hard-won, but necessary.

'But not to your new one. You are to become a

creature of the senses—all five of them. You want to touch silks and skin. You want to taste champagne and kisses. Your eyes will long for luxury, your ears for flattery, you will want to move within clouds of scent from lavish flowers and from exotic perfume. You will talk with your hands, with your eyes, with your laughter. Instinct will appear to dominate over thought.'

'Appear?' She felt breathless, her mind reeling from thoughts of silk, skin, kisses, perfume.

'Underneath you will be thinking very hard indeed, because you will be acting, and the woman you are portraying will be thinking hard too. She is not a heedless flirt, she is a determined adventuress.' He leaned forward, his forearms on his knees. 'Unless we can release the inner hedonist in you.'

'I am not sure I have one,' Jessica confessed. Hedonism required money, time and self-indulgence. The first two she could not afford, the third she dare not permit. Until now.

'In that case we will take one sense at a time and work on it. Which shall we start with? Not taste, for you have just had your supper, and not smell, because this fire seems intent on smoking. I shall have to think about hearing a little. Sight—or touch, Jessica?'

'You choose.' She threw the question back as fast as if this were a ball game and the ball red hot.

'Oh, no. You must also learn to be demanding and capricious. You will always be the one to choose, whatever the question.'

Sight sounded safest. It was probably the one he expected her to say. 'Touch,' she decided, her eyes meeting his defiantly.

* * *

He had been sure she would decide upon sight, an apparently safe sense, although he was having ideas about that. Inwardly Gareth gave Miss Gifford points for courage.

'Close your eyes.' She stiffened immediately, her fingers curling tight around the arms of the chair. 'Do you not trust me, Jessica? We are not going to get very far with this if you do not.'

Clear green eyes looked into his. For long seconds he watched her thinking. 'Yes,' she decided finally, her mouth quirking into a rueful smile. 'Although quite what I trust you to do I am not certain.' The long lashes that contrasted so piquantly with her tightly bound hair lowered, feathering her cheeks and she waited, blind, outwardly tranquil. Except for her death grip on the leather arms.

'Stroke the arms of the chair,' Gareth said, keeping his voice low. A frown line appeared between her brows, then she nodded and relaxed her fingers. 'Tell me what you feel.'

'It is smooth, warm from where my hands have been.' She felt further down. 'Cool here. It feels strong. Somehow I can tell it is thick.' He waited while she explored further. 'It is smoother here, where hands have rubbed; I can feel the grain lower down.'

Gareth felt in his pocket and pulled out the clean linen handkerchief his valet had placed there that morning. On the table beside him was a sample of heavy silk Maude had forgotten last time she had sat in this room. He leaned over and dropped both pieces of fabric into Jessica's lap. 'And these?'

She scooped them up in her cupped hands and rubbed with thumb and forefinger, then bent her head to bury her face in them. 'That is cheating,' Gareth said mildly and she raised her head and smiled in the direction of his voice.

'Very well.' She dropped the silk into her lap and concentrated on touching the linen. 'Expensive, very fine Irish linen. I imagine one could see through it. But a strong, masculine feel.' Her fingers found the whitework monogram in the corner and rubbed gently. 'Excellent work.'

'And the other?' He found he could not take his eyes off her face.

'The silk? Beautiful. A dress weight, expensive again. I imagine it is coloured, although I have no idea why.' She ran it through her fingers and sighed. 'It is alive.'

'Which would you prefer to wear?' Gareth asked. Jessica frowned. She was thinking too much still, not feeling. 'Next to your skin?' he added outrageously, intent on shocking an instinctive reaction out of her.

Jessica gave a little gasp at his effrontery, but answered, as he had hoped, without reflection. 'The silk. Utterly impractical, but like bathing in warm oil. See how it slides and slithers.' Eyes still closed, she held it out to him and he took it, warm from her hands, and let it slip through his fingers. It was no longer possible, for some reason, to sit still. Gareth got to his feet, standing in front of the chair so close their toes nearly touched.

'Will you stand up, Jessica?'

Obedient, she did as he asked. 'You are standing very near.' It was a matter-of-fact observation but he could sense the reserve behind it.

'How can you tell?'

'Your voice. And I can feel your—' She swallowed, making the chaste muslin fichu veiling her throat move. 'Your heat.'

Heat? Gareth felt suddenly as though he was burning up, the colour in his cheeks as high as that on Jessica's. He dragged air down into his lungs and kept his voice steady. 'Touch me.' It might have been steady—he could do nothing about the huskiness.

'What!' Her eyes flew open and she took a half-step back until the edge of the chair hit the back of her knees.

'Jessica, I am not asking you to make love to me…'

'Good!' She looked deliciously flustered.

'But the new you is going to touch men all the time,' Gareth explained, in haste before one of Miss Gifford's clenched hands found his ear. 'It will be part of your charm, one of your weapons. The slightest, fleeting touches. A caress with your fingertips on a sleeve, a flick to remove an imaginary piece of lint from a lapel, a handshake held just a fraction too long. You must be completely relaxed touching a man.'

'I see.' She narrowed her eyes at him, still suspicious. 'I think.'

'You think too much Jessica, just feel.'

'Hmm.' She put her head on one side, reminding him irresistibly of an inquisitive robin who has just spotted a worm. 'Like this?' She reached up and brushed her fingertips across his lapel, her movement wafting a faint scent of Castile soap and warm woman to his nostrils.

'Yes. Just like that. Now, find some other ways.'

There was a glint of mischief in her eyes now and she caught her lower lip in her teeth for a moment. The heat flooded Gareth again, this time sharply focused in his groin. If his reaction to an inexpert touch from Miss Gifford, dressed like a governess, was this, what effect was she going to have in her new guise?

'I need to find excuses to touch, and they should be so brief that the man concerned will not know if they are an accident, an impulse—or a message. An invitation, even.' She nodded to herself, then, smiling, raised her hand and brought it up to pat her fichu into order, managing as she did so to brush the back of her fingers against his. The tingle reached right up his arm. 'Like that?'

'Perfect, Jessica.'

'But I need to hold your eyes as I do it, I think, to make you even more unsure of my intentions. You must not know whether I meant to touch you or not.' The limpid green gaze held nothing but the faintest question and then she was smiling again, a polite social smile.

'Excellent,' Gareth managed, wondering what the hell was wrong with him. True, he had spent a decidedly fraught twenty-four hours, but that was no excuse for feeling like a randy eighteen-year-old simply because he was toe to toe with a buttoned-up governess.

'Oh!' She was peering up at him now. 'My lord, I do believe there is a money spider in your hair.' Jessica stood on tiptoe, reached and flicked lightly at the side of his head, her fingers just skimming his temple before they ruffled into his hair. This time the tingle went straight down to the base of his spine with predictable results. 'There.' She held up slender fingers for him to see the tiny red dot that was swinging from them. 'What luck for me.'

There was a faint ink mark on her forefinger. It would

need work with a pumice stone—seductresses did not have ink blots. Jessica blew softly and the red dot landed on his lapel and vanished into his neck cloth. *This one does...* 'You gave it back.'

'We can share it—I expect we are going to need all the luck we can get to pull this off.'

'You have not changed your mind?'

The half-hidden seductress vanished to be replaced with the governess, her expression severe. 'I said I would do it—I do not go back on my word.'

'No.' Gareth studied her straight back, raised chin, determined expression. 'I can see that.'

'My lord. Her Ser...' There was a muffled exchange from the hall. 'I beg your pardon, Lady Sebastian Ravenhurst and Lady Dereham are here. I explained that you were at breakfast, my lord, but—'

'Show them in, Jordan, bring more cups.' Resigned to yet another turbulent breakfast Gareth pushed back his chair and got to his feet as his cousin Bel and her sister-in-law Eva, Grand Duchess of Maubourg, swept into the room in a flurry of flounces. At the other end of the table Jessica stood too, schooling her knees not to knock together. These two elegant, assured, sophisticated matrons would take one look at her and laugh Gareth's plan to scorn.

'Gareth, we came at once, Maude said things have reached a crisis.'

'Thank you, Bel.'

So that would be his cousin, Lady Dereham. A tall brunette, she kissed him on the cheek, and stood aside to make room for an equally tall, rather more statuesque brunette whose deportment could have been used as a model of perfection. The Grand Duchess.

'Gareth, you poor man. Lord Pangbourne appears to have become quite irrational, even allowing for Maude's tendency for the dramatic.' Her English accent was perfect, her gaze direct. 'Your message was cryptic, but we will do our very best to help.'

'Then allow me to introduce Miss Gifford, who has agreed to play the critical role in this scheme.' Both ladies turned and Jessica sank down into her best court curtsy. She knew how to do it in theory, but she had never had to do it in practice. It was murder on the thigh muscles, she discovered, rising with relief as the Grand Duchess stepped forward and caught her hand in her own kid-encased one.

'Your Serene Highness…'

'Lady Sebastian, please. Except for court appearances, I do not use my title outside the Duchy. Miss Gifford…' she looked at her, a smile lighting up her face, '…you poor thing—what theatricals have Maude and Gareth prevailed upon you to join?'

'Good morning Miss Gifford.' Lady Dereham came to shake hands, then sank down on a dining chair and peeled off her gloves. 'Yes, we insist upon knowing all the details at once.' She lifted the silver pot before her. 'I fear we will need sustaining with considerably more coffee.'

'Templeton has become fixed in his intention to carry out the exceedingly mawkish scheme he cooked up with my esteemed parent and marry off Maude and myself.'

'Not so mawkish if you consider the land holdings,' Lady Dereham observed, stirring sugar into her cup.

'Templeton's no fool—he is dangling an estate almost the size of your own before you.'

'Quite. How can I refuse? That is the problem. He has decided I am perfect for Maude—but it is obvious that even he would draw the line at marrying her off to a libertine. Or, at least, to one who created a public scandal. He has a strange way of showing it, but he is fond of Maude and would not want her to be hurt by her husband's public infidelities.'

'His private ones would, no doubt, be of no account,' Lady Sebastian remarked wryly. A flicker of memory came back to Jessica—Lady Sebastian's first husband, the Grand Duke, had been a notorious rake, leaving a trail of highly visible liaisons across Europe.

'Exactly. I, therefore, must become not just a rake, but a very public philanderer.' Gareth reapplied himself to his sirloin, then looked up to find three pairs of eyes fixed upon him, sighed and put down his knife and fork. 'Our intention is that Jessica, who is the widow of a gentleman who performed some service for the Duchy…' he raised an eyebrow at Lady Sebastian, who nodded '…has returned to London to re-establish her life. Bel has leased her the Half Moon Street house as a favour to Eva and will introduce her to society at Maude's charity ball. Jessica, it will soon become apparent, is an adventuress at whose feet any number of gentlemen are about to prostrate themselves.'

Jessica could almost feel the effort it took the two ladies not to turn and look at her in disbelief. 'I,' Gareth concluded, 'will make a complete cake of myself over her, conduct a flaming *affaire* in the full glare of the Season and Templeton will cast me off.'

'I see,' Lady Dereham said with what Jessica regarded as almost supernatural calm. Suddenly she could see the family relationship between them—Lady Belinda was exhibiting the same calm as she had seen in Gareth in the brothel. A sort of watchful stillness. 'And our role—other than providing an *entrée* for Miss Gifford—is to be what exactly?'

'I am very much afraid that Lord Standon expects you to transform me into a dashing adventuress,' Jessica said, bracing herself for the polite laughter that must surely follow. 'A glamorous siren,' she added, heaping on the improbabilities.

Both ladies did turn at that, fine dark eyes under arched brows and amused grey ones regarded her. Neither woman laughed. They must feel it was past a joke to achieve such a task.

'Oh, yes,' Lady Dereham said. 'Hair first, don't you agree, Eva? And then see what suggests itself once we know what colour we are working with?'

'Monsieur Antoine.' Lady Sebastian nodded. 'Gareth, would you be so good as to ring for Jordan, I must send a note immediately.'

'You think it is not impossible?' Jessica shook her head. Not only did she have to appear stylish enough to be seen with leaders of the *ton* such as these, but in addition she must seem alluring and dangerous.

'I think Gareth is showing remarkable insight,' his cousin said with a mocking smile in his direction. 'Lord Fellingham was saying to me just the other day that Gareth seemed jaded; one can only be relieved that he is not so bored that he missed this opportunity.'

'Fellingham is an ass,' Gareth retorted, pushing his

plate away and reaching for the toast. 'Bored? I have estates to run, a speech to write for the House, that damned orphans' charity Maude nagged me into chairing…'

'You enjoy it, you know you do. If you did not, why did you invite them all down to Hetherington in the summer and teach the boys to play cricket?'

Gareth grimaced. 'Smashed half the glass in the succession houses, young hellions.'

'So did you when you and Sebastian were boys,' Lady Dereham retorted. 'You don't fool me, Gareth Morant—you are working hard for those orphans, and you enjoy it. But being busy does not preclude becoming jaded; this will do you a power of good.'

'We are doing this to rescue Maude from an impossible situation, not me from the *ennui* of my duties. Ah, Jordan, Lady Sebastian wishes to have a message delivered.' The butler bowed his way out with instructions to deliver the hairdresser on Lady Sebastian's doorstep in an hour equipped with sufficient tools of his trade to create a transformation. *What if he is not free?* Jessica wondered, then smiled at her naïvety. Not free for a Grand Duchess, the sister-in-law of a duke?

Jessica sat, eating her breakfast in the unobtrusively quiet manner life as a paid dependent in numerous households had taught her, and watched with the focus she would have applied to learning a new instrument.

She watched the unselfconscious grace and command of the two women, she listened to the freedom with which they conversed and the lightness with which they teased Gareth. And she allowed her eyes to feast on their clothes, on carriage dresses in the very latest stare, crafted from fabrics of quiet luxury, trimmed with exquisite detail. She looked longingly at the smart gloves, tossed carelessly to one side, the thickness of the grosgrain bonnet ribbons, the pretty clasps on the reticules. How could she even learn to treat such luxury with nonchalance, let alone seduce men to her side while she did it?

'What name will you be using?' Lady Dereham asked, cutting across her increasingly alarming thoughts.

'Name?' On top of everything else she had to lose her identity as well, it seemed. Her mind went blank.

'Francesca Carleton,' Gareth said. Three women looked at him in enquiry. He shrugged. 'It just came to me.'

'Well…' Lady Sebastian got to her feet, gathering up her possessions '…in that case it is time for Mrs Carleton to come with us.' She paused on the threshold, waiting while Gareth came round the table to open the door for her. 'Be prepared for a surprise, Gareth.' As she looked at Jessica her eyes twinkled in a smile of pure naughtiness. 'We are going to have so much fun.'

Chapter Seven

❦

Jessica sat in the closed carriage and tried not to look anxious under the combined scrutiny of the ladies opposite.

'How on earth did you become entangled in this madcap scheme?' Lady Dereham enquired, in much the same tone as she might have used to enquire whether Jessica had enjoyed a concert.

'Lord Standon rescued me from a brothel.' Lady Sebastian opened her mouth, then closed it again without speaking. It seemed there was something that would shake their *sang froid* after all. 'I am a governess.'

'I rather thought you might be.' Lady Dereham nodded.

'I was kidnapped when I arrived on the stage and taken to the brothel.' She shivered—repeating the story did not make it any less horrible. 'Gareth—Lord Standon— rescued me. Before anything too awful happened,' she added hastily. She did not feel up to explaining that she had careered down the corridor stark naked, observed two orgies and had escaped slung over Gareth's shoulder while wearing Lord Fellingham's pantaloons.

'What was Gareth doing in such a place?' Lady Sebastian enquired, interested. 'No, do not tell me, I can imagine.'

'Nothing, actually.' Jessica felt bound to defend him. 'He was accompanying Lord Fellingham and Lord Rotherham, but he was rather cross and bored by it, I think.'

'But how did you go from your rescue—for which we must be profoundly grateful—to this?' Lady Dereham was looking understandably puzzled. You did not know Gareth before, did you?'

'Like all the men of your family, Bel dear, Gareth is nothing if not ingenious.' Lady Sebastian's smile was one of pleasurable reminiscence. Jessica remembered the circumstances of the Grand Duchess's unconventional romance. 'I presume Miss Gifford is unknown in London, is presently unemployed and, being a young lady of intelligence and integrity, is a much safer partner in this deception than one of her frailer sisters.'

Jessica nodded. 'You are quite right, Lady Sebastian. Gareth, er…Lord—'

'Call him Gareth,' Lady Dereham interjected. 'And I am Bel and this is Eva. We are all going to become very good friends before this is out, I should imagine.'

Jessica cast a dubious glance at the Grand Duchess, who smiled her wicked smile again. 'Eva,' she confirmed. 'Now, you were saying, Jessica?'

'Gareth is concerned that Lady Maude is not implicated in this, in case it goes wrong, and he was also anxious not to involve anyone who might be less than discreet.'

'And what is to become of you when this is all over?'

Bel enquired. 'I imagine that reverting to being a governess again—unless in the Scottish Highlands—might be somewhat dangerous.'

'I receive a cottage and a pension.' Jessica braced herself for some critical comment about such largesse, but none came.

'Very reasonable,' was all Bel said. 'You will enjoy that better than being at the beck and call of some demanding employer and their obnoxious brats, I dare say.'

'Not all brats are obnoxious,' Eva remarked. 'My son, naturally, is an angel.' Somehow, if he took after his mother, Jessica doubted it. 'As will yours be, I am sure,' she added with a sly sideways and downwards glance at Lady Dereham's waistline.

'Eva! How did you know?' Bel laid one hand protectively over her flat stomach.

'When I saw Reynard last night he was looking stunned—I recognise the symptoms of a man coming to terms with incipient fatherhood—and you are looking a trifle pale.' Eva smiled, 'However, I suspect mine will be born first.'

'You, too? Eva, how wonderful!' The two embraced while Jessica sat in tactful silence through a confusing exchange about what Freddie would make of it, how insufferably smug Jack was, dates and something about sea air that made Bel blush.

'Jessica, I am sorry.' Eva turned to her, her cheeks flushed, her expression apologetic. 'We are neglecting you.'

'Not at all. May I offer my congratulations to you both?'

'Thank you. Oh, look, we're here. Borrow this and

use the veil.' Eva whipped off her bonnet and placed it on Jessica's head.

The door was opened, the steps let down and Jessica found herself in a wide hallway, confronting a man whom she supposed from his clothing must be the butler. With his brawny frame and broken nose he appeared to have been recruited from the prize-fighting ring. Perhaps the Grand Duchess employed him as a bodyguard as well.

'Grimstone, is his lordship at home?'

'No, my lady. I understand Lord Sebastian is at his club.'

'Excellent. This is Miss Gifford, Grimstone. You have not set eyes on her, nor have you ever heard of her.'

The butler gazed at a point somewhere over Jessica's head without a flicker of expression. 'Monsieur Antoine is in your dressing room, my lady.'

Jessica regarded the room and its occupants with some trepidation. A large dressing table draped in net supported a wide mirror and an elaborate silver-mounted vanity set. Next to it was a wash stand with ewer and basin and, standing waiting before it, was a slender, intense-looking man in a black suit, a languid-looking youth and a woman she guessed was Lady Sebastian's dresser.

She tried not to stare about her at the array of gowns draped over chairs or hanging from the blue brocade screen in the corner. Hat boxes teetered in a pile and gloves spilled out of their packaging. Bel was not so reticent.

'Eva, you must have bought out every shop in town!' She picked up a gauze scarf and ran it through her fingers.

The Grand Duchess laughed, shedding her furs and

gloves into the hands of her silent dresser. 'Thank you, Veronique. But of course I have been shopping—I haven't been to Paris yet this year. One must dress, my dear! Ah, Monsieur Antoine.'

'Your Serene Highness.' Eva did not correct him and from the elaborate flourish of his bow Jessica guessed he would have been mortified if he been unable to extract every drop of enjoyment from his contact with royalty. 'In what way may I serve you?'

'This lady, who as you see has naturally a most modest and elegant style…' *Elegant?* '…has, for reasons which I cannot reveal, to appear in society in quite another guise. Naturally, this matter requires the utmost discretion. I trust I may rely upon you?'

'A matter of state!' Eva did not disabuse the coiffeur of this useful notion. 'Our lips are sealed, your Serene Highness. May I enquire in what way *madame* should be transformed?'

'Into a lady of some…experience. A lady who will be invited to the very best parties, naturally, but one who will be *popular* with the gentlemen, shall we say?'

'I comprehend entirely, ma'am. Dashing, a little dangerous, perhaps? A lady of powerful attraction.'

'Precisely,' Bel said, perching on a stool and untying her bonnet. 'Dangerous.'

The hairdresser advanced upon Jessica with finicking small steps, his head on first one side, then the other. She tried to look experienced, dashing and dangerous and knew she was failing comprehensively to look anything but a governess out of her depth. It was an effort of will not to shift from one foot to the other under the intensity of his stare.

'If *madame* will kindly shed her pelisse and bonnet and sit here.' He gestured to a stool set before the dressing table. The dresser darted forward, removing the items and taking Jessica's gloves. Feeling as though she was going to the dentist, Jessica sat.

'Remove the pins!' The acolyte darted forward and began to deconstruct the tight, careful coiffure pin by pin, then combed out the braids. Her hair, blonde, waving and long enough to reach to her elbows, fell about her shoulders. 'Hmm.' Monsieur Antoine picked up a strand, rubbed it between his fingers, peered closely at it, then dropped it dismissively. 'A natural, most English blonde.' That did not appear to be a recommendation. Jessica seemed to recall hearing somewhere that blondes were out of fashion.

'It is a very pretty colour,' Bel said supportively.

'But not dangerous,' Monsieur Antoine pointed out incontrovertibly, beginning to prowl again. 'Not dashing.' He came close and stared into Jessica's eyes as she blinked back. 'Gold, that is what is needed, with just a hint of red.'

'Won't that be a touch brassy?' Anxious, Jessica frowned into the mirror at her pale skin and long— but blonde—lashes. What would she look like with brassy hair?

'Brassy? *Brassy?* Madame, remember, I am an *artiste*! We speak here of guineas, of glow, of subtle excitement. Of *élan*, panache!' He scowled, perhaps daunted by the reality in front of him, then made a recover. 'And curls. This demands curls. The scissors, *Albert*.'

'You are not going to cut it?' Jessica grabbed handfuls defensively.

'But of course; as it is it is impossible—the hair of a governess.' He stood poised, the scissors in hand, having delivered what was apparently the ultimate insult. 'I assume *madame* has come from the Continent…'

'I have?'

'She has,' Eva confirmed. 'The very latest French style, if you please, *monsieur*. It will grow again,' she pointed out to Jessica.

'Oh, very well.' Jessica released her grip and clasped her hands in her lap. Curls and gold it was. In for a penny, in for a…guinea. At least it should soon be over.

Two hours of snipping, washing, soaking in strange substances, more washing, combing, the application of a thick red paste, rinsing, drying and curling later, Jessica stared dumbfounded into the mirror again.

A mass of shiny guinea-gold curls framed her face in an outrageously flattering manner. The curls were short enough to cluster naturally, except at the back where they were half-teased down into flirty ringlets on her shoulder and half-pinned up to give some mass to the coiffure. The wide-eyed woman looking back must be her—after all, the eyes were green, although they looked darker and more intense than she remembered, the mouth was the same, although now it was parted in a gasp of surprise and the plain blue gown was certainly the one she had arrived in.

'Oh,' said Jessica. 'That is me?'

'It most certainly is,' Eva said with satisfaction. 'A most excellent result, *Monsieur* Antoine, exactly what I had hoped for. You will call upon *madame* daily once she is established and you will maintain this look, with appropriate variations depending on her social diary.'

The hairdresser and his assistant bowed themselves out, leaving two satisfied ladies and one stunned one behind them.

'Now,' said Bel with resolution. 'Now we shop.'

'After luncheon,' Eva said firmly, walking Jessica to the door. 'When we have made lists.'

'But who is going to pay for all this?' Jessica protested, waving a hand in a gesture that encompassed the pile of parcels and hat boxes that surrounded the three of them and the even larger list of items that would arrive from the workshops of the *modistes* and milliners they had spent the afternoon visiting. It might well be vulgar to mention money, but someone had to—Bel and Eva appeared oblivious to the amount that was slipping through their prettily gloved fingers.

'Gareth is,' Bel said. 'Now don't frown, Jessica—sorry, *Francesca*. We really must become used to calling you that or we will make slips later. He can well afford it and, if this is to be done, it must be done properly or no one will believe it. And these things are not so very extravagant, just suitable to your supposed background. Here we are, your new home.'

Jessica peered out and her wavering spirits rose at the sight of the neat narrow house with its black brick and shining door knocker and the pair of clipped bay trees by the green front door. Her own house, even if it were only for a few weeks. Somewhere that was all hers, not a plain room in someone else's house where she was regarded as barely above a servant and entered a reception room on sufferance. However difficult this task she had accepted was going to be, at least there would be a safe haven to retreat to at the end of each day.

'I have left it fully furnished,' Bel was saying as they climbed the steps and the door swung open. 'And I will leave Mr and Mrs Hedges and the rest of the staff to look after you. Good afternoon, Hedges, this is Mrs Carleton. I hope you received my note this morning and everything is ready for her?'

'Yes, my lady.' This butler was cut from a very different cloth than Lady Sebastian's ex-pugilist, but his expression as he regarded the incongruous figure before him with the dashing hairstyle and the governess's clothes was a masterpiece of tact. 'Mrs Carleton, ma'am. Mrs Hedges has prepared your room.'

'Thank you, Hedges.' Jessica had long since learned not to show that she was intimidated by superior butlers, but now she hesitated. If this really was her house now… She glanced at Bel, who gave a slight nod of encouragement. 'Could you bring tea to the drawing room, please?'

'At once, ma'am.' He moved to throw open a door and Jessica smiled, inclined her head and swept through it. *Goodness*, she thought faintly, *that worked*.

'I have left all my staff in place here except for my dresser, and that is going to be an important position under the circumstances.' Bel sank into a chair and put her feet up on a beadwork footstool. 'Ooh, why is shopping so tiring?' She did not wait for an answer, her brow clearing as an idea seemed to strike her. 'I wonder if Lady Catchpole's dresser has found a new employer.'

'Lady Catchpole?' Eva frowned. 'I do not know her.'

'She was Rosa Delagarde, one of the leading lights of the stage for the past three years, but she caught herself a baron and they married last week. Now, knowing George Catchpole, he might have married an actress, but he is going to want a command performance as a lady from her in future. I would not be at all surprised if he will insist on a starched-up dresser of the highest respectability.' She got up and went to the French writing desk at the side of the room and drew out some paper. 'I will write at once. *La Delagarde* was always turned out in the most dashing style—just what we need.'

'But would she be discreet?' Jessica wondered.

'There was never any gossip about the Catchpole romance before the announcement, and that would have made her dresser some good money if it had been leaked to the scandal sheets.' Bel folded the note, stuck on a wafer and addressed it as Hedges brought in the tea tray. 'Hedges, please see this is delivered as soon as possible.'

They sipped tea in companionable silence for a while. Jessica had no idea what was passing through the minds of her two companions, but her own thoughts were a muddle of impressions, worries and, lurking under everything else, excitement.

I am taking tea with a countess and a Grand Duchess, I have been shopping in the most exclusive shops in London and I am about to embark upon a Season of scandal with a man who has a completely reprehensible effect on my pulse rate.

'Can you dance?' Bel asked, cutting across Jessica's ruminations on just how Gareth Morant made her feel and how shocking it was that he should have such an effect.

'Yes. In theory,' she added with scrupulous honesty.

'I have taught all the country dances and so forth, but I have never waltzed, nor have I danced a cotillion.'

'A dancing master, then?' Eva reached for her reticule and extracted her note tablets. 'Another list is called for, I can see.'

At least, Jessica consoled herself as she surrendered to having her life, her appearance and her wardrobe organised, she would be able to spend this evening in peace and quiet reflection.

The door opened and Hedges coughed. The ladies turned to regard him. 'Lord Standon has sent to say that he hopes it will be acceptable if he joins you for dinner tonight, Mrs Carleton.'

Jessica realised with a start that he was speaking to her. 'Where?'

'Here, ma'am. He has sent Mrs Hedges instructions for a detailed menu.'

'Has he, indeed?' Jessica meant to sound sarcastic, but the butler merely inclined his head.

'Yes, ma'am. Mrs Hedges has sent the footman out with a shopping list now.'

No one appeared to think that she might refuse this suggestion. Or was it an order?

'And how many people is his lordship intending that I entertain to dinner this evening?'

'I understood from the note that it was to be a private occasion, ma'am.' Hedges bowed himself out.

'He is impossible!'

'Hedges? But I always found him—'

'Gareth. Impossible. What on earth are the staff to conclude from him inviting himself here for a dinner *à deux*? That we are lovers?' Bel and Eva both smiled and

Jessica felt the colour rising up her cheeks. 'Whatever he wants people to think for the purposes of this masquerade, I have no intention—'

'Of course not,' Bel soothed. 'I will have a quiet word with Hedges. He and Mrs Hedges already understand that you are helping Gareth with a tricky family problem.'

'Thank you.' Jessica brought her agitation under control with an effort. If she was going to make a public spectacle of herself with Gareth Morant, it might seem out of proportion to worry about what the servants thought, but she had to live with them for several weeks and the prospect of reading contempt or condemnation in their eyes was not easy to bear.

'What are you going to wear?' Eva put down her tea cup and looked thoughtful. 'What a pity so many of your gowns will take several days and we only have the ones we bought ready made.'

'Well, obviously I will dress for dinner, but would Gareth expect me to make a special effort?'

'I imagine that Gareth is intending to teach you the arts of dinner-table flirtation,' Bel observed.

'And remember,' Eva interjected, 'Francesca Carleton *always* makes an effort. She would not be seen outside her bedchamber less than exquisitely gowned and coiffed and with a subtle use of maquillage. Or in it, come to that,' she added, 'if she has a companion.'

That is not *going to arise,* Jessica reassured herself. *The only man I will appear to encourage is Gareth and he will not want to enter my bedchamber in any case.* After all, he had kissed her only to satisfy his curiosity and he had already seen her, stark naked and covered in goose bumps. There was no erotic mystery there. Thank goodness.

'From now on you will never appear except in character, although you will not be ready to burst upon society until Maude's ball in three weeks' time. Meanwhile, you must practise with us, with Gareth and with your new dresser until your image and your story is perfected.' Eva's smile held sympathy as well as kindness. 'I do not expect you have ever been encouraged to be thoroughly selfish, have you?'

'I have not had that luxury,' Jessica confessed. 'I have been earning my own living in a way that does not allow for mistakes or self-indulgence. Common sense, practicality and self-control are my talents.'

'But Miss Jessica Gifford, superior governess, is an act too, is she not?' Eva turned her dark, intelligent eyes on Jessica. 'It is an act you have worked on and perfected, but it is not you. What were you before you made that decision, chose that path, I wonder? If you could subdue your real self to become her, you can free something of you to become Francesca.'

Bel, nibbling on a macaroon with a faraway look on her face, was not listening. 'The pale green silk,' she pronounced. 'It needs taking in, but with a sash it will be perfect for this evening.'

'Yes, thank you.' Jessica turned, eager for the distraction from Eva's disconcerting theory. Was there really something in her of the wanton, daring creature she needed to portray?

Mama... Wide green eyes peeping provocatively over the edge of a fan, the soft teasing voice that could charm birds out of trees, the careless shrug of her shoulders when Jessica, aged thirteen, had worried about the rent being in arrears yet again.

'Oh, I'll go and smile at Mr Gilroy, darling,' she would say. 'He'll give us another week.'

Jessica had vowed she would never be in a position where keeping the roof over her head relied on her ability to smile at a man until she turned him into a fool. But then, Jessica had never had one-tenth of her mother's natural charm, so she had believed. Or had Miss Miranda Trevor, banker's daughter, learned those arts out of sheer necessity when she had run away with Captain the Honourable James Gifford and found herself living the life of a gambler's wife?

'Shall we help you change before we go?' Bel offered and the disturbing thoughts vanished, obscured by the immediate worry of what Gareth Morant, Lord Standon, was going to make of her first steps in the shoes of Mrs Francesca Carleton.

Chapter Eight

Gareth mounted the steps to Jessica's new front door with an anticipation that surprised him. He already knew that he enjoyed her company but the necessity for this masquerade was a tiresome interruption to his life and he should be resenting it. He paused, his hand on the knocker, examining his feelings.

He was not resentful, he was not even vaguely irritated. He was stimulated and he rather thought he was going to be amused. Was Rotherham right? Had he become bored and jaded with the round of careless pleasures and unavoidable duties?

The door opened and he let go of the cast metal with a thud.

'Good evening, my lord.' Hedges regarded him benevolently. Gareth decided that the staff must approve of their new, temporary, mistress. 'Mrs Hedges has followed your instructions for dinner to the letter, my lord.'

'Excellent.' Gareth shed his heavy coat and handed the footman his hat, cane and gloves. He did not know whether Jessica would have the gowns to enable her to dress for dinner yet, but he had done the occasion justice with silk knee breeches, striped stockings and his newest swallowtail coat.

'Lord Standon, madam.' Hedges threw open the drawing-room door and Gareth walked through.

'My lord.' A slender lady in pale almond green silk rose from the fireside and dropped a slight curtsy. 'A most inclement evening, is it not? I do hope you did not become chilled.'

Gareth returned the courtesy with a bow, unable to repress the smile that curved his mouth. It was Jessica, but not the Jessica who had left his house that morning, wide-eyed and in the more than capable grasp of his cousin and Sebastian's new wife.

'Mrs Carleton. It is indeed very raw out, but I took the precaution of wearing a heavy coat.'

The door closed softly behind him as he walked to the fireside. 'Please, do sit.' She extended a hand as though to show him which chair to take, pale fingers emerging from the tight ecru lace sleeves, and the tips just brushed his knuckles.

So, she had remembered one lesson from the night before. Gareth said nothing, but caught and held her gaze for a long moment as they both sat. The colour rose, charmingly, under her skin, then she laughed. 'Oh dear, I am afraid I simply cannot control my blushes.'

'They are charming,' he said, meaning it. Her hair was astonishing, the soft curls opening up her face and taking at least two years from her appearance. The severity and the attempt to look older had been deliberate, he was sure; now Jessica was the most intriguing mixture of sophistication and innocence.

'What is it?' she asked, her eyes narrowing at him. All of a sudden she was the governess again and he reminded himself that she was neither the innocent nor the sophisticate. Jessica was a respectable, intelligent woman who was making her own place in the world and had been managing that very well until the rotten underbelly of polite society had ensnared her.

'I was admiring your hair,' he said, with partial honesty. 'It is delightful—exactly the look I think we should aim at, yet it is still you.'

'I am not certain about the colour.' Gareth found himself watching the play of expression on her face: the frown as she worried about the colour, the look of rueful acceptance that it was suitable for their masquerade and then the amusement at her own doubts banishing the seriousness from her eyes. 'I know it is exactly right for our purposes. I will get used to it and it will wash out in time.'

'I like the style. You will keep that, will you not? Afterwards?' He wondered if there was any length left in it—the back was elegantly pinned up provoking an inconvenient fantasy of unpinning it.

'Perhaps.' She was silent while he wondered whether a comment on the gown she was wearing might push her from frankness into reticence. She was wearing a fine lace fichu around her shoulders. Was the subtle glimpse of flesh through the lace deliberate or modesty? He decided to keep silent on the subject, although he was admiring the effect of softly draped silk on a form he was only too aware was sweetly rounded and warm.

The memory of the sensual shock as she had hurtled into his arms in the brothel came to him with almost painful intensity and he crossed his legs, trying not to think about the lovely elegance of the line from shoulder to the swell of her hip. He was quite certain that Jessica had not the slightest idea of how beautiful her body was.

And why should she? She is inexperienced and respectable, he reminded himself sternly. He was here for one reason only, and that was to equip her for the role she was to play. And it *was* a role, not reality.

'Did you enjoy your shopping expedition?'

'Very much. Your cousins are so kind. But it is not real,' she added, echoing his thought. 'I cannot believe that it is me, sitting in all those fashionable shops, being waited upon, making decisions, choosing between ribbons for my slippers as though I have a dozen pairs already and can toss them aside the moment they show wear.'

Gareth thought of telling her that she must keep all the clothes and accessories they bought for the deception, then caught himself in time. Jessica had accepted payment for what she was doing because she was a professional woman and knew she was worth her hire. But he guessed she might have a very different reaction to accepting fine clothes and fripperies—they were too close to the presents a true courtesan would expect.

She was restful to be with, sitting there with her clasped hands, her eyes resting on him as though she was studying him, which he supposed she was. Miss Gifford was not a woman who went headlong into something unprepared. That mixture of restraint and sense, combined with the image of the girl who, stark naked and terrified, had picked a lock and set about rescuing herself from a situation where most would have been in a dead faint of horror, piqued more than his amused interest—it stirred something inside him.

'I assume that this evening's meal is so that we can explore the sense of taste?' she asked, cutting across his uncomfortable self-examination. He did not feel Jessica Gifford was so restful after all.

'Yes. The sense and sensuality of food and how you can use it for flirtation and seduction.' Her eyebrows rose. 'Are you hungry?'

'Very,' Jessica admitted. 'Have you any idea how tiring spending large amounts of money is?' Her smile seemed to glow and she gave a little wriggle of pleasure, as though someone had run a finger down her spine.

Gareth took a deep breath. He was enjoying this too much; that had to cease. It was not what he was here for, they had work to do.

'Well, being hungry before meals in public must stop at once,' he said severely. 'Food must become a luxury, a game, a tool in your armoury of seduction. Before any meal taken when men are present, you must consume something solid and sustaining at home first.'

'Dinner is served, madam.' Hedges stood holding the door while Jessica closed her lips on what he suspected was about to be a withering comment on the foolishness of fashionable life.

She stood instead and placed the tips of her fingers on his proffered forearm, glancing up at him from under her lashes as she did so.

'Very nice,' he murmured, escorting her through the door and into the dining room. Their chairs had been placed as he had requested, with hers at the head of the table and his on her right. On the white cloth there were only the place settings, a flower arrangement, a candelabra and two dishes, one before each place.

'I wanted to concentrate on one thing at a time,' he explained, holding her chair for her. Jessica sat, regarding the almost empty table dubiously.

'Oysters?'

'Do you dislike them?' He sat beside her. 'If you have no objection to dining alone with me, I will pour the wine and we can ring when we require the second course.'

'Yes. Thank you, Hedges, that will be all for the moment.' The butler closed the door behind him. 'That is a relief; I do not feel comfortable having this sort of lesson before an audience.' She lifted her fork, then put it down again. 'I've never eaten raw oysters, I have only had them in beefsteak-and-oyster pie.'

'Oysters are regarded as a highly erotic food. Look at them.' He wondered if she would understand the symbolism and watched as she studied the six open shells set out on an extravagant bed of crushed ice.

'Erotic?' Jessica murmured, lifting one shell delicately and advancing it closer so she could stare down into the fleshy folds moving gently in their briny liquid, cradled within the opalescent shell. He knew the exact moment she caught his meaning from the blush that coloured her cheeks. 'Well, really! Do men think of nothing but sex?'

Gareth had been watching her over the rim of his wine glass as he took a sip of the white burgundy. At her question he choked, half-laughing, and put the glass down. 'I'm afraid we do think about it quite a lot,' he admitted apologetically.

Jessica knew she was blushing. She put the oyster back on the plate and lifted her own glass, hoping for a little Dutch courage. 'You mean that in dining rooms all over the country people are sitting down to oysters and the men are looking at them and thinking they look like… And then *eating* them?'

Now what have I said to amuse him? she wondered as Gareth gave another gasp of laughter.

'Yes.' He did not appear capable of elaborating.

'I see.' She eyed the offending shellfish. 'How exactly does one eat a raw oyster?'

'You squeeze on a little lemon juice, then raise the shell to your lips and tip it in.' Garth suited the action to his words, chewed a couple of times and then swallowed. 'Sublime. In *very* polite company one eats it with your knife and fork, but that need not concern us.'

'Hmm.' Jessica knew she was sounding prim, although something inside her was wanting to giggle, partly because the whole idea of food as erotic seemed nonsensical and partly because she was beginning to feel as though she was in a dream, or had had far too much to drink, or both. Not that she had ever had more than one glass of wine at once in her life, but she supposed this light-headed, bubbly sensation was how intoxication felt.

She picked up her oyster, regarded it severely and tipped it to her lips. Cool, salty, fleshy and sensuous, it was like nothing she had ever tasted, and certainly not like the rather rubbery constituents of a pie. Jessica bit, swallowed, thought about it and smiled. 'It is fabulous!'

'Then let me give you another.' Gareth squeezed lemon, then lifted one from his plate and advanced it to her lips. Jessica sat back, a little shocked. 'Oh quite, absolutely scandalous behaviour, and you do not do this at polite dinner parties, not until we have reached the stage of really setting the *ton* to talking. But we might be seen sharing our oysters in a box at the theatre.'

Jessica opened her lips and Gareth touched the shell to them. 'Keep your eyes on me,' he murmured as, instinctively, her lids drooped. His eyes, as she lifted hers to them, were dark and something hot burned at the back of them. 'Just so, we are exchanging unspoken words, messages that cannot be said out loud in company. And everyone else will know that is what we are doing.'

This time she let the flesh slide into her mouth and the memory of his tongue, tangling with hers, as hot as this was cold, filled her. 'What is it?' He was instantly alert to her mood. 'What are you thinking about?'

Too startled by her own reaction to prevaricate, Jessica answered honestly, 'You kissing me', and was rewarded by the knowledge that she had both surprised and disconcerted him.

The heat in his eyes flared and she knew he was remembering too, but his voice was dry as he said, 'Those are exactly the thoughts you should be conjuring up— they will add verisimilitude to your acting.'

'Excellent.' If he thought he was going to disconcert her, he had another think coming. And in any case, she was more than capable of disconcerting herself, without his help. 'My turn.'

This time, as she held out the shell and the oyster slid between Gareth's lips she ran the tip of her tongue over her own and he almost choked. 'You are worryingly good at this,' he said when he was recovered and they laughed and ate the remaining oysters chastely from their own plates.

Jessica rang the little bell by her plate and the next course, 'A pea fowl, larded, removed with a ginger soufflé and asparagus, madam', was brought in.

The guinea fowl led to a much less disconcerting discussion about taste and texture and a good-natured dispute about the amount of port in the sauce, which Jessica lost as she had never knowingly tasted port before. She thought she had scored points by batting her eyelashes prettily and imploring Gareth to carve, because he was certain to be *so* good at it.

The ginger soufflé melted on the tongue, leaving an unexpected heat behind it. By this time she found she was paying as much attention to taste and texture, heat and cold, spice and sweetness as she had to the feel of the items Gareth had had her touch the night before.

'That just leaves the asparagus,' he remarked innocently.

Jessica eyed the thick green shafts, glistening with melted butter and the giggle finally escaped. She had eaten asparagus often enough in the past, daintily with knife and fork, casually with her fingers, the butter running down her chin; now, fuelled by the atmosphere of sensual indulgence and the experience with the oysters, she had no doubt at all what asparagus was supposed to be symbolising.

'No,' she gasped, not worrying that the end of her nose must be turning pink as she laughed or that this was not behaviour expected of either the governess, or of the lady who wore a fashionable silken gown. 'This is too funny to take seriously.'

Silence. She had overstepped the mark with the man who was, when it came right down to it, her employer.

He was paying her to take this seriously and she was giggling. What was the matter with her? Miss Jessica Gifford *never* giggled.

Eva and Bel had wanted her—expected her—to wear the gown without a fichu, to let her hair down, to rouge her lips and blacken her lashes. But her instincts had told her that the first time that Gareth saw her in public he had to see someone who would shock him in truth. His reaction must convince a jaded, cynical audience.

So she had found a fichu, pinned up her ringlets, left her face scrubbed and innocent—and laughed at the game he was trying to teach her. And now he was looking at her, his face shuttered. Those grey eyes were wet-flint dark and the mobile mouth still. Jessica held her breath, wishing she could not remember what his lips had felt like against hers, wishing she had no memory of the scent and the heat of him.

His mouth moved She saw the tip of one white, sharp, canine catch at the corner of his underlip, and then Gareth smiled at her, a slow, lazy smile that caught her breath in her throat and had the stumbling words of apology tangling into silence on her tongue. *Oh, my God*, she thought, shocking herself, *he is gorgeous.*

All he said, mildly, was, 'Sex often is very funny.'

'Oh.' Jessica, charmed out of her embarrassment, regarded him, curious. 'I thought it a subject men had little sense of humour about. That…place was so cold, so joyless. Would you ever hear laughter there? Joyous laughter?'

'Perhaps not.' Gareth picked up his wine glass, twirling it gently between thumb and fingers. 'But there are more aspects to the relations between men and women than that—and, yes, men, despite our fragile sense of self-worth, do enjoy being with a woman with a sense of humour and wit.'

'I shall remember that,' Jessica said primly, wondering whether Gareth was being ironic about the fragile sense of self-worth or whether even large, calm aristocrats had their insecurities.

'Tell me about your family.' He changed the subject abruptly as she rang the bell.

'I was about to leave you to your port and nuts.'

'You have an absorbing novel, or perhaps some stitchery to occupy yourself?' Gareth leaned back in his chair to allow the footman access to his plate.

'Neither, I confess.'

'Then stay and keep me company,' he suggested as the man placed the decanter at his side and the dish of nuts before him.

'Is that not rather…unusual behaviour for a lady?'

'Rather dashing—but then…' Gareth waited until the door closed behind the footman '…you are rather a dashing lady, are you not, Mrs Carleton?'

'So I understand. May I try some port?'

Gareth poured a little into her empty wine glass, then cracked a walnut and placed the meat on her side plate. Jessica sipped, wrinkling her nose. 'Very heavy.' He took a swallow of his, watching her over the edge of his glass. Strangely it did not make her feel uncomfortable; it was as though she had spent many an evening companionably in his company. She put her elbows on the table, nibbling the nut, her port forgotten. 'What should I be doing tomorrow?'

'What do you want to do? More shopping?'

'No!' Jessica rolled her eyes. 'I have shopped until I can shop no more—at least for a day or two. I shall wait until everything is delivered, then Lady Dereham and Lady Sebastian will come and we will go through it all and see what further accessories I need. I cannot imagine anything can be missing, but they insist there will be all kinds of things we have forgotten.'

'If you have no engagements, there are two things we need to see to.'

'Really?' Jessica frowned and absently sipped her port. The rich taste was beginning to grow on her.

'Perfume and jewellery,' Gareth said and it seemed to her he was watching her for her reaction.

'Jewellery?' she enquired coolly. There were only two sorts of women a man bought jewellery for—his wife and his mistress.

'I rather thought you might take it like that. How would it be if I promise to take it all back at the end, every last pearl? If I promise to leave you with not so much as an amber bead?'

'That, my lord, would be acceptable.' At least, it would be socially acceptable. Jessica found her heart was beating erratically with a mixture of disappointment and the thought of wearing such jewellery, if only for a short time. The picture of Gareth showering gems upon her was shamefully pleasurable—and yet she had never so much as coveted a diamond in her life. Mama's pearl set was in the bank along with her savings, Papa's signet ring and her coral-and-silver christening rattle.

Governesses did not wear any jewellery beyond, perhaps, a chaste cross. Had a few hours with this man seduced her from her acceptance of her true station in life to such a extent that she had fallen prey to the shallowness of fashionable life?

The feeling that had give risen to the giggle was stirring again and a little voice was murmuring in her ear to stop being such a prig. She was going to earn her holiday from reality; if that meant revelling in a little shallowness, then she, Miss Jessica Gifford, was going to do so with gusto.

Chapter Nine

'May I have diamonds?' Jessica asked, hoping Gareth would realise she was joking. In for a penny, in for a thousand pounds, the reckless little voice urged her, while common sense told her that aquamarines, pearls and garnets would be the sensible thing for him to buy.

'Of course. Of the finest water, naturally, although, with *your* eyes, emeralds should be your stone. But only a limited number of pieces.' Without thinking she raised her eyebrows in enquiry, surprised at his sudden lack of liberality. 'To be in keeping with your cover story. The late Mr Carleton would have earned good money from his royal service, but not so much that he could shower his wife with jewels. And perhaps you have already sold a few pieces to finance your London adventure.'

'Oh, I see.' She tried another sip of port, beginning to enjoy the warm slide of the wine down her throat. 'I am, perhaps, just a little bit desperate to find a new protector?'

'Not desperate yet, but certainly a trifle concerned. This London adventure is a big gamble for you.'

'And yet I am retaining the good will of the Grand

Duchess?' Jessica took the fresh walnut that Gareth cracked for her, frowning over the intricacies of her new character. She seemed as convoluted as the whorls of the nut.

'Eva is a continental—London society will expect her court to be a touch more…relaxed. And I am sure she will let it be known that the family owed your late husband a debt of gratitude for some service. Given the intrigues of *her* late husband, the exact nature of the service is naturally something we do not speak about. It would explain a little indulgence on her part.'

'May I ask a personal question?' What was making her so bold? Perhaps the port, perhaps the intimacy of sitting like this with a man with the curtains drawn tight against the cold, damp night and the candlelight flickering. Or perhaps it was just this man

'You may, although I cannot promise I will answer.' He smiled at her, a look heavy-lidded and amused. 'In return I will ask you again about your family.'

'Very well.' She did not have to tell him everything, after all. 'If you met this Mrs Carleton in real life, would you pursue her, attempt to become her protector?'

Would he answer? 'I don't know,' Gareth replied, his expression becoming speculative. 'I haven't met her yet.'

Very clever, my lord, Jessica thought, determined not to let him escape with word play. 'But in principle?'

'In principle, possibly.'

'Even if you were not trying to shock Lord Pangbourne?'

'Possibly.' He watched her face. 'Now have I shocked you?'

'No.' Jessica shrugged, hiding the fact that, yes, she

was a little shocked. Which was foolish. Did she think this man was different from all the rest in some way? 'It is the way of the world. Or at least, of so-called polite society.'

'And not-so-polite society, I can assure you. Enough of my moral deficiencies—where do you come from, Miss Jessica Gifford?'

She had thought about this moment and what she could safely reply. 'My father was a military man. And a gamester. He and my mother eloped and both families cut them off. He was killed in an argument over cards when I was twelve.' She paused, wondering how much more she might tell him.

'Twelve? Were you the only child?' She nodded. 'How did your mother support you?'

Tell him the truth, the shocking truth I only realised when I was sixteen? Tell him that I was raised and sent to a good school in Bath on the proceeds of Mama's great charm and thanks to the liberality of her protectors? No.

'Mama had many good friends. I was well educated and able to take all those expensive additional lessons that have equipped me for life as a superior governess. I can play the harp as well as the pianoforte, speak three languages, paint in watercolour. Mama died of a fever when I was in my final year at school in Bath.'

The protector of the moment had disappeared before his paramour was even laid in her coffin. She fought back the memories of those days when she could not allow herself to give way to her grief, days while she sold every piece of jewellery, every pretty trinket, every length of lace, buried her mother decently and bought herself the good, but sombre, wardrobe befitting her new role in life.

'And those good friends could not support you?' Gareth asked, the concern in his voice almost upsetting her careful control.

'One—a vicar—did offer to take me into his home, but I do not care to be beholden.' *And certainly not to a pious hypocrite who preached virtue to his flock while visiting Mama every Saturday night!* And there was always the fear that those men might expect her to carry on in her mother's footsteps.

Mama had done the shocking, the unthinkable thing and had sacrificed her virtue and her reputation to give her daughter a future. Jessica could only guess at what that had meant for a woman who had loved her husband, with all his faults, and who had been brought up in the strictest respectability.

'You do what you have to do, darling,' she had said once when Jessica had protested that the Honourable Mr Farrington was anything but honourable. The reality of what Mama had been to those men had never been spoken between them, the fiction that Mama was merely keeping them company was always maintained, even when Jessica dabbed arnica on bruised wrists or listened to her mother's stifled sobs late at night.

You do what you have to do. And now she was all but standing in her mother's shoes, only she was doing it to gain her own independence, once and for all, and to repay a debt to a man who had rescued her from degradation and shame.

'I see.' Gareth poured himself more wine and sat back, loose-limbed, relaxed, in the high-backed chair. 'I must confess to even more admiration for you than I was already feeling. Your independent career and high standards are to be applauded.'

'Thank you.' Jessica felt embarrassed. She knew, without false modesty, that she deserved the praise and yet it was strange to have someone recognise what she had achieved, what it had cost in sheer hard work and determination. 'Now, tell me about tomorrow.'

He smiled, obviously recognising that she was trying to turn the subject. 'I will go and buy your jewels and you and Maude can go and have your scent designed.'

'Designed?' Jessica stared at him.

'But of course. When you pass by, men will inhale, entranced, and know it is you, and only you.'

'Poppycock!' Jessica retorted roundly. 'You are teasing me.'

'Not at all.' Gareth regarded her for some moments, then stood up. 'Will you come here, Jessica?' Wary, she stood and walked towards him. 'Give me your hands.'

Biting her lip, she placed her palms in his out-stretched hands. His fingers meshed with hers then lifted, carrying her inner wrists up to his face. His breath feathered the fragile, exposed skin and her own breath caught in her throat.

'You have your own, unique, fragrance. I can smell it now, warm and female and Jessica.' His voice was husky, the words, spoken so close to the sensitised flesh, was like the brush of feathers across her pulse. 'But it is subtle, a scent only a lover will know and recognise.' *And you*, she thought, unsteady on her feet. *You will know the scent of me again.* 'We need to give you a scent the hunting male can find and then seek out.'

'That is a disconcerting thought,' she murmured.

Gareth's eyes lifted, met hers across their conjoined hands, and she thought she glimpsed the hunter there, in front of her, dangerous, more of an animal than a man. She drew their hands towards her, pulling down until his knuckles were level with her mouth, then inclining her head until she could inhale the heat from the back of his hands.

'Warmth and man and Gareth,' she murmured. His very stillness told her she had startled him, even without the sudden hammering of his pulse against her wrist. She kept her eyes on the clean lines of his tendons, the blue veins under the skin, the healing graze on one big knuckle. A man's hands engulfing hers, and yet, at this moment, who was the stronger? She rather thought it was she.

'You learn your lessons well, Miss Gifford,' Gareth said after a moment, and she admired the control in his voice. 'You are going to become a very dangerous huntress.'

'Count upon it, my lord,' she promised, releasing his fingers and turning on her heel to walk to the door. As she opened it she turned to see him still standing there watching her, a smile of reluctant admiration on his lips.

How I dared, Jessica thought, distracted, as Maude's carriage drew up in front of a small bow-fronted shop entrance. *Todmorton's* it read in spindly gilt lettering above the door. *Craftsmen Perfumers*. At a gesture from Maude she pulled down her veil and stood to follow her out of the carriage.

It had been keeping her awake all night, tossing and turning. How she had dared turn the tables on Gareth like that, behave like a woman of the *demi-monde*, how it had felt to hold him in her thrall for those long, shimmering moments while his blood raced in his veins and his skin heated in her clasp.

It was power and it was dangerous power and he was not the man to practise it on. There were *no* men it was safe to practise such wiles upon and certainly not the one with whom she had to act out this masquerade. She did not need to seduce, only to give the impression of seduction. But it was all becoming too real.

'What did you say, Jessica?' Maude turned from her contemplation of a display of giant bath sponges in the shop window. 'Did you say *frightening*?'

'Er, yes. Frightening being out like this, in disguise,' she extemporised as the footman opened the shop door for her and they entered into fragrant gloom.

'Not to worry, no one will know you veiled, and afterwards, no one could make any connection with you wearing that frightful stuff gown,' Maude reassured her, blissfully unconscious of the fact that such dreadful gowns were Jessica's everyday uniform. 'Mr Todmorton, good morning. Yes, I am in the best of health, thank you. Now, this is the friend of mine for whom we require a scent. Something unique, something *tantalising*, yet discreet. Can you help us?'

'Lady Maude, an honour to assist a friend of yours. Clarence, a chair for her ladyship and show her our new range of triple-milled soaps while she waits.' The man who bustled forwards, stirring the air into a swirling rainbow of scents as his long apron swished across the floor, was of an indeterminate age. His bald pate gleamed, his white hands were clasped across his rotund belly and his smile was wide and ingenuous.

'Madam, please, come into my workshop.'

* * *

Jessica felt awkward, sitting disguised by her heavy veil in front of the neat, professional figure of the perfumer in his workroom. She looked round, curious at its ordered rows of labelled drawers from floor to ceiling, its racks of bottles and phials and its clean, bare surfaces. She had expected to smell a riot of perfumes like the fragrant shop outside, then realised he must need to work with nothing to distract his sensitive nostrils.

'Would you mind removing your glove, madam?' With the coolly impersonal tone it was like going to the doctor. Jessica stripped off her right glove. 'And holding out your hand, palm upwards?'

It was like the encounter with Gareth last night, and yet utterly unlike. This man made no attempt to touch her, merely leaning forward until his nose was above her bared wrist and inhaling. He might, she thought with an inward chuckle, be a cook smelling the soup to adjust the chervil.

'Hmm.' Mr Todmorton sat back, nodded sharply and reached for a notebook. 'You wish for a scent for evening and for day, madam?'

'Yes.' She supposed she did, although a daring dab of lavender water, or essence of violets on her handkerchief was the sum total of Jessica's experience with perfume.

'And the impression you wish to create?'

She stared at him, failing to understand, then realised he could not see her expression for her veil. 'I am sorry, I do not quite comprehend.'

Again, she might have been with a medical man, she embarrassed to discuss some feminine problem, he entirely at his professional ease.

'Do you wish to be seductive and subtle or flamboyant? Do you wish to be unique and memorable, or merely sweetly feminine?'

'Subtle,' Jessica said hastily. 'But seductive, memorable. Definitively unique.'

He nodded, apparently unsurprised by her requests, which seemed to her contradictory. 'Now, which family? That is our first question. Florals as a main group are insufficiently memorable, and besides, will not last well on your type of skin. The woody, leather and *fougère* groups are too heavy and perhaps too masculine.' He jotted another note and frowned. 'Chypre or amber?' It was apparently a rhetorical question, as he shook his head in thought. 'Chypre. Mystery, warmth, natural depth. Floral undertones rather than moss, perhaps? Yes, I see it clearly now. I will prepare something in a *parfum*, an *eau de toilette* and a very light dilution for scenting linen.'

Jessica, who had been expecting to be offered samples to sniff and choose between, found herself being escorted to the workroom door, a decision made without the slightest involvement on her part. It was a relief, she decided, buttoning her glove again; how she would have recognised a suitable scent she had no idea, although it would have been amusing to have sniffed her way along the array of intriguing bottles.

Maude was perched on a stool in front of the counter, a predictably large stack of packages in front of her. The assistant was folding white paper crisply around what appeared to be the final box, although Maude's gaze was roving the shadowed interior with all the concentration of a huntress in search of prey.

The assistant knotted string and reached for the sealing wax as she saw Jessica. 'Well? Mr Todmorton, have you found just the thing?'

'I will *create* just the thing,' he corrected in gentle reproof. 'If you and madam return in three days, Lady Maude, I will have the first bottles ready.'

'Oh, look at these lovely little things!' Maude jumped down and went to rummage in a basin of miniature, fine-grained sponges.

'From Corfu, my lady.' The assistant knew his trade, Jessica thought, amused. 'Young girls dive for them; each is selected with great care to be perfect for cleansing the face…'

'We must have some, see how fine they are. Catch!' Maude tossed one to Jessica across the width of the little shop. A featherlight ball, it wavered in the air and she reached for it just as the door opened.

The sponge bounced off the broad chest of the gentleman who entered and he reached up and caught it one handed.

'Gar—' No, it was not Gareth, it was quite another man altogether, Jessica realised, puzzled why she had made the mistake. This man was as tall and as broad, but he was far darker, both in hair and eyes, but also in skin tone as though some Mediterranean blood flowed in his veins. She was spending too much time with Gareth, that was the trouble. Thinking about him too much led to seeing him everywhere.

Frowning over why that should be such a very bad thing, it took Jessica a moment to recall the people around her, then she saw Maude's face. There was a faint rose flush on her cheekbones, her lovely lips were parted as though she had just gasped and her eyes were wide. The gentleman, apparently impervious to this vision of loveliness, turned the sponge over in his fingers for a moment, then handed it to Jessica, his eyes sliding over her veiled face with polite indifference.

'Thank you, sir.'

'Not at all.' He inclined his head, unsmiling, giving her an opportunity to observe a nose that would have done credit to a Grecian statue, dark brown eyes and severe, well-formed lips.

There was nothing further to be said. Jessica stepped forward and placed the sponge on the counter. Maude was still standing to one side clutching an over-spilling double handful of tiny globes. 'Here, let me.' She removed them and dropped them back into the basin, her back firmly to the gentleman. 'How many do you want?'

Maude blinked at her, a frown of irritation between her arched brows. *'Move,'* she hissed.

'What?' Jessica hissed back. She could almost feel the three men staring at them. 'More, did you say?' she added in a clear voice. 'Shall we take six?' She stepped to one side before Maude could physically shove her aside as she appeared about to do, and began to select another five sponges, delving amongst them to find the ones of the finest grain. 'Please,' she half turned and spoke to the assistant, 'do serve the gentleman, we may be some time.'

'Thank you.' Again, that polite, chilly, inclination of the head. Beside her Jessica heard Maude moan faintly. *What on earth is the matter with her?*

'The order for the Unicorn, Mr Hurst?'

Unicorn?

'Indeed. And two dozen of those small sponges, if you please—send them round later. I will take the main order, *madame* awaits it.'

'Certainly.' The assistant retrieved a package from under the counter and handed it over with reverent care. 'If you will just keep it this way up, Mr Hurst.'

'Thank you. Good day.' He nodded to Mr Todmorton and the assistant and raised his hand to the brim of his hat as he passed the ladies.

The door closed behind him, the bell jangling into silence. Jessica frowned at Maude, who appeared to have been struck dumb. 'Maude, we need to pay.'

'What? Oh, put it all on my account, Mr Todmorton. *Who* was that gentleman?'

'Mr Hurst, Lady Maude. He owns a number of theatres, including the Unicorn.'

Jessica scooped up their shopping and took Maude firmly by the elbow before she could make any more outrageous enquiries about a strange man. 'Thank you, Mr Todmorton, I look forward to my new scent. Good day.'

It seemed she had not lost her touch with recalcitrant pupils. Maude was outside on the pavement before she could protest, her mouth open indignantly.

'Jessica! I wanted to find out more.'

'You cannot interrogate shopkeepers about gentlemen, Maude, it just is not done.' She broke off as the footman jumped down from the carriage and hurried to take the parcel. 'Thank you. We will walk a little. Hyde Park is that way, is it not?'

'Yes, ma'am, just along there, left into Piccadilly and a short walk and you'll be there.'

'How am I going to find out about him if I do not ask?' Maude said with crushing reasonableness.

'But why should you want to?' Jessica snuggled her gloved hands into her wide sleeves and wished she had a large muff like Maude's. The day was chill and a touch misty, but they could hardly have this conversation in the carriage for the servants to overhear.

'Why?' Maude sounded incredulous. 'Did you not think him the most attractive man you have ever seen?'

'He was very good looking, if you like icebergs,' Jessica agreed. 'But I would hardly call him the *most* attractive man I have seen. Although when he first walked in, I thought for a moment he was Gareth.'

'Gareth is a very well-looking man, but nothing to compare with Mr Hurst,' Maude pronounced reverently. 'But the name is an odd coincidence, do you not think?'

'What do you mean?' Jessica side-stepped to avoid a snapping pug being led along by a liveried footman with his nose in the air.

'Well, Gareth is a Ravenhurst—at least, his mother is. He and Eva's husband and Bel, and goodness knows how many others—I lose count, some of them are abroad—are grandchildren of the Duke of Allington. Hurst—Ravenhurst. Perhaps he is a connection.'

'Hurst is a very common name, especially in the North, I believe,' Jessica said repressively, rather spoiling the aloof effect by adding, 'That cock won't fight, Maude—you are not going to be able to get to know him on account of him being some sort of distant relative of your Ravenhurst friends. And besides, your papa is not going to want you speaking to a theatre owner, however well off.'

'His clothes were very superior, were they not?' Maude sighed, walking straight past a shop window containing an array of bonnets labelled *Fresh in from Paris* without a sideways glance.

'I did not notice.' Jessica studied as much of the lovely, determined face as she could while it was screened by a wide-brimmed bonnet. Maude looked uncommonly focused. 'Maude, I am not going through this masquerade in order to free you from Gareth just for you to commit some indiscretion with a tradesman!'

Her companion stopped dead and glared at her. 'Mr Hurst is not a tradesman.'

'Well, he certainly does not have vouchers for Almack's,' Jessica retorted. 'You have glimpsed him for five minutes—you know nothing about him! Maude, what are you planning?'

'I don't know.' Jessica sighed with relief: that sounded genuine. 'I shall have to think about it. I refuse to give up. Did you see the way he looked at me?'

'Maude, he looked at both of us as though we were part of the furniture,' Jessica said repressively. 'And you were throwing sponges about and then moaning—he probably thought you were slightly about in the head and I was your keeper.'

'Oh.' Momentarily cast down, Maude began to walk on and Jessica hid another sigh of relief which rapidly turned to one of exasperation as Maude gave a little skip. 'I must look through the newspapers and see what is on at the Unicorn. He cannot be made to think of me unless I am very much in his way, now can he?'

Gareth is going to have to sort this out, Jessica decided. It was beyond her. She would write and ask if he would take breakfast with her, then she could be sure of a private word before any of her enthusiastic supporters descended upon her for the day.

Chapter Ten

Gareth lay naked on his back on the bed, looking up into the shadows as the firelight sent them dancing over the ceiling and cornices. It was past one in the morning, but he felt too indolent to get between the sheets, too awake to snuff out the candles and sleep. He turned his head, restless, and saw the light catch the gemstones in the open boxes he had left on the bedside stand.

He had enjoyed choosing jewellery for Jessica, wished that he could see it at once displayed against her white neck, on her slender wrists. He smiled at the thought of her pleasure when she tried each item on for the first time. The smile broadened as he remembered the chill in her eyes when he had first mentioned buying her jewellery and the mischief as a purely feminine desire both to tease him and to wear such baubles overcame her.

It was amusing having Jessica to talk to, he mused, like having an unconventional friend—if one could be friends with a woman. Maude was like a younger sister, a beloved, charming, worrying responsibility. Miss

Gifford was his responsibility, too, but in quite a different way. For a start, his feelings for her were not brotherly. He was not quite sure what they were—those of an employer? A guardian? No, neither of those fitted. He would have to settle for friend.

He dragged himself up against the pillows, reached for the boxes and picked out the pieces, one by one. A pair of emerald drop earrings, edged with diamonds. Good stones, but not over-large. Tasteful and appropriate. He dropped them and lifted a thin necklace of diamonds, supple and snakelike as it flowed over his hands. Matching ear bobs. A pearl set. Aquamarines for day wear, two silver gilt wrist clasps and a gold chain.

Yes, a suitable collection of respectable jewellery for a widow with good taste, hinting that she would appreciate something better. And he did have something better.

It had been ridiculous to buy it, Gareth told himself as he reached out for the red morocco case and thumbed the catch. The lid fell back and he blinked at the fire reflected from the diamonds, the almost fierce green glow of the emeralds. It was a full parure: necklace and armlets, rings and earrings, a tiara—the sort of jewellery a nobleman bought for his wife, not what a lady such as the fictitious Mrs Carleton could ever hope to wear.

But he had seen it, seen Jessica's eyes in the shimmer of the stones, and the compulsion had gripped him and he had bought the set. Madness. He could always resell them. They were of the best quality, an investment.

Gareth set the case down and lifted the finest piece from its setting. A great diamond-cut emerald designed to be a brooch or to sit in the front of the tiara or to fasten to the necklace. It lay in his palm, the colour of Jessica's eyes when she was angry.

A glint of gold caught his eye and he looked down the length of his naked body. It was scattered with gems where he had discarded each piece. The earrings lay on his flat belly, twinkling indecently amidst the central arrow of dark hair. The diamond necklace snaked over his thigh, an unsettling contrast with hard, masculine muscle. A gold chain slithered down his chest as he shifted and he started as it caressed his left nipple.

His fist clenched over the great gemstone as he stared down, uncomprehending, at the blatant evidence of his own arousal. *Bloody hell.* What had brought *that* on? He was as rampant as a stallion and he had not even been thinking about sex. Surely to God he was not aroused by handling jewellery? That was a perversion he had never heard of before and had no wish to contemplate now.

There was a pain in his palm, as sharp as the insistent nagging in his groin. He opened his hand and glared at the emerald as though it could answer his puzzle.

'Oh, no.' The words were a whisper. The stone did not speak, but his imagination did, taking the image of the parure, decking his memory of Jessica's white, naked body with it. Only it was no memory, this was impurest fantasy, for the Jessica he could see now was not a desperate, cold fugitive. She was warm, smiling, turning to him, holding out her hands…

'*No!*' Gareth swept the sparkling ornaments to one side and rolled off the bed, pacing across the room as though to shake off an incubus that had descended upon him in his sleep. How could he? It was dishonourable, disgraceful—and downright painful.

Up until two minutes ago he would have sworn an oath on everything he held most dear that his intentions towards Jessica Gifford were chivalrous and good. He would protect her through this masquerade and then, from a distance, ensure her well being in modest comfort and security for the rest of her life. Yes, he had kissed her, but in anger—and he had not enjoyed it. Much. And she had understood about that. He hoped.

Gareth made an abrupt turn and paced back again, swearing as his naked left instep made painful contract with an earring. He enjoyed flirting with her a little as he tutored her in the arts of seduction. Of *pretended* seduction, he corrected himself. But mild flirtation was almost second nature to him—and she gave no sign of being either alarmed or confused by it. No, rather she appeared amused by the entire exercise.

It was simply that he was unused to being so close to a woman, yet not sexually involved with her, that was all. And certainly not a woman he had seen naked. He winced as his right foot made contact with the other earring and he bent to scoop them up and toss them into their case.

He hadn't had a woman for a while, that must be it. His restless pacing brought him up in front of the tilted cheval glass and he stared critically at his reflected image, glaring at his offending penis. It had, thank Heavens, subsided somewhat. How long was it since he had made love? Too damn long. The treacherous member stirred hopefully and he snarled at it as though it were an uncontrollable wild animal, not part of his own body.

Common decency insisted that he stop thinking about Jessica like that. All it would take was a little self-control. And that, of course, he had in abundance. Of course.

* * *

Jessica was sitting eating a particularly succulent slice of ham when Gareth finally arrived at Half Moon Street for his breakfast. She had risen early, having succumbed to the first clear, sharp morning for days and taken a brisk walk around Green Park with a footman trailing with reasonably well disguised resentment at her heels.

Now she was eating with an appetite, contemplating her surprising new life with some pleasure. The shock of her adventure had subsided, she was amused and stimulated by her lessons in flirtation. Maude was proving a true friend, if a worrying one. Her nerve-racking imposture had not yet begun and Jessica realised she felt as though she were on holiday.

'Good morning,' she said, observing that Gareth flinched at the brightness of her greeting. In fact, now she looked more closely, he appeared to have spent a night of either severe insomnia or indulgent dissipation. Or possibly both. 'Would you like to sit down and I will fetch you some breakfast?' He appeared to drag his gaze to her face with an effort. 'You seem a little tired.'

'Yes. Yes, I am. Tired.' His eyes roamed over the buffet, then back to the table. 'I will have coffee, thank you. Nothing more.'

She lifted the silver pot and poured, adding a dash of milk and no sugar, just as he liked it. 'Would you like some toast?'

'No. Thank you.' Gareth took the cup and sat opposite her. 'There is no call for you to wait upon me.'

It was not said with a smile. Jessica felt the sick knot of embarrassment tighten in her stomach and knew she was colouring up. She had presumed upon her position, one of the unforgivable sins for a governess. She was treating this breakfast table as though she was truly mistress of the household and not an amateur actress incompetently learning to play a part. And she had summoned Gareth to come to breakfast without a second thought. There were doubtless all kinds of ways in which she had offended and now Gareth—Lord Standon—was displeased.

'I beg your pardon, my lord.' She folded her hands in her lap, dropped her eyes to her plate and wondered how soon she might slip from the room.

'What the devil?' He grounded his cup with enough force to crack porcelain. Jessica winced. Causing him to shatter Bel's Spode morning service would simply be the last straw. 'What are you apologising for? I'm the one behaving like a bear with a sore head.'

'I was presuming too much upon my position, my lord. I should not have asked you—'

'Your *position*? Your position is the mistress of this house and as a lady—and the only one in residence—I would hope you would feel free to take charge of any meal in it and order the servants as you see fit. And what is this *my lord* nonsense?'

'I thought you were offended by my presumption. And asking you to call was indiscreet.' He smiled and the knot unravelled itself and she unclasped her hands. It was all right. And in any case, she had to get used to being liberated from the restricted position she had disciplined herself to accept in the past. She had a personality, opinions—and she could give herself permission to exercise both

'It was a touch unconventional, perhaps, but I came in through the mews and the back garden.'

'You are not usually so…tense,' she ventured. 'Or at least, not in my short acquaintance with you.'

'I am usually too lazy to be tense, is that what you mean?' His smile was wry. 'Indolent, perhaps? Normally I see little merit in losing one's temper or becoming fraught over problems. A little thought, a little calm planning and most things resolve themselves. At the risk of labouring the point, Jessica, I am angry with myself because I have miscalculated over something, not with you.'

'And that cost you a night's sleep?' she asked sympathetically, nudging the plate of toast and the butter in his direction and controlling the quirk of her lips as he reached out and took them. She risked pushing the ham across as well, then topped up both their coffee cups.

'It did. That and a…friend of mine who has a mind of his own and appears set upon directing mine along quite the wrong paths.' Gareth cut into the ham and bit into his toast with a fierceness that made her glad she was not the object of his displeasure.

'A close friend?'

'Very. A lifelong one, you might say. We are attached.' He shifted in his chair and silence fell. Jessica tactfully busied herself with buttering toast and mentally reviewing how she was going to tell him about Maude's sudden fascination with the completely ineligible Mr Hurst.

'Why are you still dressing like that?' Gareth demanded, making her jump. 'Have your new clothes not arrived?'

They had, a collection beyond her wildest dreams, gowns for every occasion. Bel and Eva might have assured her they were entirely appropriate for her apparent station in life and were not at all extravagant in comparison with others she would see, but to her they were simply luxury made manifest.

'Yes. They are all in my room.'

'Then why do you continue to dress like a governess? And your hair—you are doing your very best to turn a dashing crop into a prim nothing. You dress like a governess; no wonder you feel you should behave like one.'

'I *am* one, and I am not ashamed of it. No, please listen.' He closed his mouth again as she held up a hand. 'The masquerade has not yet begun. When it does, you will meet Mrs Carleton, for the first time, in public. You cannot risk showing you are familiar with her—I must be as much of a shock to you as possible.'

She had thought it all through as she had twisted her elegant new ringlets into stiff braids, and she knew she was right. And she also knew that she wanted to flaunt herself for him alone in her new satins and laces and watch his face, see the hot, wicked darkness come in to his eyes again as it had when he had kissed her. And that was dangerous madness, even if all it meant was that she needed approval and reassurance.

'Very well.' He sipped his coffee, then added, 'I will send round the jewellery.'

'Oh, thank you. My scent is being made up; I enjoyed that very much, although I did not have much to do— Mr Todmorton simply inhaled the air about two inches above my wrist and pronounced!'

'You mean to say you did not ransack his shop?' His mood seemed improved now, perhaps he was simply one of those men who needed several cups of coffee in the morning. Jessica nudged the jam across and rang for more toast.

'I did not. Maude did. Um…'

'Um?'

'While we were there, a gentleman came in.'

'You were veiled?'

'Oh, yes, there is no risk he could recognise me again. No, it is Maude. I am sure I should not tell you this, but I fear I have absolutely no influence with her and—'

'Who is it?' Gareth said with resignation. 'I would not worry. She will flirt, but then she is not going to come to any harm with most of the men she will meet this Season.'

'I doubt she will meet this one at Almack's,' Jessica worried. 'His name is Hurst and he owns theatres, the Unicorn included.'

Gareth cast up his eyes. 'Oh, Lord. She has always been fascinated by the theatre. Not that she can act for a groat. Whenever we are at house parties and someone suggests a theatrical entertainment, Maude has to be persuaded to be the prompter or look after the costumes.

'All of us Ravenhurst cousins seem to have an ability as actors—purely amateur, with the exception of Sebastian, Eva's husband, who was a government agent and had as many faces as Edmund Kean—and Maude says she is jealous of our skill. It is just the glamour of the theatre, that is all. It will wear off.'

'I do not think it will be so easy. She was struck dumb just at the sight of him. I suppose he is probably the most handsome man I have ever seen.' Gareth's eyebrows rose. 'If one finds icicles attractive.'

'In that case she will get frostbite.' Her worry must

have shown for he smiled, the old, lazy smile that should have reassured her and instead made butterflies dash madly about in her chest. 'Don't tell me—we are going to be making up a party to whatever is showing at the Unicorn at the moment?'

'I fear so.'

'Well, Maude will have to concentrate all her dubious thespian abilities on extracting herself from our so-called engagement before she can focus on persuading Lord Pangbourne that he wants a theatrical manager for a son-in-law.'

'True. I am refining too much upon it, no doubt. Gareth…' She found herself suddenly, ridiculously shy. He sat, politely waiting for her to speak. 'My final two lessons—sight and sound? How are those to be achieved?'

'Sight we will do today, this afternoon. I intend despatching you with Bel and Eva and Maude for a nice drive in the park. London is still a little thin of company, but there will be enough for you to work upon. When you return I shall expect a report detailing which ladies you consider to be rivals, which you should cultivate and which may be safely ignored. But, more importantly, I want you to be Mrs Carleton inside your head. I want you to look—really look—at all the men you see. Sum up each one with a view to seduction. Fix them in your mind. What might be their weaknesses, what attracts you to them, how will you approach them, how you would set out to seduce each one and how dangerous each is.'

'Gareth!' She stared, shocked. 'In cold blood, just like that? You want me to look at men and…'

'Assess them. Yes. You did a good job summing up Mr Hurst, the handsome icicle, did you not?' He drained his cup and stood up. 'Thank you for breakfast, Miss Gifford. Enjoy your drive.'

Jessica sat staring blankly at the Dutch still life hanging on the wall opposite. There had been a sardonic note in Gareth's voice, a set to his mouth that somehow told her that he did not exactly relish setting her that task. On the other hand, thinking about it, it was certainly good tactics to familiarise herself with the prominent players on the stage she was to inhabit for the next few weeks.

The ladies arrived in Bel's barouche with the top down, all well wrapped up and with hot bricks at their feet and lap rugs over their knees. Maude handed an enormous muff to Jessica as she climbed in. 'This is for you, I saw you didn't have one. They are all the crack.'

'Thank you!' Jessica struggled to control the fur muff that was about the size of a medium dog, although mercifully lighter. 'What a lovely day.'

'It is ideal for the task Gareth has set us,' Eva shifted in her seat, allowing Jessica an even better view of her pelisse with its fur epaulettes, collar and cuffs. Another Paris fashion, she guessed. 'Everyone who is anyone will be out in Hyde Park with the sun shining like this.'

Reluctantly, for she was enjoying the crisp air and the sun on her face, Jessica settled her veil securely and they set off. 'If necessary, I shall introduce you, rather vaguely, as Miss Smith,' Bel explained. 'Just bow slightly. People will assume you are a companion, or a visiting relative.'

'A poor relation,' Jessica murmured, smoothing a hand over the skirts of her plain brown pelisse.

'Precisely. We do not want anyone putting two and

two together and making five when I launch Mrs Carleton into society,' Eva said with a crisp decision that made her sound, for the first time, like the Grand Duchess she was.

The carriage swung through the gates into Hyde Park, the driver reining back to steady his team as he insinuated it into the mass of carriages and riding horses that thronged the wide tan-covered drive. 'Very thin,' Bel observed, sounding disappointed. 'We shall have to do the best we may.'

Jessica was glad her veil hid her unsophisticated amazement at what her companions obviously thought was a quiet day in the Park. Bel was already waving and bowing to acquaintances.

'We need to concentrate on the men,' Maude reminded her *sotto voce* as a landau containing an elderly lady drew up alongside.

'Three nephews,' Bel murmured back. 'Lady St Margaret, how do you do!'

Carriage after carriage stopped, oblivious to the traffic jam they were creating around the Dereham carriage. It was rapidly becoming obvious that Bel was a leading light in London society and that Eva was a star, the ladies simpering and looking conscious as they carefully addressed her as *Lady Sebastian*, the exciting words *your Serene Highness* trembling on their lips.

'You are going to be lionised,' Bel commented after they had disposed of a particularly effusive matron.

'All the better for our purposes,' Eva replied with a sigh. 'But such a bore. Ah, now that's better, here are some men at last.'

Three uniformed officers on raking cavalry mounts

reined in beside their carriage, doffing their hats. Maude smiled, causing a noticeable effect. 'Lady Sebastian, may I introduce Major Aulbarre, Captain Lord Heathcote, Captain the Honourable Charles Grahame?' Bel deferred to Eva. 'Gentlemen, I believe you know Lady Maude? Oh, yes, and Miss Smith.'

Amused, Jessica graded the depths of bows. All three managed suitably deep inclinations for Eva, despite their high pommels. For Maude they all imbued their greetings with implications of admiration, and, in the case of the Major, deep homage. Jessica received two nods and a thin smile from Captain Grahame.

As they rode off, having expressed their eager anticipation of the first ball of the Season, four pairs of feminine eyes studied their retreating figures, then turned back. 'Captain Grahame is a very good-looking gentleman,' Jessica ventured, feeling it was an inadequate assessment.

'Too much so for his own swollen head,' Bel declared. 'And not enough money. Lord Heathcote is the man to concentrate on from that little group.'

'I thought him haughty,' Jessica demurred.

'Indeed he is, and well connected, rich and highly competitive. What we want is someone to create a stir when Gareth makes his move to secure your favours.'

'Surely we do not want to provoke a duel?' Jessica was horrified. 'Someone could get hurt!'

'But it wouldn't be Gareth,' Maude assured her. 'I am sure he is an *amazing* shot.'

'We do not want things to go that far.' Bel had gone a little pale. 'I have endured the suspense of one duel, I am not going to put up with another.'

'A duel? What happened?' Maude was, predictably, agog. 'Who was fighting over you? Was it Ashe?'

'Yes, and I am not going to tell you who the other man was, so it is no good asking, Maude. They both deloped, thank goodness, but I swear it put ten years on me, waiting for the result.'

'But—' Maude broke off and directed a wide smile to their left. 'Lord Bourton, good day! Grandfather was a West Indies merchant, father made a baron, but the son has a shocking reputation for the ladies,' she summarised in a murmur into Jessica's ear.

Again, Jessica was ignored, but this time she made herself disregard that and study the man driving the high-perch phaeton. His dress was slightly extreme to her, admittedly still untutored, eye. His horses were flashy and his air of self-consequence considerable. Having said all that, he was certainly a strikingly good-looking young man, if one ignored a definite weakness about the chin.

'Pretty,' she observed two minutes later as he drove off, attempting to get his fidgety team under better control. 'And spoiled. He won't like it if he does not get what he wants.'

Half an hour later she had resorted to jotting notes, unable to hold so many names and faces in her head. Goodness knows, it would cause a scandal if her notebook ever fell into anyone else's hands—her observations were nothing short of libellous.

Her head was spinning, but she appreciated Gareth's idea in setting her this task. She had never done more than glance indifferently at a gentleman; staring at one was quite out of the question. And she had certainly never assessed them in the light of seduction. Now she felt she could cast a bold eye over any man she met in the course of her masquerade.

Even the man riding towards them now.

'Well,' Jessica observed with heartfelt appreciation, 'now that is what I call a truly handsome man.'

'So do I,' Eva said, a smile twisting the corner of her mouth. 'But he is out of bounds for your games—I am married to this one.'

Chapter Eleven

'**O**h my goodness! That is Lord Sebastian?' Jessica subsided in blushing confusion as the man brought his raking chestnut sidling up to the barouche. 'I do apologise!'

Eva smiled wickedly. 'There is no need to apologise, my thoughts on first seeing him were considerably more explicit.'

Lord Sebastian Ryder looked fit, lean, and, in some indefinable way, dangerous. His grey eyes were fixed on his wife's face and Jessica took a shaky breath. What would it feel like to have a man look at her like that? Eva reached out her hand and he bent and caught it, pressing a kiss on the inside of her wrist before releasing her.

'My love. Maude. Bel, my wicked sister, what are you up to? I sense mischief.' Bel shot him a reproving glance and inclined her head reproachfully towards Jessica. Jessica did not make the mistake for one moment of thinking he had not noticed her already. 'And Miss Jones, I assume?'

'Miss Smith, my lord,' Jessica answered, suppressing a laugh. She liked Eva's husband, she decided.

'Indeed you are,' he agreed gravely. 'And what course is this barque full of beauty bound upon?'

'We are collecting men for Jessica to study,' Maude explained, provoking a grin from his lordship and a mortified gasp from Jessica.

'Heaven help the entire male sex if you three are hunting,' he observed with every appearance of sincerity. 'Here comes another poor victim for you to add to your tally. Good day, Morant.'

'Gareth!' *Oh Lord, I spoke aloud.* Jessica was aware of Maude's rapid, intelligent glance that appeared to penetrate her veil before flickering away as Gareth came to a stop next to Lord Sebastian.

'Ryder.' There was respect, even affection there between the two cousins, she noticed, struggling to keep her attention on observation and to still the ridiculous flutterings inside that Gareth's unexpected arrival had provoked. What was the matter with her? He was hardly going to test her on her observations here and now.

Think, look, she reproved herself as though she were a slow student failing to grasp the principles of sketching. *Are they alike?*

She could tell that Lord Sebastian was Bel's brother—there was a similarity in colouring and in the way they smiled, the turn of their heads. There was nothing of Gareth that immediately spoke of a relationship, yet when you saw all three together she could sense the kinship.

How wonderful to have that easy familiarity, that tie, she thought wistfully.

Gareth turned from making bantering remarks about his cousin's new horse and fixed his gaze on Jessica's veiled figure. 'Are you having a successful drive, Miss Brown?'

'Smith,' Sebastian corrected helpfully.

'Not really,' Maude interjected. 'Jessica thinks that you two are the only handsome men she has seen all afternoon.'

'Maude! I said no such thing.' Jessica struggled to keep both the schoolmistress and the flustered innocent out of her voice. 'There were Lord Bourton and Captain Grahame, and any number of pleasant gentlemen.' There, that was said with a light-hearted, sophisticated air. 'And I made no observation whatsoever about Lord Standon,' she added, ruining things.

Lord Sebastian grinned at her, but mercifully made no comment, Eva choked back a laugh and Gareth gazed at her, disconcertingly expressionless. Surely his feelings were not hurt? 'Never say I instructed you to flirt with married men, Miss Smith.'

Jessica had got her breath back, although why she had been feeling slightly winded in the first place she could not say. 'Certainly you did not, my lord,' she retorted. 'And I was not flirting with Lord Sebastian— my remarks about his person were made while he was well out of earshot.'

Sebastian gave a shout of laughter, making a nervous chestnut hack being ridden past them shy away and several dowagers turn their heads to see what was occurring. 'Miss Smith, I am flattered. Morant, I have a suspicion you have been bested.'

'I am certainly constantly being surprised,' Gareth countered. 'And find myself quite off balance. I had no idea that the bombazine bodices of our educationalists hid spirits of such independence.'

'Jessica does not wear bombazine,' Maude protested indignantly, making them all laugh.

'We should all be wearing overcoats,' Bel said with a shiver. 'I think it is time to be turning back; the day has turned quite raw.'

Gareth gave instructions to the coachman and the group turned towards the gate, joining a log-jam of other vehicles whose occupants had obviously become as chilled as Bel's party.

'This is such a miserable time of the year,' Jessica observed. 'The nights draw in so early and the air is so damp and chill most of the time. I find it hard to keep up my spirits, especially if I am teaching children who do not have any natural liveliness.'

'Oh, but I think it is one of the best times.' Maude was adamant in her contradiction. 'The start of the Season. There is something magical about going out in the cold and the dark and then into a house lit up with hundreds of candles and warmth and noise.'

'Did you have no chance of a come-out?' Eva asked.

'No.' Jessica shook her head. More questions; well meant, kindly, but full of pitfalls. 'My mother died. We were already not well off. I had my living to earn.'

Gareth glanced down, wishing he could see Jessica's expression beneath the heavy veil. She was not comfortable with being questioned about her past, he had noticed it when he had asked. It was not something to her own discredit, he was sure. Perhaps simply the memory of hard times and past slights.

His grey hack sidled and snorted, not liking being kept to a slow walk in this crowd of horses and vehicles. Normally he would have touched his hat and ridden on, out of consideration for his mount, if nothing else, but now he soothed it with his voice and stayed where he was. Sebastian would stay too; concern for his newly pregnant wife showed in his every glance in her direction.

Love and marriage changed a man, Gareth mused, blanking out the conversation in the barouche now the talk had turned to hats and Jessica had relaxed. He would never have dreamed he would see Ryder dancing attendance on a carriage full of ladies. He was a man more at home bluffing his way through the courts of Europe on secret government business or sliding like a pike through the murky waters of some back slum. At least, Gareth corrected himself, not unless one of the ladies was a spy or there were stolen diamonds secreted in the upholstery.

Or take Sebastian's brother-in-law, Ashe Reynard, Viscount Dereham. He had returned from Waterloo, a hardened military man and a devil-may-care rake by all accounts. He had encountered Bel—under circumstances that made them both grin reminiscently, but which they steadfastly refused to discuss—and the next thing anyone knew, he was leg-shackled, faithful and a pillar of society.

It was enough to make a man nervous. Neither of them had been intending to fall in love, let alone get married. That, apparently, was not enough to protect you. Gareth grimaced, guiding the grey through an opening gap and managing to hold it for long enough for Bel's coachman to get past and clear of the gate. Why was he even brooding on the subject now? He had his careful scheme in place to save him from having to marry Maude and he was under no particular pressure to get married at all—there were male Morant cousins a-plenty if he managed to fall off his hunter and break his neck. It was all this talk of flirtation and Jessica's worries about Maude's unfortunate *tendre* for the unsuitable Mr Hurst, that was all.

He turned in the saddle and raised a hand in farewell before trotting off down Park Lane with a view to a leisurely bath before that evening's promised card game at the club. There wouldn't be many free evenings for idleness in male company once the Season opened with Eva's ball and he was plunged into his false flirtation with the lethal Mrs Carleton.

The sound of hooves right behind him had him turning his head. 'Ryder?'

'Bel says to tell you that she is making up a party to the opera tonight and do you want to come? Miss *Smith* will be there, I gather; she said something about the fifth sense if that means anything to you.'

'Opera.' Not his favourite form of entertainment—he enjoyed the music, but not the fuss and feathers that went with it. On the other hand, it would be an excellent opportunity to talk to Jessica about the place of sound in seduction.

'All right, I'll come.'

'Our box is well placed,' Ryder offered as consolation as he turned his black gelding to make his way back through the traffic. 'Bring your earplugs.'

Jessica had never been to the opera; it was not something that a governess would have the slightest excuse to accompany her charges to and she certainly could not afford to go on her own account.

'What do you think?' Eva stood in front of the long glass in her dressing room and regarded her reflection critically. 'Madame Hortense assures me it is in the very latest French mode.'

A white silk slip dress plunged from beneath a miniscule blue satin bodice which was cut so low and ended so high under the breast line that it barely contained the Grand Duchess's bosom. From the short sleeves of the bodice gauze under-sleeves billowed out to be caught in at the wrist by the pleated gauntlet cuffs of white kid evening gloves. Her dresser settled an immensely long silk stole, embroidered white on white, about her shoulders, remarking critically as she did so, 'You won't fit in that much longer, not with the young gentleman growing at the rate he is.'

'I think it is lovely,' Jessica assured her. No one, looking at Eva's slim but curvaceous figure, would guess she was expecting. 'The hat, er…headdress is certainly original.'

'I was not sure about it.' The round cap topped with small white plumes perched on top of Eva's head like some sort of exotic crown.

'It makes you look very regal,' Bel contributed, peering over Eva's shoulder at her own reflection in a confection of silk, tulle and bird-of-paradise feathers with some complacency. She had collected Jessica and driven her to Eva's so all three could go with Lord Sebastian as escort. Lord Dereham, Bel's husband, was still out of town.

Jessica guessed Eva knew she was being teased, for she merely looked down her nose and refused to be drawn.

'Will it not seem very odd that I am veiled?' Jessica asked. She had assumed that the simple dark blue silk gown she owned would be suitable and that a veil might not look out of place. Now, seeing the splendour of the other two in their opera dress, she had doubts.

'I shall say you are my companion and in mourning,' Eva said.

'And attending the opera?' Jessica was dubious.

'By my command,' Eva said imperiously. 'Any eccentricity is excused foreign royalty, I have discovered. Even when I insist that here I am simply Lady Sebastian, no one pays it any account. Very tiresome.'

There was a discreet tap at the door. 'Lord Sebastian's compliments, ma'am, but are you going to be all night? Not that he has any objection to missing the first three acts, he says.' Grimstone remained outside, so whether he was keeping his face as straight as his voice could only be imagined.

'We are coming now.' Jessica followed behind, clutching Eva's fan and the reticule that Eva's dresser thrust into her hands at the last moment.

Lord Sebastian helped Bel and Eva into the carriage, then turned to Jessica as she waited on the doorstep. 'You look very well this evening, Miss Smith, but I suggest you lower your veil now.' He followed her in and sat down carefully beside her, taking care not to crush the folds of her skirt. 'I confess to some curiosity at seeing Miss Smith shed her disguise and emerge as Mrs Carleton.'

'I am not so much curious as very apprehensive,' Jessica admitted. 'The suspense is beginning to prey on my nerves and I would welcome the thing starting.'

'Only ten more days,' Eva assured her, 'and then the Season begins with my ball.'

Gareth was waiting for them at the box. Jessica, jostled by the chattering throng and the focus of many an enquiring stare, despite her position by Eva's side, let out a sigh of pure relief at the sight of him.

He stood and she went to him instinctively, laying one hand on his forearm and whispering, 'I am so glad to see you!'

He seemed to understand without further explanation, for he turned her slightly and showed her a chair in the deeper shadow where the edge of the curtain was caught back. 'Sit there,' he suggested. 'You can put back your veil, no one outside the box will be able to see you.'

It was not until he patted her hand that she realised she was still touching him—*clinging more like*, she chided herself. Her palm lay on the warm black cloth that covered the supple muscle beneath and she snatched it away. She made a business of lifting her veil over the careful top knot that she had created to be as unlike her new hairstyle as possible while the glow in her cheeks subsided.

Sebastian sat at the furthest side from her with Eva next to him and then Bel. Gareth moved his seat away from Bel and into the shadows with Jessica. 'We can whisper,' he said, leaning sideways in the straight gilt chair until his shoulder just brushed hers.

'I have never been to the opera before,' she confided. 'What will they be performing?'

'Mozart, the *Marriage of Figaro*.'

'Oh, how interesting. I have played some of the music on the piano, but it is not the same.'

'How does music make you feel?' Gareth had no need to make such an innocuous question a secret, but he kept his voice low. It felt as though the two of them were hiding in this sheltered corner. Jessica shivered, surprised at herself for enjoying the *frisson* the thought brought with it.

'Feel?' She frowned at him. 'If it is challenging, then it is interesting to master. Familiar tunes are soothing.'

She could not see the expression in his eyes, but she could tell from the enquiring tilt of his head to one side that he was puzzled. 'And that is all the emotion music evokes? No passion, romance, nostalgia, *joie de vivre*, sadness?'

'Church music has the power to evoke reverent feelings.'

He made a noise somewhere between a snort and a laugh. 'Reverent feelings is not what we are about here, Jessica. Listen to the music, hear the emotion. You are not a governess any longer, bound to get up a piece exactly so as to be able to teach it. Open your mind and your heart to it. Never mind the plot, just *feel* and then tell me about it. Remember, you are to become a creature of emotion.'

Intrigued by the intensity of his directions, Jessica murmured, 'I will try.' She understood Italian and knew the story, so following the progress of the opera would not be hard and she could concentrate on the music. The orchestra tuning up, the swelling noise of the audience taking their places, filled her with an anticipation that was almost nervous. Or perhaps it was Gareth's closeness, the heat of his body reaching hers through the thin silk only inches from his shoulder.

'Can you see all right?'

She nodded, craning to see the empty stage, the flickering lights, the blur of faces in the distant boxes on the other side of the auditorium. There was applause as the conductor walked out, raised his baton and the overture began.

By the time Figaro strode on to the stage, Susanna dancing at his heels and trying on her new hat, Jessica was lost in the enchantment of the scene. The chattering from the stalls, the laughter from one of the boxes where a group of young bucks were entertaining their *chères amies*, failed to break the spell.

She listened, amused, as Figaro, convinced that the count had immoral intentions towards his fiancée, begins to plot. 'If you want to dance, my dear little count, I'll play the tune for you on my guitar…' she sang softly under her breath.

'You can translate?' Gareth asked, his breath whispering in her ear.

'Yes. Figaro is going to teach his master a lesson. Hush, here comes Marcellina.'

They laughed together over Cerubino's love-lorn sighings. 'I talk of love when waking, I talk of love when dreaming…' Jessica sang, her voice reaching only Gareth's ears. He leant closer, slid his arm along the back of her chair to lean in towards her. 'He's so sweet,' she whispered. 'So silly and young and romantic.'

'You will have to deal with equally silly young men soon,' Gareth teased as the characters came and went on the stage, entangling themselves deeper and deeper in their misunderstandings.

'But you will deal with them for me?' Jessica turned to look at him, anxious.

'Oh, yes. The young sprigs and the old roués and the dangerous rakes.' His eyes were amused, yet intent. Surely the flames that flickered in them were simply a trick of the light? 'I will protect you, Jessica, never fear.'

'Thank you,' she whispered.

'You are mine, after all,' he added, turning a little to look at the stage, leaving her confused and oddly breathless…*Mine* in the little drama they were going to enact, or *mine* in the sense of his responsibility now? Or something else entirely?

She forced her concentration back to the stage where the village girls were singing the praises of their undeserving count and Figaro was teasing Cerubino with scary stories of what he could expect in the army. Whether it was the composer's skill or Gareth's instruction to let herself feel, but Jessica realised all her emotions seemed to be on the surface.

She quaked for poor Cerubino, yearned with him for his hopeless calf-love. She felt Susanna's anger at the count's amorous intriguing and cheered on Figaro's plans for his master's come-uppance. But most of all her heart was aching for the countess's unhappiness.

Beside her she was aware, constantly, of Gareth's closeness, of him sharing the experience with her. From time to time they half-turned to one another, exchanging a smile.

Then she realised the point the opera had reached.

'Who—?' Gareth began to whisper.

'Hush!' Without thinking she raised her hand and touched her fingertips to his mouth. 'It is *"Dove sono"*. So beautiful…' The countess, alone, her heart breaking, began to sing as Gareth's breath warmed her flesh.

'*Dove sono*…where are the beautiful moments of sweetness and of pleasure, what happened to the promises of that lying tongue?'

Chapter Twelve

The aching loveliness of it silenced even the young bucks in their box. The voice floated high and pure and sad through the crowded space and Gareth turned to watch Jessica's face.

Her eyes were closed, her lips curved in pleasure at the exquisite sound, but her eyelashes were tipped with tears, glinting in the light like tiny diamonds. The countess sang the last, heartbreaking, line and stood for a moment, then left the stage. Gareth, without being able to understand a word of it, found himself caught in Jessica's emotion, bending closer as she gave a little sigh.

Her eyes fluttered open as the count and Antonio began the next scene, but it was clear she was still in that last aria and so, caught in the shimmer of her eyes, was he. Her hand, still raised from where she had silenced him with that featherlight touch to his lips, brushed his cheek as she lowered it.

They were so close he would hardly have to bend his head to kiss her. He wanted to, wanted to comfort her, as though she, not the countess, had been betrayed. For a long moment they were still, locked in the music.

'That is so sad,' she murmured. 'She loves him, forgives him, yet she knows he will betray her again and again. Her only hope is that, by remaining loyal to him, his ungrateful heart may change.'

'He will not change,' Gareth said. 'She is doomed to be betrayed.' He drew his handkerchief from his pocket and passed it to her. 'Your lashes are wet.' For a moment he thought of pulling her against his shoulder to hold her while she recovered from the emotion, then he controlled the impulse.

'Oh!' Jessica took the linen and dabbed at her eyes. 'I had no idea how it would affect me. When I read it, I thought her foolish to persist in loving him, but hearing it, you can understand that she will love him until death, despite everything.' She sat with the fabric crumpled in her hands, then handed it back. 'Thank you.'

Gareth reached for the handkerchief, his hand closing over hers. It was small and warm and vulnerable within his grasp and he simply held on, letting their joined hands rest on the arm of her chair. He felt her fingers curl against his palm, then relax as her attention was caught again by the unfolding story and her hand remained linked with his.

Jessica came to herself with a start as the curtain fell for the interval. She was pressed close to Gareth, her hand locked in his, her head almost resting on his shoulder. With a little gasp she sat up. Her veil, falling to her shoulders, snagged on his lapels and she freed her hand before the others, who were beginning to stand up, could see. Whatever had come over her?

'We will go and visit the Hetheringtons' box opposite,' Eva announced. 'She is beckoning and it will be safer than having goodness knows who coming in here.'

'Jessica and I will stay.' Gareth stood to set back the chairs. 'Could you have them bring us refreshments? I do not think it wise for her to be mixing too much.'

'But—' Alone with him, with all those emotions still surging around inside her? Jessica felt as light-headed and foolish as Cerubino, and about as reliable.

'You are probably right.' Eva nodded. 'I'm sorry, Jessica, I should have thought. But you will not be bored with Gareth's company.'

Boredom was the least of her concerns. Jessica assured her friends that she would be perfectly fine and resumed her seat.

'How do you feel?' Gareth spun a chair round at right angles to her secluded niche and straddled it.

'Flustered,' she confessed, too shaken at her own feelings to conceal them. 'The emotion of that music simply carried me away. Was it Mozart's genius, or was it hearing it performed so well?' *Or was it you?*

'Both.' Gareth ran a hand through his hair, wreaking havoc with his elegant style, and Jessica realised that he too had been affected, although he was not going to admit it as readily as she. 'And you had given yourself permission to simply experience it—not as a task to learn about, not as a piece to study.'

'Do you think the countess is a fool?' she asked abruptly, realising as she asked it that the question had been lurking there at the back of her mind. 'To love such a rogue, even though she can see him so clearly for what he is?'

'No.' Gareth frowned. 'No, I do not. I do not under-stand her, but I do not think she can help herself. A year ago, perhaps I would have dismissed her as weak. Now—' He broke off, the frown still creasing between his brows.

'What has changed for you?' More comfortable now the focus was off her and her feelings, Jessica twisted round in her chair so she could look at his face more easily.

'Seeing Reynard and Sebastian fall in love.' The frown vanished as he spoke of his friends. 'You haven't met Reynard—Lord Dereham—yet. But when you do you will see, he and Bel are like Sebastian and Eva: utterly devoted, totally as one.

'They are two of the bravest men I know,' he contin-ued, frowning. 'And two of the most self-reliant. A soldier and a secret agent. And yet now they have given themselves something to fear, something that would bring them to their knees—the thought of losing the women they have fallen in love with. You only have to watch them when they look at their wives.'

'As you say—it is love,' Jessica pointed out, secretly amused by his bafflement.

'Yes, but they did not seek it. They were not looking to get married—and yet they were struck down with it like a fever.'

Jessica laughed. 'There is no need to make a normal human emotion sound like a dangerous disease!'

'It might as well be—it attacks as remorselessly and without warning,' he retorted grimly. 'Look at them now. Both Bel and Eva are expecting. Reynard and Sebastian are more afraid than they have ever been in their lives— at best their wives are going to have to endure childbirth, at worst, they may lose them. What were they thinking of?'

'They are in love; wanting to have children together is perfectly normal for people in love.' Jessica shook her head at him. 'It is perfectly normal for married people who are not in love, come to that.'

'Getting married should be a rational process,' Gareth grumbled, defeated by her logic, but refusing to leave the subject. He got to his feet to unlatch the door at the sound of a knock, took a tray from the waiter and locked it again. 'Then people go falling in love in a positively irrational manner.'

'I have not met Lord Dereham, as you say.' Jessica took the glass of champagne he handed her and sipped thoughtfully. 'But Bel seems very happy, and Eva and Lord Sebastian obviously are, so love cannot be so bad, can it?'

'It is unpredictable. They are well suited, I will admit. But what if the person you fall in love with is utterly unsuitable? Or married? Or does not love you in return?'

'Then you have to learn to live with it somehow, I suppose—or in the case of an unsuitable love, throw convention to one side and marry them anyway.' She shrugged, smiling. 'I don't know, I have never fallen in love. But don't worry, it may never happen to you.'

'Falling in love or suffering a broken heart?' Gareth grinned back at her. Apparently he had shaken off his gloom at the prospect of an erratic god of love firing off random arrows at blameless noblemen.

'Either, I suppose.' She tried to imagine Gareth with his bachelor world, indulgently organised to suit his every whim, turned upside down by the eruption of love into his life. He was no pampered sybarite, she knew he had a well-developed sense of duty and worked hard for

his estates, his charities and dependents, she had seen
him and heard Maude talk of it.

But Lord Standon had no one's will to consider but
his own and marriage, let alone love, would change all
that. It would probably do him good, she told herself
robustly, trying not to feel a twinge of envy for the
unknown but fortunate young lady concerned. 'You are
going to have to act it soon when Mrs Carleton comes
into your life.'

'What you will be seeing then, my dear, will be an
exhibition of unbridled lust and desire.' Gareth produced
a comical leer.

Jessica failed to suppress an unladylike snort of
laughter, but she still wanted to probe this scandalous
relationship she was supposed to be participating in.
'So, you do not intend to be feigning love?'

'The Mrs Carletons of this world are not the sort of
women the Earl of Standon would marry.' He said it so
matter of factly that Jessica was taken aback. It almost
felt as though she—and Mama—and not the fictional
adventuress had been snubbed.

'Indeed? Then let us hope, for your sake, that the next
time you come across such a lady in reality, Eros is
looking in the opposite direction,' she retorted tartly,
annoyed with herself for caring. 'Making statements
like that could be tempting fate.'

And letting her concentration slip so that she half-
believed this was real life and not fantasy was even
more dangerous. Gareth was an attractive man and one
as far beyond her reach as a royal duke. Finding herself
enjoying his company, feeling a *frisson* when he came
close enough for his breath to caress her skin was

madness. She, Jessica Gifford, was a spinster governess. She now had the opportunity to become a lady of modest independent means and that was the height of her ambition. Anything else was for three-o'clock-in-the-morning dreams or the hazy aftermath of an orgy of novel reading.

Gareth topped up her glass, apparently unmoved by her warnings. 'I shall learn by my friends' downfall and simply not permit myself to become attracted in the first place.'

'I see,' Jessica said, her face straight despite this ludicrous masculine logic. *As if it were as simple as that!* 'So, are my lessons in the senses complete now?'

'The theory is, certainly. It all boils down to feeling, emotions, sensuality. Now you will have to practise. I will look forward to seeing your progress when I return.'

'You are going away?' Jessica wondered at her own feeling of alarm. It was ridiculous. She had Bel and Eva to support her, Maude's frivolous encouragement, a respectable house to lodge in and her own wits to rely upon. But the feeling of calm strength that had reached her from him in the brothel and had led her to trust him was weakening to her own self-reliance.

'Not for long, and only into the country to my estate on business. I will be back just before Bel's ball.'

Jessica gave herself a mental shake. She had never depended upon a man before—certainly not dear Papa— why was she weakening now? Gareth feared falling in love; she should fear this kind of feminine weakness.

You should be ashamed of yourself, Jessica Gifford, she scolded inwardly. *All it takes is a pair of broad shoulders and steady grey eyes and look at you! You are employed by this man to carry out a task. An unconventional one to be sure, but a task. If he had left me to instil deportment and the French tongue into a pair of schoolroom chits, I would do it without needing more than his initial instructions. This is no different. I do not need protection, I do not need support. I most certainly do not need further tuition!*

She had lectured herself into a state of resolute independence when he stood to answer another tap at the door. The orchestra was filing back in and beginning to retune their instruments, the interval was almost over.

'Whatever have you two been arguing about?' Bel asked, amusement rippling through her voice.

'Nothing.' Gareth looked puzzled. 'Nothing whatsoever.'

Bel looked at Jessica. 'Well, if I were one of Jessica's pupils, I would be feeling highly apprehensive at the moment. I remember that look from my governess all too well—it's the one that accompanies the lecture on frivolity and slacking.'

'I am neither frivolous nor slack,' Gareth responded amiably. 'Jessica is naturally of a more sober disposition than you are, cousin.'

'I was mentally lecturing myself,' Jessica interposed as Bel seemed ready to settle down and tease Gareth. 'I am allowing myself to enjoy this life of leisure and pleasure far too much.'

'No fear it will last,' Lord Sebastian observed with a sly smile at his wife as he held the chair for her. 'Eva and Bel will drag you from ball to party, from reception to masque, from dress shop to milliner, all in the name of doing your social duty.'

'Or, in my case, in the cause of this masquerade I will be enacting.'

'I am so looking forward to it,' Eva said with a pleasurable shiver. 'I do so enjoy a masquerade.'

The days before the ball slipped by with terrifying speed. Word of the charity extravaganza spread like wildfire throughout the smart set who were pouring into London for the start of the Season and invitations were eagerly anticipated, angled for and, in some cases, blatantly solicited.

'Could you believe your ears?' Maude was saying with horrified amusement to Eva as the pair of them were shown into the Half Moon Street drawing room a week before the event. 'Good morning Jessica darling.' She pounced, hugged, her cold cheek tingling against Jessica's warm one for a moment, then tossed her floss-trimmed bonnet onto the sofa. 'That odious shabby-genteel Mrs Harrington—'

'Harrington-Smythe, Maude, *please*,' Eva corrected with a wicked smile.

'Harrington-Smythe, then, as though that makes her manners any better.' Maude stripped off her gloves and went to perch on the fender to warm her hands. 'She positively bounced up to me in the Exeter Exchange—'

'If you will patronise such a middle-class emporium,' Eva interrupted, 'what do you expect?'

'Dagger-cheap silk stockings, that what I expect,' Maude countered. 'We don't all have your limitless dress allowance, Eva. Anyway, up she comes, bold as brass and says, "My dear Lady Maude, I am so looking forward to your wonderful ball!" Gush, gush, smarm.

"But I can't imagine what has happened to our invitations. I said to the girls…' Maude opened her eyes wide in cruel parody, '"Mark my words, girls, they'll have gone astray in the post, for Lady Maude will be wanting all her friends to support her efforts for those brave soldiers.' And then she said with a silly simper, "Even if they are just rough common men." I nearly boxed her ears.'

'What did you say?' Eva hooked a toe under a footstool and put her feet up with a grateful sigh.

'I said that it was not my ball because, after all, I was just an unmarried girl and naturally couldn't be hostess at such an event—you would have been *amazed* at how demure I sounded, Jessica—but I knew Lady Sebastian and the Grand Duchess had drawn up the most exclusive guest list so I had every confidence that all my most *particular* friends would be invited.'

'Cat,' Eva remarked appreciatively.

'It isn't that I mind her husband being a coal merchant or her frightful taste in puce satin gowns, and I'll take anyone's money for my rough, common soldiers. It is just that she toad-eats so,' Maude complained. 'Her poor daughters would be perfectly acceptable if only she didn't dress them in pink silk on every possible occasion and frizz their hair.'

'I'll invite them to a masquerade,' Eva promised. 'But never mind them, how are you, Jessica? Are you quite prepared for your grand opening scene?'

She exhaled a long breath and smiled ruefully. 'I think so.' Listening to Maude's airy talk of who was in and who was out made her realise just how ignorant she was of this whole gilded, privileged world—and how easy it would be to blunder over the simplest thing, let alone her pretence of being a dangerously seductive adventuress.

'Don't worry,' Eva reassured her, her sharp eyes apparently spotting more apprehension than Jessica thought she was showing. 'You must remember that you have been out of the country for years—if you do something you realise is odd, just say *Oh, that's how we do it in Maubourg*. And you will look the part—that is nine-tenths of the battle.'

That was true, Jessica thought, grateful for the reassurance. Even though she was keeping to her modest gowns and her severe hairstyle for the moment, the knowledge that the silks and the lawns and the cashmeres were hanging in her wardrobe, and the glimpses of her guinea-gold hair, made her feel a different woman already.

She was practising her seductive arts too, not certain whether she was glad or sorry that Gareth was not there to see her improvement. Without him she felt fidgety and supposed it was the lack of his guidance she was missing. Yet at the same time the strange tension she felt when he was near was gone and she found her concentration was much better. Altogether it was very odd, and she had a sneaking suspicion that the memory of that kiss was responsible for her conflicting feelings about Gareth Morant.

She had secured the services of Lady Catchpole's ex-dresser and Mirabelle spent much effort demonstrating the uses of the fan in flirtation. Jessica spent an hour a day perfecting each trick—the slow unfurling to draw the eye, the seemingly thoughtless use of the closed fan to draw down the line of one's neck or across the bosom of one's dress. Then there were the messages that could be sent—resting the fan on one's heart, peeping over it half-open, running fingers across the ribs, slapping it into the palm—they were all to be learned.

'You have just told me that I am ugly, that you want to talk to me and I am breaking your heart,' Mirabelle had observed critically only that morning. 'What did you intend to say, Mrs Carleton, ma'am?'

'That you were making me jealous looking at other women, and that I could not be with you as I was being watched,' Jessica confessed, sending them both off into peals of laughter. 'More practice,' she said ruefully. 'Show me again.'

After much thought they had decide to tell the dresser the false story of Jessica's identity and to enlist her help in fitting her new mistress for the task of finding a protector in London society as though that were Jessica's true purpose. It was too risky to let her know the truth, however discreet she had been in Lady Catchpole's employ, and the effort of keeping up the pretence in the house did help fix in Jessica's mind who she was now supposed to be.

Dancing lessons had progressed well, Bel's daily lectures on everything from orders of precedence to who was sleeping with whom and the latest *on-dits* about the royal family were dutifully absorbed and Jessica took every opportunity, heavily veiled, to drive out with one of her three new friends, observing the rich and the famous and the merely pretentious as they flaunted their finery through the fashionable promenades and the shops.

She even had the opportunity of practising her new skills and wiles on real men, for Bel and Eva volunteered their husbands for intimate dinner parties in the Half Moon Street house.

'It is a pleasure to meet you, especially here.' Lord Dereham, bowing over her hand, had a wicked smile that sent appreciative shivers all down Jessica's spine, despite the presence of his wife, smiling, equally wickedly, in the background. 'This house has many very happy memories for me. But it is you we must concentrate upon, is it not, Mrs Carleton? I have been brought up to date with this scheme you are all hatching to rescue poor Maude from Gareth's clutches and I understand that Sebastian and I are under orders from our wives to flirt outrageously with you.'

Jessica had blushed rosily, despite her very best efforts to look sophisticated and unconcerned by the attentions of two of the best-looking, most sophisticated and certainly the most teasing males she had ever come across. It was difficult at first to respond to their allusive jokes, their elegant compliments, dropped carelessly into the conversation, the half-serious repartee that had her laughing and blushing. But then she grew in confidence, applied her intelligence to the situation and found she could turn the tables on them with increasing confidence.

'Ah, if I had a heart to lose, ma'am,' Ashe Reynard, Lord Dereham, said in apparent seriousness, gazing deeply into her eyes while she gazed limpidly back. 'But, alas...'

'You had many of them to squander last night, my lord,' Jessica retaliated pertly. 'I saw you lose hand after hand of them at the piquet table. How could I trust you to look after mine any better?'

He chuckled at that, confiding later to his wife—

who promptly reported it back the next day to Jessica—
that no unattached man was going to be safe and he had
grave doubts about some of the married ones at that.

So her confident words to Eva were almost the truth.
She would look the part, she could act the part—but
could she convince the world that she had it in her power
to make Gareth Morant, Earl of Standon, fall head over
heels in love with her?

There were only days before she would find out.

Chapter Thirteen

Once more her nostrils were full of overwhelming smells and her ears with the braying of excited voices. For a brief, panicky, moment Jessica shut her eyes, trying to blank out the memory of that descent of the brothel staircase into the heat and stir of a room full of lascivious men.

'Mrs Carleton, ma'am? Are you all right?' *What is his name?* Jessica struggled to recall. It was only an hour after Eva and Bel had taken their places at the head of the receiving line and it was already obvious that their charity ball was going to be a complete crush. Which might signal its overwhelming success, but meant equally that Jessica's head was spinning.

'Quite well, Mr Hamilton, thank you. It was just the noise. I have been living quite retired, you understand.' She summoned up a brave smile and was rewarded as he patted her lightly on the arm with his white gloved hand.

No, these sensations were different—it was the well-bred laughter of ladies, the noise of the *ton* all trying to make themselves heard above the hubbub without actually shrieking, the scent of flowers and expensive scent. There was no coarse laughter here, no stink of male sweat and cheap perfume and cigarillo smoke.

She, Miss Jessica Gifford, governess, was at the opening ball of the Season of 1816 and was enjoying the giddying knowledge that she was the focus of considerable male attention. She could not believe it, after so short a time, but her dance card was almost half-full, three gentlemen were at her side, vying to entertain her with their witticisms and compliments, and a fourth had hastened off to fetch her a glass of champagne.

'I cannot believe you ever succeeded in living retired, Mrs Carleton,' the youngest of her attendants said with an attempt at a knowing smile. As he was all of nineteen, this was not entirely successful. 'Wherever you are, the gentlemen will beat a path to your door.' He leaned closer and whispered, 'Your bedchamber door.'

'Lord Chevering, that is a very naughty suggestion,' she pouted, rapping him lightly on the forearm with her fan. He blushed and smirked. *This is ridiculously easy, they are such idiots!* 'You forget, I was under the protection of her Serene Highness.'

She glanced towards Eva as she spoke. The Grand Duchess was in laughing conversation with an ambassador, someone who had been pointed out to Jessica as a High Court judge and two leading politicians. With her uncanny knack of seeing all that was going on Eva caught the glance and smiled, a small, wicked sign of encouragement.

'And you will be delighting us with your presence for the entire Season, ma'am?' That was the third gentleman, Sir Oscar Remington, who appeared more delighted with his view down the front of Jessica's alarmingly low-cut gown than with her personality.

'I expect so—I have been made *so* welcome.' She unfurled her fan and shot him a slanting look over the top of it. The fan also had the advantage of covering up her bosom, at least temporarily.

'It is a pleasure to welcome such a lovely new face into our midst.' Sir Oscar moved a little closer, managing to crowd out Mr Sayle, who had returned with her champagne. 'And one belonging to a lady of, shall we say, experience? Not yet another of the naïve young ladies who are flocking here for their first Season.'

'Experience, Sir Oscar? Oh, thank you, Mr Sayle.' She took the glass from the flustered gentleman with a smile that made him blush and sipped. 'I have no experience of London society, I fear. Why, I was the merest child when Mr Carleton married me and whisked me off abroad in the late Grand Duke's service.'

'Of life, dear lady, of life.' Sir Oscar was definitely getting too close and she had not been expecting such a full-frontal approach quite this early in her debut.

'Oh, yes. Life.' She sighed soulfully, half-turning so she could gaze into Mr Sayle's eyes as she drank deeply from her glass. 'Life is so full of…opportunity, is it not?'

'I should say so,' he agreed enthusiastically, his voice changing to a more discouraging tone. 'Oh. Hello, Grahame.' One of the riders Jessica recognised from her first carriage expedition to the park appeared, clicked his heels and executed a bow, which gave her ample opportunity to admire his dress regimentals.

'Won't you introduce me to the new star in our firmament, Sayle?' Jessica bit the inside of her lip, uncertain whether to laugh or sneer. She was looking very well, she knew that without false modesty. The combined efforts of her supporters had sent her out looking as attractive as she had ever felt herself to be. But the ballroom was full of much lovelier ladies than she. The reason that she was surrounded by men was that she was giving out signals that she might flirt, might be indiscreet, might even, if the incentive was right, be *available*.

'Mrs Carleton, may I present Captain Grahame.'

'Captain.' Jessica dipped a slight curtsy, leaning forward, just a little, to give the captain a glimpse of those features so much admired by Sir Oscar. How she was managing all this without a blush of shame she had no idea. It was as though she had donned Francsca Carleton and her dubious morals along with her silken gown.

'Madam! Your devoted servant.' He even had a thin moustache, which he brushed up with the back of his finger as he spoke. It was either a nervous mannerism or an attempt to look dashingly military. 'Might I have the honour of a dance—or more than one?'

'You'll be lucky,' Lord Chevering blundered in, earning himself a glare from the captain for his gaucheness. 'Mrs Carleton won't give us an aye or a nay, no matter how we plead.'

'Now you are being naughty again, my lord,' she chided, tapping his cheek with her fan and provoking a delighted laugh and a crimson blush. *Really, after a classroom of inattentive small boys, this is almost too simple!* 'You know a lady must be careful with the dances she gives—think of my reputation, gentlemen. I am not certain I will be dancing at all this evening.'

The thought of what Mrs Carleton's reputation might

be produced a glazed expression in four pairs of male eyes and a glare from a starched-up dowager sweeping past close enough to catch, if not the words, at least the atmosphere of innuendo.

Jessica repressed a sigh. This was all very well, but a whole evening of it, even with dancing, was going to prove tiresome. She chided herself; it might be ridiculous, flirting with a group of over-amorous gentlemen, but at least she was being very well paid for it and had the prospect of a good supper and a snug house to go back to. It could have been the draughty house in the wilds of Northumberland with the 'eccentric' daughter, or the chaos of a home full of ill-disciplined boys to contend with.

And even though she had to put up with—no, encourage—their dubious attentions, there was no danger they could go any further than that. Lord Sebastian and Lord Dereham were there, unobtrusively watching over her. And soon Gareth would be here and the masquerade could begin in earnest.

But where is Gareth?

Jessica shifted a little so she could watch the part of the room just beyond the receiving line. Maude was there, her father Lord Pangbourne at her side, jovially making conversation with the new arrivals about the work his daughter and her friends were doing for the wounded soldiers. He was a good-hearted man, she acknowledged, even if he had such a blind spot about Maude and Gareth.

The orchestra in the ballroom through the wide arch had stopped playing light airs and were tuning up for the dancing and there was still no sign of Gareth. Maude was behaving with poise and decorum, dutifully standing at her papa's side and laughing at all his sallies. If she was on the look-out for Mr Hurst, to whom she had insisted the committee send an invitation, one could not tell.

'Ride with you?' She pulled herself together and focused on what the Captain was saying. If she was not careful, she was going to blunder through sheer inattention. 'How kind, but I am afraid I do not have a riding habit in my wardrobe.' She plied the fan again, delighted at how versatile it was proving to be. 'But I hope I might see you in the park while I am driving out. I am certain you must look so dashing on your charger.'

He laughed at her flattery, assuring her that he had left his charger behind in barracks. 'No, I will be exercising my hunters, ma'am…'

His overconfident voice faded in her ears as some sense sent all her attention towards the door. *He is here.*

There was a stir around the receiving line, Maude stiffened and Lord Pangbourne beamed as Lord Standon turned from a laughing exchange with his cousin and strolled towards father and daughter.

Oh, but he looks wonderful. Maude, Bel and Eva seemed to dismiss Gareth as merely a *well-looking man*, and to be sure he was no match for Sebastian and Ashe in pattern-book good looks. But as she watched him stroll across to Maude, smiling at acquaintances as he crossed the parquet floor, she thought him their equal in masculine presence and in virile elegance with his broad shoulders and slim waist and long easy stride.

That deceptively lazy smile hid a decisiveness she had seen in action, the humour a seriousness and sense of honour and obligation that both she and Maude could be grateful for, and the broken nose and rugged chin lent character that, in her opinion, matched Lord Sebastian's saturnine looks and Lord Dereham's blond glamour.

Then she saw the laughter lines crinkle round those clear grey eyes as he greeted Maude and something twisted inside her. She had not seen him since he had left for his estates over a week before. It was agreed that it would seem most natural if they did nothing to rehearse this supposedly first encounter and the realisation of how much she had missed him hit Jessica with a force that almost overset her. *What is the matter with me?*

Then, *I desire him*, she thought, aghast. She fought for poise, attempting to rationalise her feelings, but they would not be ordered or controlled. *At least it will help my acting*, she thought wildly as some part of her managed to chatter on inanely to the circle of men around her. She watched out of the corner of her eye as Lord Pangbourne beamed upon Gareth's head, bent over Maude's dance card.

Gareth sketched a gesture to one side of the room and Jessica guessed he was saying he would escort Maude in to supper later. Her father must be delighted with this show of attentiveness; he was probably choosing the hymns for the wedding service even as he stood there, poor man.

Gareth, laughing at something Maude had just said, shifted position and began to scan the room casually as though looking out for acquaintances. The group around her shifted, blocked her view, moved again. Jessica knew the moment he saw her, felt the grey eyes lock with hers, saw the laughter ebb out of his face.

They could all act, the Ravenhurst cousins, he had

told her. But were any of them good enough to force the blood from their own cheeks? Gareth had gone white.

Maude said something to him, her hand on his arm, but he walked away from her as though she had been an importunate street hawker, straight across the room to where Jessica stood in her circle of bucks and beaux, as direct as if they had been alone in the room and the crowded reception hall clear space.

Startled looks followed him, ladies drew their skirts back, affronted by him brushing past them without ceremony. A man began, 'Ah, Morant, I need to talk— ', but was ignored. They had wanted to cause a stir—it seemed they were about to brew a scandal.

Maude was overacting to a ridiculous degree, Gareth thought, bowing low over her hand with an ex- aggerated courtesy that had Lord Pangbourne beaming with pleasure.

She gazed at him wide-eyed with an expression of simpering adoration on her face that almost had him laughing aloud. 'Maude, my dear. You look ravishing tonight.' And so she did, the minx, no doubt in the ex- pectation that her unsuitable theatre fellow was going to put in an appearance. She was doomed to disappoint- ment. Gareth had done some investigating and Hurst was not given to attending *ton* parties. Work appeared to be his world and he had made no attempt to break into society, despite wealth and looks that would doubtless have won him an *entrée* of sorts.

'Now, how many dances are you going to allow me?' he teased. 'Or have they all gone, snapped up by other lucky fellows?'

'As many as you like,' Pangbourne put in. 'No need to stand on propriety, Morant, everyone knows the way the land lies, eh?'

'Three, then?' He took the proffered card and filled in a country dance, a waltz and the supper dance, making a production of it, drawing the attention of the gaggle of matrons and chaperons who were covertly watching them. The gossip mills would be working overtime; within minutes word would spread that the long-awaited betrothal was on the verge of being announced.

Someone else was watching him, he could feel it. Not a hostile gaze, but one of an intensity that brought the hair up on his closely barbered nape and sent a *frisson* of anticipation down his spine. *Jessica.*

'So, we are agreed on supper?' he asked, turning slowly to sweep the room with an apparently casual glance.

He couldn't see her. Frowning, he searched again and then a knot of men by one of the large flower arrangements shifted, parting to reveal a single woman in their midst. She was looking at him.

In the part of his brain that was reminding him how to act as a sophisticated gentleman, Gareth knew his jaw had dropped. He shut it, but no amount of inculcated poise and manners was going to stop him staring. *Jessica? It has to be, but...*

He was moving without conscious volition, vaguely aware of Maude's voice, sharp, behind him, 'Gareth!' and of Pangbourne spluttering.

She isn't beautiful, something said inside his head. *But she's enchanting. I want her.* This was not supposed to be happening, he thought in the kind of daze he had not experienced since he was in his teens. He chose the ladies

who received his admiration, he wasn't dragged into
something by the parts of his anatomy that were even
now overriding his brain with painful intensity. This was
a carefully staged simulacrum of instant attraction, it
was not supposed to be a genuine *coup de foudre. Not
for a prim governess with a talent for common sense...*

Not beautiful. He clung to that thought, vaguely
aware that his sleeve was brushing too close to someone.
She was looking directly at him, although her lips,
warm, rose pink, were moving, talking. Her face, framed
by the artfully tumbled curls, was pale and her eyes as
clear and transparent as spring water. Everything about
the simple sheath of almond silk that turned her figure
into a graceful column said cunning artifice, glamour,
and yet the woman he saw radiated a kind of clarity and
honesty that stopped the breath in his throat.

Not beautiful. 'Damn it—' Someone was irritated
with him, he realised vaguely, striding towards his goal.
He didn't care. All he cared about was managing to
drag air down into his lungs so that he could articulate
when he got to her.

'Madam.' *Thank God. I can speak, and it is Jessica
and she looks perfect—and if this pack of bucks, bloods
and coxcombs has so much as laid a finger on her...*

'Sir.' She dropped a curtsy nicely calculated to
indicate that she had no idea of his rank and to show
off an expanse of milk-white bosom.

Gareth choked back an order to get into the retiring
room that minute and make herself decent. 'We have
not been introduced, ma'am. Grahame, if you would
be so good?'

'Of course.' Captain Grahame, too wise to show his

chagrin, did so with apparent good grace. 'Mrs Carleton, may I present the Earl of Standon? Standon, Mrs Carleton has returned from Maubourg with Grand Duchess Eva. Her husband was in service with the Duke.'

'The late Grand Duke and my late husband,' Jessica clarified, carefully making her widowed status quite clear. 'My lord, you are related to Lord Sebastian, I think?'

She was wearing the pearl set. Gareth had a sudden memory of the necklace slithering down his own naked body and an image of how it would look if he unfastened it now and let it slide over those milky curves, down into the shadowed valley of her low-cut bodice. 'Indeed. We are cousins, ma'am.'

It was a miracle he was making any sense, he thought. He had expected to have to guide a nervous Jessica through this first momentous meeting, yet she seemed the calm one, if he discounted how wide her pupils were, and the fluttering of the pulse in the angle of her throat.

Why had he not expected this? He had assured her over and over again that she would be perfectly convincing in her role as seductive adventuress, and he had not been lying to her. But faced with the sceptical, upright, prim governess, he had somehow not been able to imagine the full impact of the woman in reality.

'You will dance with me,' Gareth said curtly.

Jessica's eyes widened at the tone, then she tapped him on the arm with her fan in mock reproof.

'So hasty, my lord! I was just telling these gentlemen that I may not dance at all this evening.'

'You will dance with me, ma'am,' he said evenly, stepping closer and lifting the wrist from which the tiny gilded dance card and pencil dangled.

'You are very forceful, sir.' Jessica smiled, cat-like, apparently basking smugly in this masculine attention. Only Gareth, he was certain, saw the question in her eyes, the nervousness at his tone. 'One each, then, gentlemen. Lord Chevering asked first…'

'You misunderstand, Mrs Carleton.' Gareth untied the gold cord card and took the dance card between forefinger and thumb of each hand. 'You will dance with *me*.' The thin card ripped as he tore it across and then again, the pieces showering to the floor.

'Dammit, Standon!' Captain Grahame took a step forward, his face darkening. 'The lady—'

'The lady has no objection. Has she?' Gareth asked softly, staring deep into Jessica's eyes. For a moment the clear green clouded with panic, then her gaze sharpened, focused and she smiled that pussycat smile again.

'My lord!' The fan swirled open and she looked over the top of the cream-and-gold lacquer with something like devilment. 'I yield to your command. Gentlemen, I confess I find myself swept off my feet—perhaps another evening when you find yourselves more…persuasive?'

She laid her hand on Gareth's proffered forearm and, with a dimpling smile to either side, allowed herself to be led towards the ballroom. Gareth concentrated on relaxing, sauntering, trying not to look like a man expecting to have a challenge hurled at his back at any moment.

None came. The room seemed hushed. Eyes were following them, he knew without looking. He had his scandal.

Chapter Fourteen

'**W**hat do you think you are doing?' Jessica demanded in a hissing whisper. 'I thought there was supposed to be a gradual onset of your infatuation over several meetings, not you acting like the Grand Turk in the middle of the reception room! La, my lord!' she remarked more loudly as they passed a group of goggling matrons at the entrance to the ballroom. 'I swear you have quite undone my resolution not to dance.

'And I never thought I would hear myself say *La!* either,' she added bitterly, *sotto voce*.

What *was* he doing? A very good question. He could hardly respond with the truth, that he was in the grip of an attack of mind-numbing lust, or she would probably flee the room screaming.

'I saw the opportunity to create an effective scandal immediately,' Gareth improvised. 'Why shilly-shally about?'

'Why, indeed?' He could almost hear Jessica's teeth gritting as they came to a halt on the dance floor. 'I do wish you could have warned me, though. My heart was in my mouth—I thought you were about to provoke a challenge just then.'

So did I. Gareth took his place at her side at the head of the set as other couples followed them on to the floor. He tried to ignore the sensation of curious eyes burning into his back and looked down instead to meet Jessica's sideways glace. To an onlooker she would appear to be looking up at him flirtatiously, but he could see the governess-look in her eyes. For some reason it did nothing to diminish this heat that was surging through his veins, pooling in his belly.

The music struck up and they linked hands across their bodies and began to lead the set down the room. In the manoeuvre Jessica's knuckles accidentally brushed the front of his thin silk evening breeches, with predictable results. Gareth fought to think of cold horse troughs and Parliamentary reports.

They reached the end, separated, turned to face each other in concert with the other dozen or so couples and Gareth made himself focus on the steps and on strategy, although he rather feared he was beyond that. Beyond tactics even, he told himself with wry humour. He had probably reached the stage where improvisation was all that was going to save the day.

It was their turn to step forward and promenade again. 'Do remember we have only just met,' Jessica murmured, smiling with every appearance of enjoyment and pressing rather too close for propriety as they turned.

Yes, there was that. He was feeling so overset by that lightning strike of desire that he was in danger of forgetting the overall plan. What was the most convincing thing for him to do next? Retire into some secluded, but visible, corner and flirt, seemed the answer.

The dance was interminable. Jessica applied her mind to her recent dancing lessons and turned and skipped, dipped and linked hands, reciting the steps in her head as though she were conjugating irregular verbs.

People were still staring; she could feel the touch of their eyes like the press of fingertips on her skin. And Gareth—had he any sense of the wave of desire that had swept through her when she had seen him? It was difficult to think of that, and the dance and the person she was supposed to be, all at once.

'Thank Heavens that is over,' she murmured with heartfelt relief as he led her to a *chaise* in a curtained alcove.

'Champagne.' Gareth clicked his fingers at a passing waiter and snagged a full bottle and two glasses from the tray. 'Here, drink this.'

'On an empty stomach?'

'Pretend.' He sat down beside her and she was overwhelmingly aware of the size of him, so close and hot on the fragile piece of furniture. 'I have taken your lure, the hook is in my mouth, now you have to reel me in.'

'You make it sound as though you are a hapless victim of my toils—and that is what you are supposed to be, is it not?' Jessica took an incautious sip of the wine and choked. 'But you did not seem very hapless back there, Gareth, believe me. And none of those gentlemen thought it either. Some of them were very capable of putting their weaker brethren in their place, I saw them do it earlier—but they hardly dared twitch when you snatched me from under their noses.'

Gareth tossed back his champagne and refilled his glass, his eyes roaming the room, as though alert for any raiding party intent on regaining his prize. It seemed to her that he was controlling his breathing.

'In fact,' Jessica persisted, 'you felt very domineering and masterful and positively scary.'

That brought his attention back to her with a jolt. 'I am sorry!'

'No, please do not apologise,' she said earnestly, fixing her eyes on his face. 'Actually it was most…stimulating.' The flush stained her cheeks as her own words registered and she opened her fan, making rather a business of it, and waved it in the hope of a cooling draught. 'I must be getting into the part rather too much.'

There was a silence, one that crackled with unspoken questions and, on Jessica's side at least, rather too much horrified self-awareness for comfort. Gareth was holding her gaze and she watched, fascinated, as the stormy grey eyes darkened and his lids drooped into a sensual stare that had the goose bumps prickling wildly up and down her spine.

Then he smiled and she let her breath go with an audible gasp. 'I hadn't realised what a dangerous game this acting is,' he said lightly. 'Do you think when Kean is playing Macbeth, he goes home at night with the urge upon him to murder kings?'

Jessica felt the blood ebb and flow in her cheeks. Did he mean that he realised she wanted, in truth, to be his lover or that he wanted to be hers? Or both? Or neither? What to say? How to ask?

Words, for once, failed her. She was saved by an amused voice remarking, 'You *have* set the cat amongst the pigeons, Gareth.' It was Bel, eyes twinkling with mischief. 'Eva has sent me over to ask what the devil you are playing at—her words—and on the way I was accosted by Lord Pangbourne demanding to know what I thought was the best thing to do in the face of your apparent brainstorm.'

'Oh, Lord.' Gareth looked conscience-stricken. 'Maude.'

'You did snub her quite outrageously,' Jessica put in. She felt guilty, too—from the moment she had set eyes on Gareth, nothing and nobody had mattered. But what he had done was a very different matter than the gradual erosion of his supposed engagement to Lady Maude— he had swept the whole thing away with one stroke and very publicly at that.

'Actually, Maude is perfectly fine,' Bel reassured them. 'She is doing the rounds, stirring the pot and assuring everyone—in the strictest confidence, naturally, which means it will be all over town by tomorrow—that she always knew you were a rake and a libertine at heart, but could never convince her father of it. Her tale is that she had been browbeaten into acceptance of your forthcoming proposal, but now that you have exposed your true nature for all to see, she is deeply relieved.'

'That is a mercy. Thank goodness Maude is so uninhibited.' Jessica sank back against the hard bolster cushion. 'Our mission has been accomplished, it seems.'

'Yes, but you cannot stop yet,' Bel pointed out. 'It would be obvious that it was a ploy if you suddenly vanish and Gareth returns to being his usual well-behaved self.'

'Couldn't I vanish and he could brood for a few weeks in dark despair like a Byronic hero?' Jessica suggested.

'No, he could not,' Gareth interjected, getting to his feet with an energy that sent those wretched goose bumps going again. 'He would feel a complete idiot. He, since you two insist on discussing me in the third person, is going to carry on his rakish way with Mrs Carleton for a good while yet, believe me.'

'Heavens.' Bel blinked at her cousin. 'You look just like Sebastian when roused.'

Gareth gave a snort of laughter, rather spoiling his domineering stance. 'Is that a compliment?'

'Oh, yes,' Jessica assured him. 'Ladies will tell you that such masculine forcefulness is most attractive.'

The look he gave her was sceptical, as though he suspected her of teasing him, but there was a heat lurking behind it that made her swallow hard. 'That damned fellow Byron, I suppose.' He shot a wary look over Bel's shoulder. 'We are attracting attention again.'

'I am sure we are. I shall go now, radiating distress at having my diplomatic mission spurned and tell Eva within earshot of, I think, Lady Greyshott, that I very much fear her protégée is in the process of seducing our cousin from the paths of righteousness.'

'Will she have to appear to cast me off?' Jessica worried.

'No, she will shrug and drawl something like, *Nonsense, it is only masculine urges, quite natural, dear Gareth is such a rake*—causing Lady Greyshott to have the most enjoyable fit of the vapours—and everyone will laugh sycophantically at her outspoken foreign ways.'

'Off you go, then,' Gareth urged her, 'and we will take to the floor again, radiating defiance.'

'I must confess to feeling decidedly shaky,' Jessica admitted, wondering whether it was the situation or the fact that she was achingly aware of Gareth's body so close to hers. She found her eyes were fixed on the play of long muscles under the thin silk breeches and wrenched them away.

He filled her wine glass and passed it to her. 'More champagne,' he ordered. 'We will dance the next waltz and then, I think, we will leave.'

'Leave?' It came out as a squeak. 'Together?'

'Definitely more champagne.' He laughed at her. 'Don't look so appalled, Jessica—people will wonder what I am suggesting to you.'

'I doubt they will be wondering! I am sure their imaginations can supply an answer perfectly well,' she countered. 'Leave for where?' A couple passed their alcove, glancing in. She hastily adjusted her expression and raised her glass in a teasing toast, clinking it against the rim of his and holding his eyes until the inquisitive pair were gone. They were visible to virtually the entire room, she reminded herself, hoping that her face reflected sophisticated dalliance and not any of the other, real, emotions she was experiencing.

'I wish them well of their lurid fantasies,' Gareth said, raising a hand to brush an errant curl back from her cheek. The touch made her shiver and she turned her head fractionally, following the caressing fingers. 'In fact, I will take you home to Half Moon Street. And your chaste bed,' he added.

Was that an ironical twist to his lips as he said that,

she wondered, or a wry one? The thought of her own chaste bed held no appeal whatsoever, she realised, shocking herself profoundly. Gareth's no doubt thoroughly unchaste one, on the other hand…

'Shall we?' He stood, holding out his hand.

*Oh, yes, please…*Jessica forced a smile, put down her glass and placed her fingers in his as she got to her feet. Was he wondering why she was no doubt as pink as a peony? She hoped her scandalous thoughts were not written plain on her face for him to see, or that, if they were, he simply thought that she was overacting her part.

It was a waltz—it would have to be, she thought with a kind of resignation. The dance that would keep her in his arms throughout, the dance that would hold them face to face while she struggled to act the wanton and yet not let him see the truth of her desires in her eyes. It seemed, unless in her inexperience she was very much mistaken, that this situation had aroused Gareth to the state where he had no need to act his part. *But is it me, or is it simply male competition, the hunting urge, the need to best the other powerful males? And if it is me—surely not?—what then?*

'Why so solemn?' he murmured, taking her in his arms as they reached the floor. It seemed that the other couples left a space around them, despite the crush. Rejection—or was it that prurient curiosity demanded more room to watch?

'I am worrying about my steps,' she confided with earnest dissimulation.

'No need.' Gareth gathered her closer, his hand at her waist making her draw herself up, breathe in sharply, as surely as the strictest corset. No wonder unmarried girls needed permission before waltzing! 'I have you, just follow my lead.'

They swept into the dance and she was lost from the first note, the first step. Gareth was close—too close for propriety—he was strong, he was dominant and once again she found herself yielding to that in the most disconcerting manner.

They moved as one—in truth, she had little option. If she had fought against his direction, she knew he would simply have lifted her off her feet and carried her on with him, her skirts swirling round his long legs, her breasts crushed to his chest. As they almost were now, Jessica realised, thankful that at least this close stance meant she could not see his face.

Dizzyingly seduced by the music, the gliding sway of the dance, of Gareth's body hot and strong and close, Jessica could not have said coherently where she was in the room, or even if she was on her head or her heels. But Gareth, it seemed, was fully in control of things. As the last notes died away she came to herself and realised they were at the reception-room end of the ballroom and, as she glanced around, close to Eva and Lord Sebastian, who were standing talking to a group by the door.

'Make your farewells.' Gareth released her, then, taking her elbow, guided her towards the Grand Duchess. Heads turned. Jessica caught a glimpse of Maude, colour flying in her cheeks, standing just behind. Their eyes met and one of Maude's lids dropped in an unmistakable wink. She was enjoying herself.

'Your Serene Highness.' Jessica curtsied and Eva turned, one eyebrow raised in haughty amusement.

'My dear Mrs Carleton, you are enlivening our staid English ballroom, are you not?'

'Ma'am?' Jessica achieved a look that she thought combined injured innocence with knowing roguishness. 'I do hope not, although I confess to finding it all very new and strange. Might I be excused, ma'am?'

'A headache?' Eva enquired, tongue almost visibly in cheek.

'Yes, ma'am. Lord Standon has most kindly offered to escort me home.'

'I am sure he will look after you,' Eva said blandly. 'Will you call tomorrow afternoon?' It was a command.

'Yes, ma'am, thank you.' Another curtsy and they were walking away, out of the ballroom.

Gareth's carriage was a haven of blessed quiet and privacy after the staring eyes and whispered speculation. Jessica lay back against the squabs and sighed with relief. 'Oh, my goodness, how are we going to keep this up for weeks?'

'One appearance at a time,' Gareth said, folding himself down on to the seat opposite her. 'There is no need to put you under such pressure next time—a drive in the park is probably the logical progression.'

'And am I supposed to be under your protection by then?' she enquired, grimacing slightly at the euphemism.

'There is nothing to prevent you appearing to look around for a better offer.' Gareth sounded calm about the prospect.

'Indeed? So you can call someone out in defence of your property?'

'Is that how you see yourself?'

'It is how the world is being asked to see Mrs Carleton.'

'And you dislike that?'

'I most certainly dislike the sensation for myself, even though it is pretence.'

'And what exactly is it that you dislike, Jessica? The exchange of money for sexual favours I understand you would recoil from. But do you dislike also the idea of male possession?' There was something less calm about him now, although she could see as little of his face as she could that first evening, escaping from the brothel.

'Possession? Yes, that I do not find easy to accept. I have been independent for too long, my lord, to see it as anything but a form of servitude. Should I ever find myself in a relationship with a man, I would need equality of thought and action.'

'You are in a relationship now, with me,' he pointed out, his tone reasonable. Once again she was visited with the impression that he was controlling his breathing.

'You are my employer, Gareth. I expect to follow your direction, so far as I feel morally able to do so.' It was a shock to realise that she too was having to steady her diaphragm so that she could speak steadily. He was not touching her, yet it felt as though his scent and his presence enveloped her.

'Ah. The governess is back in control again, I see, not the actress who was swept up in her part.'

'I was not the only one swept up,' she retorted, unable to deny what he had said.

'True. But I do not have an inner governess.' He said it lightly, as a joke, but she could not hear from his voice that he was smiling. 'We are back already.' He leaned forward to look out of the window. 'All in darkness except the fanlight. Have your staff deserted you?'

'I told them to go to bed and leave a shielded lamp in the hall. I do not expect to need to call my dresser for this gown and I do not see why they should lose their sleep.'

The groom was opening the door and pulling out the steps. To her surprise Gareth jumped down before her, holding out his hand to help her alight. 'I'll walk back, Griffin,' he called up to the driver.

'Very good, my lord.'

Jessica stood on the pavement, her hand in Gareth's, watching the retreating vehicle. 'I have my key in here somewhere,' she said, freeing herself and delving in her reticule.

'May I come in for a moment, to discuss our plans for the next few days?'

It was most improper, but then who was there to censor her—except herself? And he was her employer, after all, and she had to be clear in her mind just how things were to proceed now.

'Certainly.' Jessica handed over the key and allowed herself to be shepherded over her own threshold into the dimly lit hall. 'I will just turn the lamp up.' She moved to do so, caught her heel on the trailing edge of her mantle and stumbled against Gareth.

His arms went round her, supporting her. And then he was no longer holding her up, he was crushing her against his chest and his mouth, hot and hungry and utterly irresistible, was on hers. And to her shock and delight, she was kissing him back.

Chapter Fifteen

$\infty\!\!\!\!\!\curvearrowright\!\!\!\!\!\infty$

The feel of him, the scent of him, the need for him, were all familiar things, it seemed. Her body knew what she wanted without her conscious awareness. Her arms were around Gareth's neck, her fingers sought out the point where his hair was clipped close into his neck, knowing by instinct that their pressure—*just there*—would make him gasp against her lips. Her own lips parted easily under his and the thrust of his tongue into her mouth was not shocking, only deeply arousing.

Wanton, she touched her tongue to the invader, teasing, inciting, gasping as the heat spread down, down her breasts, peaking her nipples, down to her belly, down the insides of her thighs. She ached and she knew that only his body, his hands, would stop the torment and yet she wanted him to increase it, push her further.

The world spun somewhere beyond the darkness of her closed lids, dizzying her, but she was held tight, pressed back until his body moulded against the length of her and her shoulders were hard to the wall. Jessica threw her hands wide, groping for stability, for something to lace her fingers into and hold on to against the sensation that was sweeping her up.

The handful of hard, prickly stems made her cry out, jerking her back to reality as effectively as a thrown bucket of cold water. 'What? What's wrong?' In the half-light, his eyes black, his mouth swollen, Gareth looked primeval, ready to fight whatever had attacked her.

'Holly,' Jessica gasped, shaking her hand free of the arrangement she had set in the vase only that morning. 'Oh. Gareth.' She was still crushed against the wall, his chest rising and falling with the hard breaths he was controlling. 'Gareth—we shouldn't…'

'No. We shouldn't,' he agreed, his voice husky. He didn't move.

'I don't know what—'

'It's called desire,' he said flatly, his hands tightening on her waist.

'Gareth—I'm a virgin.' She was panting, aware of every inch of him against her, aware of the heat and hardness pressed to her stomach. Somehow, with a desperate effort of will, she stopped herself rubbing against him.

'Yes. It is all right, Jessica. I won't—'

'But I wish… Oh!' She buried her face in his shoulder. She wanted him desperately, knew she must not lie with him, yet the will was simply not there to push him away, walk away.

'I wish too,' he murmured against her hair, his grip suddenly gentle. 'So much.'

The gentleness almost undid her. Jessica felt tears prickling the back of her eyes as she reached up and encircled his shoulders with her arms again, nuzzling into his neck.

'Hell,' he muttered under his breath and scooped her

up in his arms, shouldered the door open and carried her through into the dark of the drawing room.

'Gareth!'

'Shh,' he soothed, setting her down on the *chaise*. 'I want to kiss you, Jessica, that is all, just kisses, I swear.'

Just kisses. There was no *just* about it. How could something like kissing be so complex, so rich? It seemed like a simple thing, an exchange of touch, but Gareth made it an intricate bartering of breath and of heat, of taste and of touch. Somehow he had shed his coat, her own fingers were tangled in the once-immaculate folds of his neckcloth, searching for the skin beneath. And then he released her mouth.

'Ah…' Jessica sank back against the cushions, trembling. He had stopped as he had promised, he would leave her now. But how was she to move again when her body was limp and yet tense all at once, when the aching demand for more—anything, something—racked her?

Then his lips found the warm, sensitive skin beneath her ear and he began to kiss and lick down the column of her neck as she arched her head away to give him access, then up to catch the lobe between his teeth, biting gently until she sobbed his name and he murmured reassurance in words she could not catch, words that both soothed and inflamed her.

The torment of his mouth trailed down, over the curve of her breasts, down until his tongue could flicker around the point where the peaks dipped into the dark, perfumed valley between them. His hands were moving and Jessica was suddenly aware that the bodice of her gown was open, that only the fine lawn of her chemise was veiling her nipples, thrust up to meet his questing mouth by the boning of her corset.

'Gareth!' She did not know whether it was a protest or a plea, but as his lips fastened on the tip it became a mindless whimper of pleasure. The strange tension racking her intensified, deepened, became more complex as his tongue laved first one aching nub and then the other. *Only kisses*, she told herself in the part of her rational mind that was still struggling against sensation and instinct. *Only kisses*.

Then he nipped her right nipple between his teeth, so gently as she arched up beneath his weight. His tongue flickered, stroked the imprisoned, aching flesh and everything came undone, unravelled, as though something had both imploded and exploded inside her all at once. There was light, there was darkness, there was Gareth's voice a long way off and then there was nothing but a long, delicious fall into utter limpness.

'Jessica?' She lay in his arms in total abandon, her eyes shut. In the shaft of light from the hall he could see her lips were parted, sweetly curved. Colour stained her cheeks and her breast, her heart beat against his palm like a wild thing. 'My God.' Gareth stared at her, awed and a little shaken. How could he have guessed that she would be so sensual, so responsive? He had touched her nowhere but her breasts. His palms curved protectively under their weight, cupping them as she moaned.

'Hush, sweet.' He bent and kissed her, then stood on legs that were strangely unsteady and went to get the lamp from the hall. She blinked in the light as he brought it in, the picture of sweet wanton disarray on the sensu-

ously curving *chaise*. He knelt beside her and gently re-
arranged her bodice lest she be embarrassed when she
came to herself.

'Gareth? What happened? What was that?' She sat
up, pushing her tumbled hair back from her face and
reached out a hand to touch his cheek as though to
reassure herself that this was not a dream. Or, he thought
with a sudden twinge of conscience, to confirm that it
was all too real.

'It was a climax.' She blinked at him. 'An orgasm.'

Her blush showed that she understood what he was
saying, even as she shook her head in puzzlement.
'But—we didn't make love.'

'No.' Gareth sat back on his heels, fighting the
instinct to get up and go, flee before this became any
more complicated, get somewhere alone where he could
think. But if course he could not. This was Jessica; she
was completely inexperienced and she was his responsibility. 'That was most unusual. You are a sensual
woman, Jessica. A very sensual and responsive woman.'
He let the back of his hand trail up her forearm and she
shivered. Gareth pushed on, determined to make things
clear. 'Normally that would not happen until we had
become considerably more intimate.'

'And you promised we would not.' She frowned,
causing a little line to appear between her brows. He
half-lifted his hand to smooth it away, then stopped
himself. 'I'm sorry.'

'*Sorry?* Jessica, it is deeply flattering to a man that
a woman would respond so when he caresses her.'

'Really?' She sat up more, interested, her embarrassment giving way before her habitual instinct to learn.

When he nodded, she smiled and something knotted tight inside him, reminding him that he was deeply aroused and completely unsatisfied. Something must have shown in his face, for the frown reappeared. 'What about you?'

Gareth did not pretend to misunderstand her. 'It will pass, you do not need to concern yourself.'

'You won't go to that horrid brothel?' she worried.

'No, I promise not to.' He got to his feet and went to the mirror, taking the lamp to set on the mantelshelf while he retied his neck cloth.

In the glass he could see her swing her legs down from the *chaise* and twitch her bodice properly closed. 'Gareth—this isn't going to happen after every time we appear together, is it?'

'Certainly not!' He jabbed himself painfully in his Adam's apple with his tie pin and swore under his breath. 'We both got rather carried away with the atmosphere and the playacting.' *Only it wasn't playacting, that's the damnable thing. I want her, I want her in my arms and in my bed and it would not take much to have her there.* He looked up and met her eyes in the reflection. *And she'd hate me for it afterwards. I cannot, must not ruin her.*

'Yes, that must be it,' Jessica agreed. 'Does reacting like that mean I am naturally wanton?'

'No,' Gareth said firmly, racking his brains for an analogy that would stop a virtuous, chaste lady worrying about such things. 'It just means that you have an innate talent—like good pitch for music, or a true sense of colour.'

She shot him a somewhat quizzical glance, but did not question him further, simply stating, 'It is going to feel very awkward when I meet you again.'

'No more so than if we had both become rather tipsy and had shared indiscreet confidences,' he said easily, getting into his coat again. Without his valet's assistance it was not a speedy business and provided a welcome distraction from Jessica's unsettling observations. 'I will come and collect you to go driving at half past ten tomorrow, if that is convenient.'

'Yes, whatever you think is best.' She stood too, smoothing down her skirts with an unconsciously graceful gesture that had him hardening all over again. 'I have been summoned to Eva's presence in the afternoon, if you recall.'

'She will probably give us marks out of ten for our performance at the ball,' he joked, one hand on the door knob. 'Can you bolt the door after me?'

'Yes, I can reach.' She joined him in the doorway, too close for comfort, her subtle scent rising from her heated body, almost overwhelming to his sensitised nerves. 'Good night, Gareth.' The brush of her fingers on his cheek burned and he turned abruptly, wrenched the door open and stepped out into the blessed cold dampness of the night.

Jessica sat primly in the drawing room, her gloved hands folded in her lap, her saucy bonnet on the *chaise* beside her. She had made herself come and sit on the offending article of furniture while she waited for Gareth, unsure whether it was a form of penance or a piece of outrageous self-indulgence to place herself where last night's earth-shattering improprieties had occurred.

She could not be said by even the most charitable observer to be in the best of looks, she decided, glancing up at her own reflection in the overmantel mirror. One could not drink champagne at one's first, very stressful ball, then indulge in outrageously immodest behaviour with a gentleman and in consequence spend the night tossing and turning, wrestling with conscience and desire, and expect to escape without dark shadows under one's eyes and a wan complexion.

There was no doubt that Gareth would have slept perfectly well. He was, after all, a sophisticated man of the world. Jessica had worried a little about his feelings. She, at least, had experienced that exquisite, shattering, release; he had not. He had promised not to visit the brothel, and she knew, although she had no right to have asked it of him, that he would take that as a promise to visit none of them. Would the chill night air have had a calming effect on his passions? She had heard that immersion in cold water had that effect on a man. But of course, one could not ask.

Unable to sit still any longer, she jumped to her feet and began to pace. She had realised, as the clock had struck four that morning, that there was no doubting that she desired Lord Standon—it was not simply the heated delusions brought on by their playacting. In fact, she was probably suffering from some sort of infatuation for him. This was a shameful thing for a well-conducted, rational, professional female of her age to be admitting to, but one might as well be honest with oneself.

The chief thing was not to let him guess. Despite his reassuring words, he would naturally have the impression by now that she was a wanton who was not fit to undertake the education, moral or academic, of young ladies. If she were to disabuse him of that—and for some reason it was particularly important that Gareth

Morant thought well of her—she must be a model of rectitude from now on.

Which was going to be a problem, considering that she was dressed in a clinging garment that could, at best, be described as dashing, and was supposed to be spending the next hour appearing to flirt heavily with him in public.

Gareth himself was, of course, an experienced man and would not be thinking anything of what had passed—other than to hope, she supposed, that she was not foolishly besotted with him.

He was very prompt. Jessica snatched up her bonnet as the knocker sounded and went to stand before the mirror to fix it.

'Lord Standon, madam,' Hedges intoned from the doorway.

Her theory had been that it would be less embarrassing to make eye contact in the mirror. It certainly solved the question of the correct etiquette. How *did* one greet a gentleman in whose arms you had shuddered into ecstasy? With a brisk handshake? A kiss on the cheek?

'Good morning, Gareth,' she said instead, tying the satin ribbons under her chin with a jaunty bow and taking her time patting the curls at her temples into place.

'Good morning.' He sounded perfectly normal. A little cool, perhaps, although he smiled as their eyes met. 'You are very prompt.'

'I was thinking the same of you.' She picked up her gloves and reached for her reticule.

'I have taken the liberty of instructing my man of business to call upon you.' He picked up her pelisse and held it for her to slip into. His hands were efficient, adjusting it at her shoulders, and then he stepped back and lifted her vast muff, waiting while she did up the buttons.

'Thank you. But why?'

'I thought you would want him to start looking for a house for you. You can discuss which towns or parts of the country you feel might be suitable and he can start a search right away. You will want everything arranged in advance of the end of the Season, I am certain.'

'Of course. How thoughtful,' Jessica knew her tone was colourless and forced a polite smile. Inside, a hot ball of mortification gathered in her stomach. *He wants to make certain I leave as soon as this is over. After last night he wants to make certain I understand my place and am reminded of our bargain.*

'Not at all. His name is Wayman. Tell him everything you feel is important in the house you want—number of chambers, gardens and so forth.'

'Thank you.' Jessica led the way to the door. Gareth had not appeared the slightest bit discommoded by the sight of the *chaise* even. It just went to show that he placed no importance upon what had happened, other than as a warning that Miss Jessica Gifford had to be neatly, and generously, disposed of after the Season was over. 'Where shall we drive?'

'Hyde Park, I think. We want to make the maximum impact. That is a most fetching ensemble, if I may say so.'

'Isn't it?' She managed a much more creditable smile at his admiration. The outfit was cut far too tight in the bodice for comfort, had far too much ruching and laces around the neck and hem for modish restraint and the bonnet was positively pert. The overall effect was that

Mrs Carleton wished to attract as much male attention to her person as possible without actual indecency.

'What a handsome rig!' The rakish sporting carriage standing at the kerb had three black geldings harnessed unicorn in the shafts with a small tiger in red-and-blue striped jockey jacket at the head of the lead horse.

It attempted to bite him as they emerged and he dodged the big yellow teeth, grimacing at his employer. 'He's a right limb of Satan, this one, guv'nor. I told you how he'd be if you gave him lead position.'

'He will be fine, Jimmy.' Gareth handed Jessica up on to the buttoned leather of the seat. It was dyed deep blue to match the wheels, which were picked out in red like the rug he tucked around her knees. He got up beside her, gathered the reins into his left hand, took the whip in his right and nodded to the tiger. 'Let them go.'

With a muttered epitaph about the lead horse, the lad scampered round and swung himself up behind as they clattered over the cobbles down to Piccadilly.

Gareth had his hands full—even Jessica, with next to no understanding of horses or driving, could see that. The lead horse was, indeed, set on rebellion and the two behind were nervous of its plunging and head tossing. 'See, guv'nor?' Jimmy observed from his perch. His accent was pure London. 'Said you should put Nightshade up in lead.'

'If I thought this lady was interested in your observations, Jimmy, I would encourage you to continue to lecture me.' Gareth lifted his hand slightly and used the whip—the merest flick—and the leader settled. The turn right into the busy highway was accomplished safely and Jessica let out the breath she had not realised she was holding. 'As it is, you will kindly hold your tongue.'

There was a faint *humph* from behind Jessica. She glanced sideways and caught the twitch of a smile at the corner of Gareth's mouth. Not a tyrant with his servants, then. But, having seen him with his butler, she had not imagined that he would be. 'What is the name of the lead horse?' she enquired, grateful for a safe topic of conversation.

'Nero—not very original, given his colour. Although I am considering renaming him Beelzebub.'

'But Nero was a tyrant,' Jessica pointed out. 'It does indicate his character.'

'He is not tyrannising over me,' Gareth said with gritted teeth as the animal took vast exception to a sedan chair and did its best to get a leg over the traces. There was a short battle from which Gareth emerged the undoubted victor.

'You drive very well.' It was a safe conclusion that any man would be gratified with female admiration for that skill.

'Flattery, Mrs Carleton?'

'Of course,' she teased demurely. The hot knot of mortification inside had dissolved slightly, although she still felt as though every nerve was exposed, she was so alert for the slightest hint that Gareth was thinking about last night and worrying about her feelings for him. But it was not flattery. His hand was strong and sensitive on the reins, his reactions almost supernaturally sharp as he assessed the crowded thoroughfare ahead for triggers for the horse's skittish bad temper.

'Here we are.' He guided the team between the park gates and up the long carriage drive a few yards before reining them in. 'Down you get, Jimmy.'

'Wait here, shall I, guv'nor?' The lad jumped to the raked tan surface and stood, head tilted up under his peaked cap, waiting for his orders.

'Yes. Don't get into any trouble.' Gareth drove off, apparently oblivious to the snort of derision from his tiger.

'He worships you,' Jessica observed.

'I rescued him from a back slum, had him scrubbed up, beat the worst of the swearing out of him and let him do what he adores, be with horses. Of course he worships me,' Gareth said cynically.

'How did you come across him?' she asked, ignoring the cynicism for the moment. She would not let him get away with that, but now was not the time to challenge it. 'Do you often frequent back slums?'

'I do in pursuit of cutpurses who knock a lady into the gutter and make off with her reticule. I drove straight into the rookery after them. The alleys are narrow—too narrow for a horse-drawn vehicle, as I rapidly discovered. I got in as far as I could, then jumped down and took the whip to them. By the time I got back Jimmy was holding the team, swearing at all comers and offering to black their daylights if they laid a hand on my prime 'uns. I can tell a natural with horses when I see one. He told me—in between biting the coin I'd given him as a reward—that he was an orphan. So after we got the team backed out I threw him up, brought him back and he's been with me ever since.'

'That was good of you,' she said warmly, putting a hand over his gloved fist on the reins. Gareth went still, his eyes steady on his team. With care, Jessica lifted her hand away and placed it in her lap. 'You are a generous employer.'

'It is in my own interests to be so.' Still refusing to warm to her praise, he steered the team right along one of the tracks.

'Indeed? As it is in your interests to chair that charity for orphans that I have heard about? The orphans who you invite down to your country house and allow to play cricket on your lawns?'

He smiled, accepting that her persistence had defeated him. 'Very well, I am a paragon amongst employers and the foremost philanthropist in the land.'

'Now I never said that!' Jessica laughed and suddenly all was right with the world again.

Chapter Sixteen

❦

Gareth's grin broadened at her teasing and the shadows of the morning fled, leaving her relaxed and happy.

The timing of this show of harmony could not have been better. A barouche containing two heavily befurred matrons was approaching them and Gareth dropped his whip into its ring to be able to raise his hat to them. He was answered by two frosty nods and stares of penetrating disapproval. 'They are having a good look while they are about it.' She was not sure whether she was affronted or amused.

'Of course. The sight of a scarlet woman is always a source of titillation. Good morning, Lady Bathlomew!'

'They do not know that I am scarlet,' Jessica protested. 'I may be merely extremely forward or simply ignorant of correct behaviour.'

'They live in hope of a rich scandal broth,' Gareth said with a chuckle. 'Mere ignorance is not at all entertaining. Here come some of your gentlemen admirers—I expect you to exert your best efforts to make them extremely jealous of me.'

Or possibly the other way round, Jessica thought with a flash of rebellion. If he felt for her one iota of what she was beginning to feel for him… She removed one hand from the muff and waved coyly at Lord Chevering on his flashy bay. At his side Mr Sayle looked, in her opinion, far more the gentleman on a neat hack, his simple riding dress in contrast to the younger man's padded shoulders and nipped-in waist.

'Good morning, gentlemen! See how fortunate I am—Lord Standon is letting me drive behind his lovely team.' She distributed a sunny smile between them, but let her fingers rest fleetingly on Gareth's wrist. Two pairs of eyes followed the gesture.

'If I had know you wished to drive, Mrs Carleton, I would have called for you myself,' Lord Chevering declared.

'Driving what?' Gareth enquired with interest. 'Good morning Sayle.'

'I should have acquired a rig,' the young man blustered while his companion acknowledged Gareth's greeting.

'Oh. You don't have a carriage, Lord Chevering?' Jessica enquired with a little *moue* of disappointment. 'I suppose it would be very expensive.' She lingered a little on the last word.

'Perhaps you would care to ride?' Mr Sayle enquired diffidently. 'I have just acquired a very pretty grey mare you might like to try.'

'I shall be mounting Mrs Carleton myself,' Gareth interjected firmly. There was, of course, nothing wrong with the statement, unless one counted its proprietorial tone, but there was a certain something about the exchange of glances between the three men that left

Jessica feeling she had missed the point. And then she got it—and did not know how she managed not to turn beet red. He didn't mean mounting her on a horse, he meant mounting…. *Oh, outrageous!* And there was no way she could punish him for it without revealing that she understood the *double entendre*.

'Well, I would like Mr Sayle to show me his grey mare,' she said pettishly.

'Mrs Carleton, I have just said you will ride my horses.' Gareth's tone was ominous.

'I shall ride what I like,' she returned brightly, with a twinkling smile at the other men as if to invite them to admire her show of rebellion. 'You do not own me, my lord.'

That put the cat amongst the pigeons, she thought, suddenly enjoying herself, and knowing full well she was treading on dangerous ground, on the shifting sands between reality and their make-believe. 'Indeed not, ma'am,' Gareth said calmly, 'but just now I *am* in the driving seat. Good day to you, Chevering, Sayle.

'What in blazes do you think you are dong?' he demanded, the minute they were out of earshot. The sunshine seemed to vanish again. What was the matter with the man? He had seemed to welcome her teasing, they had agreed that she needed to flirt with the other men—now he was being a dog in the manger. Where had his sense of humour gone?

'I was shopping around,' Jessica replied in a sweet tone designed to infuriate. 'Don't you think it would be a little suspicious if I surrendered to the charms of your wallet without inspecting any others?'

'You are showing a suspicious talent for harlotry,' Gareth retorted. He sounded as though he meant it.

The amusement that had been bubbling up vanished. He was angry, and, suddenly, so was she. Presumably he was jealous, despite the fact that this was all a hoax. *Typical man*, she thought bitterly. She wanted to hurt him, but she did not understand why, although it was somehow connected with what had happened last night and the snub he had dealt her that morning.

'I am using my intelligence, my lord. That was one of the reasons you selected me, was it not? And I have listened to the advice of your cousins and your friends about how I should behave. Or do you think I have somehow misrepresented my character to you?'

'No, I do not,' Gareth said, breaking off to swear under his breath as Nero, sensing his driver was distracted, shied at a dead leaf blowing in the wind. He got the animal under control again. 'I said a talent for harlotry, not experience. After last night I am quite clear that I am dealing with a virgin spinster school teacher, if I ever doubted it.'

'Oh!' It was the exact truth—that was what she was. But it sounded like an insult—and when she thought about what had passed between them only hours before, Jessica decided it most certainly was one. 'Stop this carriage this instant, my lord!'

'Why?' His attention was still on the sweating horse, who had seen a yapping lapdog and was gathering his haunches under him for another display of temperament.

'Because I intend to get down.'

'What? You cannot do that here—' he took the whip out of its holder and caught the horse a glancing touch on the shoulder. At any other time Jessica would have admired his skill at missing the other horses.

'Yes, I can. And don't beat that poor horse.' She dropped her vast muff to the floor, gathered up her skirts and jumped, taking advantage of Nero deciding he was going to stand stock still in the middle of the carriage drive.

'Je—Mrs Carleton, get back here!' Something of his mood must have reached the team, for they suddenly stopped their tricks and stood placidly, as though butter would not melt in their mouths.

Jessica snatched her muff out of the carriage, thrust her hands into its snug depths and stalked to the pedestrian path at the side of the carriage drive, nose in the air. She had no intention of walking off out of the park and finding her own way home—even Mrs Carleton would not walk the streets of London unattended. No, she just wanted to teach Gareth Morant a lesson. She would find Jimmy and talk to him until Gareth turned the team—which, given the press of carriages, was going to take him a while—and came in pursuit.

The tiger was leaning against a tree, whittling a stick with an evil-looking knife and whistling tunelessly between his teeth while he watched the world go by. 'Jimmy?'

'Eh?' He dropped the stick and stood upright, staring at her. 'Where's the guv'nor, mam?'

'Coming.' Jessica waved a hand in the vague direction of the carriages. 'I felt like walking, but of course I cannot do so without a footman. Will you escort me?'

'Me, mam?' He tugged down his frogged jockey jacket self-consciously and produced a gap-toothed grin. 'Cor.'

'How old are you, Jimmy?' Jessica began to stroll along, keeping an eye out for Gareth. It wasn't that she wanted to provoke him to compete fury exactly...

'Not sure. Fourteen?' he hazarded, trotting along at her side.

'And what do you want to do when you grow up?' His brown eyes were sharp and intelligent and his movements alert; he was a bright child, she decided.

'Be head stableman for the guv'nor. Lord Standon,' he corrected himself. 'Old Franklin'll be past it by then, I reckons.'

Probably Old Franklin was a hale and hearty thirty-year-old, but Jessica refrained from saying so. Jimmy was proving an excellent distraction from having to worry about what Gareth was thinking and what she was feeling.

'Can you read and write, Jimmy? Do your figures?'

'No, mam.'

'Hmm. Well, you will need to if you are going to run a big stables.'

The lad pushed his lower lip out dubiously. 'Ain't no one to teach me.'

'I shall mention it to his lordship. There is sure to be someone on his staff who can teach you.' She wished she could do it herself, it would be a delight to work with such cheerful intelligence.

'Jimmy!' It was Gareth. The team, looking remarkably docile, was drawn up by the side of the path. 'What do you think you are doing?'

'Being a footman, guv'nor.'

'Naturally I could not walk in the park unescorted,' Jessica observed demurely, keeping a wary eye on his lordship's countenance as they walked over to the carriage. The lad helped her up, then scrambled to reach his perch. 'Jimmy has been very obliging.'

'The lady says I should learn my letters, me lord.'

'Mrs Carleton,' Gareth corrected. 'It is very kind of her to take an interest,' he added drily.

'Jimmy has ambitions. He will not achieve them without his letters and his numbers. Surely there is someone on your staff who can teach him? It need not interfere with his work.'

'You are quite correct, ma'am. Jimmy—you will tell Watson I said he's to teach you. And work hard, he's got a broad palm for slack lads.'

'Yes, guv'nor!'

'Get down here and run back to the house. I won't need you again today.'

He tooled the team out of Hyde Park, up Piccadilly and into Green Park. Watching his face, Jessica had the uneasy feeling she was in for a lecture. Well, if he didn't want her taking an interest in his servant, he only had to say so.

'Where are we going?' she ventured.

'Somewhere peaceful where I can be assured you will be attempting neither to seduce young gentlemen nor to tutor my tiger.' Gareth spoke with a satirical edge to his voice, which might have masked either amusement or irritation.

'I miss teaching,' Jessica said, suddenly discovering that it was true. 'He is a nice lad.'

'Yes.' There was a long pause while Gareth was apparently engrossed in pointing his leader precisely to enter a narrower track leading into a grove of trees. He reined in and thrust the whip handle into its stand before looping the reins around it and shifting in his seat to look at Jessica squarely. His face held the calm expression she had come to think of as typical of him, but there was something in the depths of his eyes she was not certain she could read. Puzzlement? Surely the very ordinary Miss Gifford was not a source of confusion for Lord Standon?

'What, exactly, was going on back there?' he asked. She opened her mouth to speak and he held up one hand. 'No. I know what we each did, what we each said. But why? We were both angry and I wish I understood why.'

'I was annoyed by your *double entendre*,' Jessica admitted before she had time to think about where that might lead.

'My—ah.' He grimaced. 'Providing your mounts?'

'Mounting me,' she corrected grimly.

'I did not think you would understand.' He was, at least, looking reasonably penitent.

'I may be inexperienced, but I am not quite the innocent you imagine Gareth. I can work things out without a diagram. And my business is words.'

'Yes. Apparently so.' He stared past her left ear for long enough for her to begin to fidget. 'My instinct is to warn them off,' he said abruptly.

'Because of our masquerade?'

'Because you are under my protection.' He grimaced. 'Not that I was doing a very good job of protecting you last night. Which I suppose is what is playing havoc with my temper,' he added thoughtfully.

'You hardly ravished me,' Jessica pointed out. 'It does take two.' What devil got into her she did not know, but she added, 'I enjoyed it. I would have liked to do it again.'

If she had hoped to take him completely aback, she

could not have succeeded better. For once, Lord Standon was deprived of a ready answer. 'That would be unwise,' he said at length, with the wary air of a man talking a dangerous lunatic down off the edge of a roof. 'It is not always easy to keep such things within bounds.'

'Oh, I didn't mean I thought it *wise*,' Jessica assured him. 'Or fair to you, of course—please do not think I am not very well aware of the extent of your self-restraint. I just meant it would be nice.'

'Nice.' For a moment she wondered if he was about to lecture her, then Gareth threw back his head and laughed, a full-blooded, genuine shout of amusement that had the horses sidling. 'Miss Gifford, I am beginning to wonder whether my life was simply very dull before I met you, or whether I simply did not understand how to enjoy it.'

Jessica's green eyes were amused but cautious as she watched him gain control of himself. 'I doubt it was dull, my lord,' she said drily. No, of course it hadn't been— he did not need her to remind him that he had a privileged and enjoyable life. But before he had not had the stimulus of Miss Gifford's cool regard, the novelty of being on the receiving end of unspoken disapproval or the delight of sparring with a woman who was not only intelligent but who held him in no awe whatsoever and who stirred his blood like none he could recall before.

Gareth made himself focus on Jessica's words and the feelings behind them and not on the ache of need settling low in his belly. She was, as they had discovered last night, a highly sensual young woman. It was no wonder she wished to explore that sensuality further. She trusted him; he did not flatter himself that she had been waiting for Prince Charming all her life and he was the answer to her dreams

'So nice that we had best be careful over the next few weeks,' he cautioned. 'It was not just pleasant for you. I enjoyed it.' The little smile that twitched at the corner of her mouth made him want to lean in and taste her. That taste had not left him, he realised, since their first encounter when the scent of her naked skin had filled his nostrils and his lips had touched her hair. He had kissed her and told himself that was the end of it; but last night had proved it was not. His reactions to the other men proved it too. He was jealous.

'Men are unreliable creatures, too driven by our base animal instincts to rely on.'

'I trust you,' she said simply, her dark lashes sweeping down to veil her eyes. He wanted to touch them with his tongue tip, was swaying towards her even as he thought it.

'Then your much-vaunted common sense is at fault, Miss Gifford.' Gareth sat bolt upright. 'We are close now; we will become closer. We must paint the picture of a couple who are not only on the verge of lovemaking, but who are lovers in fact. And the moment we are alone we must draw back from that, suppress the instincts that tell us to indulge in that sensual pleasure.'

'You are afraid that if we fail, then there is the danger of—' She broke off frowning, the fullness of her lower lip caught for a moment by a sharp tooth as she bit it in thought. 'Of an emotional attachment on my side.'

'I—' It was what he did fear. That and the fact that one

did not seduce innocent young ladies of good birth and then pension them off as one did a discarded mistress.

'I am an educationalist, Gareth. I thought I simply wanted the freedom to be my own woman and not be at the beck and call of an employer. Now I know I still wish to teach, but on my own terms. I am not looking for a lover or a husband.' That was said with surprising emphasis. 'But that does not mean I wish to renounce the company of men.'

'I did not think it was my company you desired,' he said, teasing, and was rewarded by a blush and a dimpling smile.

'Gareth! I meant that I am not asking that we become lovers—certainly not. I am just saying that if something like last night happens again, I am not going to go into a decline about it. Nor would I presume upon it to make demands.'

Her intention, he realised with a sudden insight, was to reassure him as much as herself. 'We are alert to the strains this strange playacting puts upon us now,' he said, choosing not to answer her words directly. 'Thank you for being so frank; we can act our roles more easily now, I think.'

'Providing you do not provoke any gentlemen into a duel,' she retorted tartly.

'I shall try not to,' he promised, gathering up the reins and heading the team back the way they had come. 'We had better give the impression that a liaison has begun as soon as possible then.'

'No one will dare to challenge you for what you have already claimed?' she asked.

'I would hope not.' Both Sebastian and Ashe had

fought duels. He never had and had no desire to do so.
But if anyone harassed or insulted Jessica, he would
have no hesitation in meeting them, he realised with a
shock. 'The evening we met I was complaining of being
bored,' he added inconsequentially, and beside him
Jessica laughed richly.

Chapter Seventeen

'**Y**ou have made an excellent beginning,' Eva said warmly. Far from the strict Grand Duchess who had ordered Mrs Carleton's presence that afternoon, she was lounging on a *chaise*, her hair down, clad in a sumptuous negligée and surrounded by fashion magazines.

'Are you unwell?' Jessica enquired, puzzling over why Eva appeared to be resting at three in the afternoon.

'No.' She placed a hand over her stomach and grimaced. 'Merely very sick this morning. I am fine now, but I am humouring Sebastian, who is flapping around as though the house were on fire. This is a man who climbs down sheer castle walls on the end of a rope and conducts knife fights in French alleyways, mind you. I thought it was women who became mildly addled with pregnancy, not their husbands, but Bel says Ashe is just as bad.'

'Lying on a sofa nibbling almond biscuits and reading *La Belle Assemblée* isn't such a sacrifice,' Jessica suggested.

'I don't know why I bother with fashion journals—

I won't fit into a thing soon. But never mind that, Bel and Maude will be here in a minute and we want to hear all about it.' On her words the boudoir door opened to admit the friends, Maude beaming. She dropped her muff and flew to embrace Jessica.

'You were wonderful! Papa is beside himself. He pressed a fifty-pound note into my hand this morning and told me to go and do some shopping to cheer myself up.' She sank elegantly into a chair and spoiled the effect by pulling off her bonnet, heeling off her shoes and curling her feet up under her.

'Yes, but you told me he said to buy something to dazzle Gareth in, so he hasn't given up,' Bel pointed out, entering more moderately and giving Jessica and Eva a peck on the cheek.

'No. Though he keeps moaning about how he was mistaken in him, and what a disappointment he is being and how he must take him in hand.'

'I'd like to see that,' Jessica observed appreciatively.

'I have talked him into inviting Gareth to the theatre tomorrow night. I suggested a nice party in our new box— you and Ashe and Eva and Sebastian and Gareth and me.'

'Would that be your new box at the Unicorn?' Eva asked. 'How did you persuade him to rent that?'

'I didn't. That's what I've spent my fifty pounds on.'

'So cheap?' Bel was peeling off her gloves, but looked up in surprise.

'Lord, no! I've had to raid my quarterly allowance as well. But it isn't the Opera House, after all.'

'And what will you tell your papa when he asks why his present has gone on that?' Jessica asked. She did not know if Maude had confided her infatuation with Mr

Hurst to the others, and realised she had not when she received a mischievous smile in return, but no mention of the theatre's owner.

'I told him I was taking a great interest in drama. He is too worried about Gareth to question it at the moment.' Maude helped herself to an almond biscuit and settled back. 'Anyway, we must warn Gareth to refuse on the grounds of an earlier engagement, and then he must take you. I have hired the box opposite for the evening.'

'An excellent plan,' Eva approved. 'What is the piece?'

'Goodness, I have no idea.'

Jessica picked up *The Times* from the table beside her and scanned the columns. 'Here we are. *The Duenna* with Mr Sinclair as Carlos and Miss Stephens as Clara. With a farce and other entertainments.'

'Oh, that's a Spanish romantic comedy. The men will hate it,' Bel observed. 'But it is a good plan. Now, Jessica, we are all dying to know—what happened last night?'

'You saw. I flirted with various men and then Gareth arrived and we were together and caused something of a stir and then we left.' Was she blushing? She hoped not.

'But what came over him?' Maude demanded. 'It was wonderfully effective, all that masterful stalking about, but that was not how we had planned it. I was completely taken aback.'

'Exactly. Everyone was taken by surprise, including me, so it seemed more realistic.'

'Realistic is certainly the word.' Eva sounded amused. 'And what happened after you left?'

'He took me home.'

'Indeed.' Eva narrowed her eyes and Jessica plastered

a bland smile on her face. 'Gareth appeared really quite…attracted.'

Bel cleared her throat and tipped her head warningly towards Maude, who caught the gesture. 'Are you asking if he seduced Jessica?' she demanded.

Now she was blushing, she could feel the heat. 'He kissed me goodnight,' she said repressively. 'It was to help get us in the mood.' The other three bit their lips, struggled with themselves and then burst into laughter. 'Oh, you know what I mean!' Jessica said crossly.

'Yes, of course,' Eva agreed, getting her giggles under control. 'Did you enjoy it?'

Jessica glared, on the point of refusing to answer. Then the urge to confide got the better of her. 'Yes.' They all stared expectantly. 'He was very good at it.'

'Goodness.' Maude stared at her. 'Gareth? I never thought of him like that.'

'Well, I suggest you do not start now,' Jessica said in her best governess tone. 'We can do without any further complications.' The stab of jealousy that shot through her at the thought of Maude in Gareth's embrace shocked her. If he ever stopped thinking about Maude like a younger sister, then why wouldn't he fall head over heels for her? She was so lovely. But should she encourage Maude or—

'I wouldn't dream of it. Gareth? I love him dearly, but he is so sensible,' Maude said firmly. 'And old.'

'*Old?*' Jessica stared at her. 'He cannot be thirty yet. I am sure he is no older than your Mr Hurst.'

'He has a loyal defender,' Bel observed. 'Maude, have you got the theatre tickets for Jessica and Gareth?'

'Oh. No, I left them in my reticule on the hall table.'

'Better go and get them now while we think of it.' Bel got to her feet. 'I wanted to ask Eva's housekeeper something, I've just remembered. I'll come with you.'

'Has Bel just tactfully removed Maude for a purpose?' Jessica demanded as the door shut behind them.

'I expect she feels I should give you a little warning about men.'

'Gareth has been a perfect gentleman,' Jessica said hotly, remembering with shame her fears about finding herself in the power of a nobleman.

'Of course. And you are a very intelligent and well-conducted gentlewoman. Which is exactly how I would have described myself before I first came into contact with a male Ravenhurst.' There was a reminiscent smile playing around Eva's lips. 'All I will say is that if you ever need any...assistance, I am here for you.'

Jessica sat staring at her own hands, which seemed to have twisted her handkerchief into a corkscrew. The knotted tangle seemed simple compared to the swirling thoughts that jumbled her brain. Ruthlessly she unpicked them. She was employed, for a generous fee, to impersonate Gareth's lover. *Impersonate, is the key word.* And she had discovered a strong physical attraction to him. In fact, if she were to be honest with herself, a *tendre* for him. And he had implied that he was not precisely indifferent to her. And now Lady Sebastian was implying that Jessica's situation was in some way comparable with hers when she met Lord Sebastian. *But they are married now...* What was Eva suggesting? That such a thing was a possibility? Or that she might let herself believe it and would need help in extracting herself?

The latter, of course. She had just been given a

friendly warning, not that she needed one. Governesses did not marry earls, even if they wanted to. Which she did not. Life was hard enough without idiotic daydreams.

'Thank you,' she said with a bright smile. 'I am very grateful for your support in all of this. I was saying to Gareth this morning that I miss teaching already; I am sure I do not know how I would get through to the end of the Season without your help, and Bel's, of course.'

'You miss teaching?' Maude came back into the room. 'Here are the tickets for the box before I forget. But teaching? Really? I would hate it—when I think of the trial I must have been to my poor governesses, I shudder at the thought of things being reversed.'

'I miss it so much I wish I could teach Gareth's tiger his letters.' Jessica tucked the ticket away safely. 'What should I wear tomorrow night?'

'Good God.' Gareth stood stock still in the middle of the drawing room and stared at her.

'What's wrong?' Jessica cast a harried glance at the mirror. She had thought the ivory moiré-silk evening gown rather lovely, although she was nervous about moving too abruptly or taking in a deep breath, the neckline was so low and her lacing so tight.

'Wrong? Nothing. You look spectacular.' He was stalking round her, inspecting every angle. 'Fantastic. I am going to have to go armed to keep off my rivals, I can see.'

'Nonsense.' Jessica felt quite flurried. True, the hairdresser had spent the afternoon on her hair and her dresser had exerted every trick in her considerable repertoire—Jessica had drawn the line at the attempt to pad out her bosom with what Mirabelle described as *chicken fillets*—but she knew she had none of the natural beauty that Maude or Eva or Bel wore so naturally. A silk purse may have been temporarily created out of the sow's ear, but she felt it was but smoke and mirrors.

'Jessica, truly, you look exquisite. Look at yourself.' He turned her to face the mirror, standing behind her so his face reflected back at her over her own shoulder. As she frowned, he frowned too. 'Stop looking doubtful! You have got to sweep into that box, utterly confident of your own beauty and your own powers. You have bagged me. I am at your feet. You have secured your earl. This is your moment of triumph.'

'I do not know if I can do it!' Panic, far worse than the nerves before the ball, swept through her. 'I do not know if I can sit in one of those boxes, lit up, stared at, the focus of everyone's attention and act that.' His hands, cupping her naked shoulders, tightened. 'I will go stiff, freeze, I know I will.'

'Then we had better unfreeze you.' Gareth turned her until she stood facing him toe to toe, the ruffles at the hem of her skirts brushing his shoes. 'We have spent all night and all day making love, I imagine. Let us see if we can look like it.'

He bent and took her lips before she could form the question. The word *how?* was swallowed up as, open mouth to open mouth, he drew her to him. There was no need to coax her lips open, no need to tease her tongue into playing with his. He filled her, bold and demanding, mimicking the ultimate possession that the pressure of his pelvis against her belly promised. And she answered him, all thoughts of freezing up banished. Her tongue moved with his, teased his as he explored her, then, boldly, licking past his lips into the heat of his mouth.

He had been drinking brandy. It flamed, hot, on her tongue as she flicked the tip against his teeth, then withdrew a little, teasing his lips. The needy sensation she had experienced before surged through her, stronger now, she realised, because she understood what it was demanding, what it would lead to.

They stepped back together, speaking together. 'I think—'

'We ought to—'

'Stop,' Gareth finished. She had succeeded in over-turning his usual amused calm. The man who faced her looked aroused, looked dangerous, for all that he had freed her when he must have known she was far too carried away by his kisses to have resisted him.

'Yes.' Jessica nodded vigorously, then grabbed for a loosened ostrich plume slipping from her elaborate coiffure. 'I imagine we look adequately, um…'

'Bedded?' he suggested with a grin, relaxing. The dangerous predator was still there, though, she thought with a delicious secret shiver. *What would it be like to be kissed by Gareth if he truly desired you? If he loved you?* 'Do you need any help with that feather?'

'No, I have it.' Jessica jabbed the pin in firmly, making her eyes water. 'Oh, I shall be so glad to let my hair down!' Was that a growl or was he simply clearing his throat? 'We had better go, don't you think? Maude thought it best if we enter our box just after they have got settled in theirs and she says they will leave her house just about now.'

* * *

They sat opposite each other in the carriage, chatting easily about neutral subjects as the wheels rumbled over the wet cobbles. It was hard to believe that only minutes before they had been in each other's arms. Jessica was beginning to feel she had regained her composure as they drew up and the flickering light from the massed torchères outside the theatre illuminated the interior of the vehicle.

Gareth stood, pulled her to her feet and pressed one hard, intense kiss on her lips, holding it until the groom threw open the door and let down the steps. Blushing, torn between indignation and bliss, Jessica tottered out and into the theatre on Gareth's arm.

'How could you! I can hardly walk, my knees have turned to jelly.'

'That's quite the nicest thing you have ever said to me,' he teased as they handed their cloaks to a waiting attendant. 'Is Lord Pangbourne here this evening?'

'Yes, my lord. His lordship has brought a small party—you have just missed them.'

'Perfect.' Gareth shepherded her through the foyer and up the stairs to the first floor.

'Have you been here before?' He seemed to know his way as he walked along the curving wall punctuated with numbered doors, checking against the pasteboard slip in his hand.

'Yes, when you told me about Maude's interest in Hurst. I wanted to check that this was at least a respectable theatre, if there is such a thing.'

'And is it?'

'It appears to be. And a very profitable one, by all

accounts. Here we are. Are you ready?' He opened the door, making as though to seize her again, and Jessica was laughing as she walked through into the box.

The light, the noise, the crowd hit her like a blow as she emerged from the shadowed passageway on to what seemed to be centre stage. It was smaller than the Opera House, and there she had been able to hide behind a curtain. Here, their box seemed to thrust out towards the tiers of others with their red and gilt and flaring lights. Heads turned, eye glasses glinted as they were lifted, a buzz of speculation went around, cutting through the clamour as people recognised Gareth.

Opposite, Maude started, her hand flying to her mouth, her gaze transfixed on Gareth's face. 'She should be in melodrama,' he murmured, amused, as he took his time arranging their chairs and seating Jessica. Alerted by his daughter's gesture, Lord Pangbourne turned from speaking to Bel, his jowls quivering with indignation.

'Oh dear, I do hope he is not going to have a seizure,' Jessica said, concerned.

'Not he. The man thrives on combat and indignation. It looks as though he is going to walk out—that really would make the gossip columns—no, Eva is being firm with him.'

Puffing indignantly, Lord Pangbourne subsided into his chair, folded his arms across his substantial stomach and proceeded to glare at their box. 'Everyone is looking at us,' Jessica hissed.

'Excellent.' Gareth lifted her hand and began to kiss her fingers elaborately. 'Could you possibly look as though you are enjoying this?'

'Oh, sorry.' Jessica ran her free hand through the

thick hair at his temples, then cupped his cheek, gazing at him adoringly. 'I want to giggle.'

'Then fan yourself vigorously and tell me how magnificent I was this afternoon in bed.'

'That, my lord, is taking playacting a little far.'

'What if there are lip readers out there?' he suggested, straight-faced.

'Oh, Gareth darling, you were magnificent in bed this afternoon,' Jessica gushed obediently. 'And you are teasing me.'

'Yes, but no one has said that to me recently.'

'Outrageous man!' She couldn't help laughing at him. 'I don't believe that for a minute.'

'I am flattered that you have such a high expectation of my performance.'

'I have a high expectation of what a mistress would expect to say to her paramour, whether she meant it or not.' Jessica snapped her fan shut and fetched him a reproving tap on the knuckles. *Expectation? He speaks as though* we *will become lovers.*

Gareth captured it, unfurled it and used it to shield their faces. 'Ouch, that was Miss Gifford, governess, at her most severe. And I do not have one just now.'

'No mistress?'

'No, not at the moment. Too much hard work, too expensive and I am too lazy.' He restored the fan to her as the snuffer men began to extinguish candles and dim lamps until most of the light was focused on the stage. Jessica bit her lip in thought. Was that why he was so passionate with her? Simple frustration? That was a flattering thought, to be sure! It was certainly one well suited to dampening down over-heated imaginings on the part of inexperienced ladies thrown into intimacy with London bucks.

And thinking of bucks… she squinted through the gloom at the box opposite as the door opened, admitting a tall figure and a fleeting shaft of light. 'Is that Captain Grahame?'

Gareth, who had bent and was trailing kisses along her neck, tilted his head to look. 'I think it is.' He went back to nibbling.

'Stop it! No one can see.'

'I can taste. And you will be nicely pink and flustered when the lights come back up.'

'I will be that without what you are doing now, my lord! Be sensible and think about Captain Grahame. Is he courting Maude, do you think? Because if so, I should warn her about his character. His conversation with me was positively warm.'

'No need, surely, given her infatuation with Hurst? No, he appears to be Pangbourne's guest—they have their heads together.'

'Does no one ever watch the play?' Jessica tried to concentrate on what was taking place on the stage. Gareth had abandoned her neck, but had taken her left hand in his and was playing with her fingers. 'Obviously not,' she answered herself, looking round at a burst of catcalling and waving from a group of rakes towards some of the more scantily clad members of the chorus. 'People are still staring at us.'

'Good. Just enjoy the play and gaze adoringly into my eyes from time to time,' Gareth recommended, cheerfully ignoring her unladylike snort.

Gradually she became less self-conscious, forgot the

raised eyeglasses and the gossip and relaxed into the play, whispering comments in Gareth's ear, clutching his hand at moments of high drama, finding again the easiness in his company she had found at the opera.

The curtain falling for the interval brought her to herself to find Gareth on his feet opening the box door. There was an exchange with someone she could not see, then he turned back, frowning, a folded paper in his hand.

'It is a note from Maude, asking me to met her urgently.' He peered at it in the dim light of the box. 'Dreadful scrawl, I hardly recognise her hand. She wants me to go to the balcony overlooking the main foyer.'

'She is still in her box.' Maude was talking with animation to Lord Sebastian.

'Probably waiting to see if I move—she won't want to stand there by herself. I had better go—goodness knows what Pangbourne is planning now.' He looked down at her. 'Will you be all right for a few minutes? Lock the door of the box, I'll knock.'

Jessica slipped the catch over and went to watch Lord Pangbourne's party. Maude was still in her box, although now she was standing towards the rear. Minutes passed; Maude stayed where she was, apparently unable to find an excuse to slip out.

A tap on the door made her jump. She had not realised how tense she had become without Gareth there. The catch was stiff under her kid-covered fingers. 'I don't think she was able to get away—' she began as Captain Grahame slid into the box, shut the door and leaned back against it.

'My dear Mrs Carleton. I must congratulate you upon

the speed of your conquest. Lord Standon is notoriously selective in his choice of *belles amies*.'

'What do you want?'

'Why, to deliver a message. And a warning.' His smile beneath the pencil-thin moustache held no warmth whatsoever.

Chapter Eighteen

'A warning, Captain Grahame? You mean a threat? I must ask you to leave—I have no wish to entertain you, and for your own sake I would strongly recommend that you remove yourself before Lord Standon returns.'

It was the same haughtily confident tone with which Jessica had faced down the tipsy husband of one of her employers, bent upon ravishing the latest unfortunate governess to cross their threshold. In that case he had retreated in confusion and had written her a glowing reference in the morning. Somehow she suspected the captain was not going to be so easy to handle.

'I have no intention of lingering—not now. I am sure we will have the opportunity for mutually profitable conversations in the future. But for now, I am bearing an offer from Lord Pangbourne.'

'He is rather older than I was looking for in a… friend,' Jessica said coolly.

Captain Grahame flushed with irritation. It seemed she was not being as compliant as he had expected. 'I would suggest you are not quite so flippant, ma'am.

Lord Pangbourne offers you two thousand pounds to leave London and Lord Standon and not return.'

How would Mrs Carleton react to that? I want to slap his face—but would she? 'Paltry,' Jessica drawled. 'He will need to do better than that Captain, and you may tell him so. What is your warning?'

'That two thousand pounds or not, leaving London would be good for your health—and for Standon's.' He handed her a rectangle of embossed pasteboard. 'My card. I suggest you do not think about it for too long, my dear.'

He was gone before Jessica could react, or fully take in the threat. She looked down at the calling card, then stuffed it into her reticule as the door opened again. 'I thought you locked this.' Gareth strolled in. 'No sign of Maude—I suppose she was unable to find an opportunity to slip out.'

'I did lock it.' Jessica sat down, feeling oddly flustered. 'I thought I heard you knock just now.' *Why was she lying to him? Why not tell him what had just happened and have the satisfaction of seeing him punch Captain Grahame's unpleasant smile off his face? The offer of money doubtless came from Maude's father, but she doubted that bluff, direct, man would threaten a woman with violence. And Gareth?*

'Captain Grahame is still over there,' she observed, gesturing towards the Pangbourne box. He must have slipped back in while she was talking to Gareth. 'He looks the sort of man who ends up getting called out by outraged brothers.'

'He does the calling out—you might almost call it a hobby of his.' Gareth sat down next to her, picked up her fan and began to waft it back and forth. 'You are quite flushed.'

'So he has fought many duels?'

'Four, to my knowledge.' He put down the fan and opened the programme. 'Wounded his opponents badly in all of them: he's a crack shot and a seriously good swordsman.'

'Oh.' Jessica managed not to gulp. 'How unpleasant. Do you duel?'

'Never have.' Gareth had found what he was looking for and was studying the cast list. 'Thought I recognised that man in the bad wig—saw him last week in something.'

'Why not?'

'Why not duel?' He smiled at her. 'You are very bloodthirsty all of a sudden, my sweet. I have never been provoked enough to issue a challenge and I appear not to have provoked anyone else sufficiently either.'

'Are you a good shot? Or better with a sword?' she persisted, trying to sound as though it were an idle interest.

'Adequate at both, I suppose. Sebastian is a better shot than I am and Dereham a better swordsman.' The curtain went up to the accompaniment of a drum roll from the orchestra and Gareth settled back in his chair, the question of duels apparently dismissed from his mind.

He was probably being modest, Jessica tried to reassure herself. Gareth was not the sort of man she would expect to boast of his prowess at anything; he would simply get on and demonstrate it. A flash of heat through her body reminded her just how effectively he had demonstrated his abilities at love-making. She forced her mind away from that seductive memory and back to the present.

Given what Gareth had just told her about Captain

Grahame's predilection for duelling, it seemed she was not mistaken in believing he was issuing a direct threat to Gareth. Should she warn him? But then he would probably go straight off and challenge Grahame for threatening her and that would trigger the very thing she wanted to avoid.

My sweet, he had called her. But then, *All of us Ravenhurst cousins seem to have an ability as actors*, she reminded herself of his words when they had been discussing Maude's fascination with Mr Hurst and the theatre. Why was she thinking about that now? Jessica shifted her position a little so she could watch Gareth's profile. He was smiling at something happening on the stage—she had lost all track of the entertainment, wild horses might be rampaging through for all she knew—his body big, powerful and relaxed.

There was a natural masculine elegance about him that came from inside as much as from the form of his body. He would be a powerful physical force if angered, but he did not spend his time picking fights like the captain, he used his wits to deal with difficult situations. Like her rescue from the brothel or the way he concealed Maude's presence when Lord Pangbourne had burst into the breakfast room.

Jessica could not imagine Gareth ever wanting to hurt anyone, let alone risk their life. Captain Grahame, on the other hand, must enjoy it. It was probably only the sanction of having to flee abroad if he killed his man that kept him from doing so. A hideous image of Gareth lying bleeding, his life ebbing out on to the crushed turf came to her, wiping away the reality of the man sitting beside her. *I love him. I can't—I must not—Oh my God, I love him…*

* * *

'Jessica?' Gareth turned at the sound of the gasp. 'Are you all right?'

'Hiccup,' she apologised, scrabbling in her reticule. 'My goodness, it has made my eyes stream.' She was being uncharacteristically clumsy with the strings of the purse. Gareth fished in his pocket and proffered his own handkerchief. 'Oh, thank you.' He could not see her face from behind the large linen square, but her voice sounded oddly muffled.

'Would you like a drink?' There were no more hiccups. Jessica finished mopping her eyes, blew her nose and folded up the handkerchief with great care.

'No, thank you. I was so nervous I was picking at my dinner, and then I thought I must eat, so I rather bolted it. I deserve indigestion for being so silly. I will have this laundered and returned to you.' She fidgeted with the reticule some more, finally succeeded in opening it and pushed the handkerchief inside.

The curtain came down, making her jump as the audience, despite their previous inattention, broke into applause and calls for the actors. 'Oh dear, I missed the end.'

'Never mind, we did not come for the play. I think that was quite a successful evening, don't you?' He clapped as the actors parted, revealing the tall, unsmiling figure of the manager who bowed to the audience. 'Is that Hurst?'

Jessica seemed to pull herself out of some abstraction and peered down at the stage. 'Yes, that is he.'

'Handsome fellow,' Gareth remarked, eying the tall, broad-shouldered figure with the austere, sculpted face. 'I can see why Maude is attracted.'

'He reminds me of you,' Jessica said.

'Me? Good God, my sweet, look at him! The man's off some classical frieze—you have noticed my nose, I assume?'

She smiled, faintly. 'There is nothing wrong with your nose—on a man. You are the same shape as he is. The same build. From the back I thought he was you that first time.' The smile vanished and was replaced by a blush.

Startled, Gareth looked down again. She noticed the way he looked? His figure? She compared him to the man on the stage and thought him as well built? A glow of purely masculine smugness ran through him and he grinned at himself for feeling it.

'I think you are all about in your head,' he said frankly. 'Are you feeling better?' She did not look it. The animation of earlier had gone and now Jessica looked strained and reserved. He was asking a lot of her, he told himself, filled with self-reproach. He was used to being stared at, gossiped about. She was not.

'Yes, I am fine. What would you like to do now?' Her head was up, her shoulders back, the smile on her face again. *My brave Jessica. I know what I want to do now.*

'Take you home. We have done enough for one night, I think.'

'Very well.' She placed her hand on his arm as they came out into the passageway, smiling and flirting with each other as they passed other couples on their way to the head of the stairs. She saw the Pangbourne party the moment he did, her fingers gripping on his forearm so tightly he thought she would be unable to relax them.

Breathe, smile he heard her murmur under her breath and the grip relaxed, her chin came up. Maude gave a theatrical start at the sight of them, them swept past, almost treading on Jessica's toes, eyes averted. Her father glowered at them both before escorting her down the stairs, his jowls quivering with indignation. Eva and Sebastian, Bel and Ashe followed, all four nodding coolly as they passed. And then he felt Jessica's grip tighten again. Captain Grahame, elegant in full regimentals, the insolent smile on his face that had Gareth longing to hit him, bowed.

'My dearest Mrs Carleton, how pleasant to see you again so soon. Standon, one must congratulate you upon setting society on its heels—so very unlike you, one would have said.' He bowed again and was gone, jogging lightly down the stairs to catch up to his party.

'What did he mean, *so soon*?' Gareth demanded, prioritising insults in his head and finding that Grahame's sniping at him was as nothing compared to the intimacy with which he addressed Jessica.

'I have no idea.' Jessica removed her hand from his arm and began to walk down the stairs. All the colour had gone from her cheeks and Gareth stepped across to take her elbow, anxious that she might faint. 'He was being provocative, no doubt. He appears to have succeeded. Thank you, I can manage.'

'Has he been pestering you?' Gareth persisted as they stepped out into the night. With the high collar of her velvet evening cloak up around her face, she seemed ethereal, fragile. Where had the strong-minded governess gone? This woman looked as though she would break in his hand, flinch at a hard word.

'No! Gareth, please do not hector me.' That was clear and decisive enough; perhaps appearances were deceptive. Gareth apologised, guiding her towards where his coachman had positioned the carriage. At times like this, in the midst of a jostling throng, the man was worth every penny of his generous wage.

'I did not mean to. The man sets my hackles up.'

'As he no doubt intends,' Jessica observed. It appeared she was once more back in control; perhaps whatever had ailed her had been set to rights by the crisp night air.

This time, instead of sitting opposite, he sat beside her on the soft plush. It would take almost half an hour to get back to Half Moon Street at this time of night, with frost on the cobbles and the streets full of the night-time crowds. Time to hold her in his arms, repeat those kisses that had so fired his blood earlier that evening.

He turned, just as the flambeaux outside the theatre illuminated the inside of the carriage like daylight. It only lasted a moment, but it was enough to see her profile: pure, pale and stark. She looked like a woman who had received the worst of news, something so bad that she was beyond crying out with the pain of it, but instead must sit still and silent, absorbing it.

'Jessica?' He reached for her in what was now virtual darkness.

'No! Please, I am not…we should not…' She got her voice under control. 'I am not in the mood for kisses, my lord. There is no one here for us to deceive.'

'You are tired,' he said, wanting nothing more than to wipe that bleakness from her eyes. 'I just want to hold you. Relax.' He put his arm around her shoulders and pulled her to him. 'There, now.'

For a moment he thought she would resist him, then

she came to him with a little sigh as though in sur-
render, curled against him, soft and trusting. And something inside him changed, welled up and gripped his
breathing so that for a long moment he could only sit
there, eyes wide open on the shadows, his senses full of
the sweetness of her. It was like lemon blossom, he
thought. Utterly fragrant, yet with the promise of a sharp
tang behind it. *I love her.*

'Gareth.'

'Yes?' *I'll tell her; I must tell her. Surely she feels
something for me? Surely she cannot lie so trustingly
in my arms, surely she would not have shuddered into
ecstasy like that if she did not feel something—?*

'When is your man of business calling? Mr Wayman,
is it not?'

'You want him to call?' It was an effort to drag his mind
away from the fantasies it was weaving to deal with this.

'Of course.' She sat up, leaving him feeling bereft. 'I
need to have this settled—we discussed it and you were
quite right. I think I will feel better when I know what
I will be doing next—it will be easier to deal with the
stress of this masquerade when I can be planning for
getting back to normal.'

'Normal?' It was as though she had slapped him.
'What you said you wanted was very far from what has
been normal for you up to now.'

'Yes, but I do need to work. I realised that, talking to
Jimmy. This will give me the opportunity to be my own
mistress, to choose who and when to teach.'

'This scheme of ours is so distasteful to you, then?'

She turned to him, surprise at his question in every
line of her silhouette. 'Of course. I made a bargain and

I will fulfil it, but I never pretended that I thought it would be a pleasurable experience.'

Irrational and unreasonable anger at her, anger at his own foolish, emotional weakness swept through him. She had insinuated herself into his heart and his soul. His body ached for her. The fact that she had not intended to do so, had done nothing other than scrupulously follow his orders, did not matter. She had burrowed under his carapace of calm, his ordered world, his cynical observance of other peoples' emotional turmoil, without any effort at all. And he had invited her into his life—he had as good as commanded her to make him fall in love with her. He had, in fact, wished this upon himself.

Through a red haze that seemed to fill his vision, Gareth reached out and yanked on the check string. The carriage rumbled to a halt and the trap flipped open. 'My lord?'

'Home.' The trap shut and the carriage moved off.

'To your house? Why?'

'Because I have something I want to show you.' *Show her? Coward, you dare not risk telling her, dare you? She will throw the words in your face, demand to be taken back to Half Moon Street and drag those damned awful stuff gowns out of the wardrobe again. She'll plait up her hair and pick up her schoolbooks and flee and you'll never see those emeralds burning on her white skin, never... But I'll be damned if she can ever say again that these few weeks had not given her any pleasure.*

'Show me?'

'Yes.' He felt her withdrawal, as thought she understood what he intended, yet she did not move.

'Very well.' She sat in silence while the carriage

moved through the streets, her hand raised to hold the strap as it swayed around corners. 'Only once, to last for ever,' she murmured, so soft he would have thought he had imagined it, if it had not been for the puff of her breath on the cold air. So soft that he surely could not have heard the note of resignation in the six words.

The butler opened the door wide, ushering them into the warmth and light of the hall. 'Good evening Jordan.' The butler took their heavy cloaks and Gareth's tall hat.

'Good evening, madam. My lord?'

'Nothing, thank you. You may lock up and retire. I do not require Malvern either.'

'I will apprise him of that, my lord. The decanters are in the library.'

Jessica gazed at Gareth from under her lashes. His mood had changed abruptly during the carriage ride and now she could not read him, other than to understand quite clearly that he had brought her here to make love to her.

If she said *no*, he would take her back home, she knew. But she did not want to go: there was the rest of her life to sleep alone, the rest of her life to reach out in the dark and find no one there. And the rest of her life to remember what it felt like to make love to the man she loved.

Why he was doing this, now, she did not understand. Was it a reaction to Captain Grahame's sneering insolence, a male need to make her unequivocally his? Or had he sensed, perhaps at some level too subtle to realise with his conscious mind, that she was his now and would welcome him?

'Would you like a drink?' He was watching her,

something more serious in his eyes than she had ever seen before. It puzzled her—she had been expecting the heat and the desire she had seen before

'Dutch courage? No.' It was tempting, to drink a glass of wine to help her toss her hat over the windmill. But she wanted all her senses tuned to him with nothing to cloud them. She smiled at him and knew it was a poor, shaky effort. 'My legs are wobbly enough as it is.'

'In that case, you give me the perfect opportunity for some masculine showing off.' He grinned as he bent and scooped her off her feet. It seemed his mood had changed again. There was a note of recklessness in his tone as though he, not she, was the one taking the risk.

'Gareth!' Oh, but it was good, held so strongly against his chest. Despite her protest, Jessica let her head fall to his shoulder and relaxed into the grip of his big hands. 'I am not some skinny little thing—'

She broke off as he began to climb the stairs. 'Are you suggesting I am not strong enough? I am wounded. You are a very satisfying armful of woman, my sweet; I will not drop you.'

'I never feared you would,' she murmured as he shouldered open a door at the first-floor front and set her on her feet. It was unmistakably his bedchamber, she could tell that even with a quick glance round by candlelight. There were piles of books on the floor by the chair and on the bedside stand. The pictures that covered the walls were an eccentric mix of size and style and subject. The colour scheme was dove grey and a stormy bluish-purple that found echoes in his eyes and there was the faintest scent of Castile soap, citrus cologne and leather.

And against the wall, opposite the heavily curtained

window, stood a bed. The dark bedcover was turned down to reveal the stark white of linen, the pillows were heaped up as though ready for their owner to lie back comfortably with a book in his hand, the firelight played over the richness of the walnut headboard.

She was staring at it, the image of Gareth lying there so strong that when the real man spoke, just behind her, she jumped. He rested his hands on her shoulders so she could not turn and face him as he spoke. 'I want to make love to you, Jessica. I want to pleasure you, to show you how it can be. I will be very careful—you need not fear…consequences. But if you have any doubts, any at all, say so and I will take you home.'

'At any point?' she asked, testing him.

'At any point.' He was standing so close behind her that she could feel the heat of him down the length of her body. Deliberately she leant back so they touched and felt the shiver go through him.

'That is asking a lot of you. I understand that it is very difficult for a man to stop when things are…' she searched for a phrase, '…well advanced.'

'Difficult and uncomfortable,' he acknowledged, his mouth muffled in her hair. 'But this is you, Jessica. I promise.'

'Then show me,' she said simply, turning into his embrace and burying her face into the soft linen over his breast.

Chapter Nineteen

$\sim\!\!\infty\!\!\sim$

Gareth had shed his coat while she was staring at the bed and now, as her palms slid round his chest and down his back she could feel the shape of him clearly, the complex strapping of muscle over his ribs, the dip into the fluid line of his spine, the way his torso narrowed to slim, tight, hips.

'You are beautiful,' Jessica breathed, wondering at how good it felt just to touch him, to caress the man she loved.

His chuckle as his hands slid down her back made her smile. 'Deluded, poor creature,' he murmured, husky with desire. One hand flattened against the small of her back; the other came up to cup her breast. 'You are wearing too many clothes.'

'So are you.' The buttons came free with her tugging, the shirt slid back over his shoulders, leaving him golden in the firelight. 'Oh.' He looked so much bigger, broader, more powerful, standing before her half-naked. But there was not time to be alarmed; the urgency of his hands with the fastening of her gown distracted her and she wriggled and turned to help, feeling nothing but relief as it slid down to puddle around her feet. Her pet-ticoats followed, then she was standing in front of him in corset and chemise, stockings and slippers. She must look ridiculous, Jessica thought, biting her lip.

Gareth did not appear to think so. He was staring at her. His lips moved soundlessly. *Thank you, God? Surely he did not just say that? One nervous, inexperienced school teacher is not much of a blessing...*

'What shall I take off next?' she asked into the silence. Instead of answering, he reached out one hand and touched her cheek as though to reassure himself she was still there. It unnerved her, that Gareth should suddenly appear so tentative, so uncertain. She had relied upon him sweeping her off her feet before she had time to think.

A log shifted and fell, sending up a shower of sparks. Jessica kicked off her slippers. 'Gareth—you are making me nervous.'

'Relying on me to sweep you off your feet?' he asked with uncanny perceptiveness. 'Give me a moment to recover from the shock of being given what I wished for.'

She frowned at him, puzzled, and then he had gathered her up in his arms and she had no time to explore his words, only to gasp as he set her down by the bed and set to work on her corset strings. They came free in seconds, the boned garment tossed aside as the chemise was whisked over her head, and then she was on the bed. The slither of the satin bedcover under her bare bottom was a shocking reminder of the brothel, but the momentary panic vanished at the sight of Gareth standing beside the bed, naked and—

Jessica shut her eyes. Tight. He was *magnificent*. Terrifying—but magnificent. She wanted to touch him. She wanted—utterly immodestly—to kiss him, kiss him *there*.

'Don't be frightened.' The bed dipped, she was pulled against him. She realised he was using her own body to shield her from the sight of his arousal. That had the equally disturbing consequence that she was pressed to it, to all of its heat and hardness.

'I'm not,' she protested, wondering if he would be unutterably shocked if she reached between their bodies and held him as she wanted to do. 'I'm…impressed.'

That surprised a snort of laughter from him.

'I'm sorry. Are virgins supposed to shriek at the sight of a naked man—or faint dead away?' she enquired, worried now, although it was becoming difficult to hold any thought but that she wanted Gareth very badly indeed and that if he did not do something in a minute, *she* was going to have to.

'I don't know—I have never been to bed with a virgin.' His hands began to move again, stroking down the length of her back, down over the curves of her buttocks, then cupping them, pulling her against him. *Oh, thank goodness, at last.* 'You may shriek if you like.'

'I would rather you kissed me.' He took her mouth on her words, rolling her over so he was above her, his weight on his elbows, his knees pressing her legs apart so her body cradled his. *We fit so well*, she thought hazily, sinking into the whirlpool of sensation that his mouth, the teasing brush of his chest hair on her nipples, the outrageous, demanding pressure at the junction of her thighs, all threw at her.

He shifted, moving lower, and she gave a gasp of complaint until his mouth found her nipple and his hand eased between their bodies to caress into the damp tangle of curls. He nipped and licked and then one long finger slid into the wet, hot folds and touched her, insistent, demanding. 'Come for me,' he said, the words vibrating against the hard, aching peak of her nipple and the world splintered, only this time with an intensity that broke her, tossed her limp and gasping on to some foreign shore where she had never been before.

She came to herself to feel him sliding up her body, cupping her face in his hands so he could kiss her trembling, parted lips. 'Have you any idea how arousing it is, the way you respond to me?' He was pressing against her, down there where the whole core of her being was opening for him, and she moaned against his lips.

'Gareth, please.'

It felt so strange, and yet so inevitably right. He was too big, yet she never doubted he could sheath himself safely within her. The pain, when it came, made her arch to take him deeper into her heat and when she opened her eyes to see him poised above her, his eyes closed, his face rapt, even that sharp pang vanished in awe. 'Gareth?' *I love you, I love you...I cannot tell you...*

His eyes were dark and stormy and fierce as his lids lifted. She saw his Adam's apple move as he swallowed once, hard. 'Jessica?'

'I'm all right. Rather more than all right.' His face relaxed, just a little, at her earnest tone and the corner of his mouth twitched. 'May we move?'

'Oh, yes. We may.' He kept his eyes open on hers as he began, the rhythm slow and powerful and achingly deep. Jessica shifted beneath him, searching for the perfect angle, seeking to become totally one. A building ache made her gasp, move restlessly against the steady discipline of his movements .

'Slowly, my sweet.'

'Yes…no. *Gareth*.' This time she came to herself to find him still moving within her, his eyes intent as he gazed down into her damp, stunned face.

'Come with me this time,' he asked her, beginning to drive the pace, spinning the sensations through her. Weakly she shook her head; surely nothing more was possible? 'Oh, yes, again Jessica.' He shifted slightly, his weight greater as he moved one hand, sliding it between their bodies again, finding that small, desperate core that ached for him, reaching it as he drove harder until she cried out, arching upwards, her fingers raking his shoulders her breasts crushed to his chest.

She was aware, just, of him leaving her body, of him pressed to her, shuddering, and then of sinking, drifting down within Gareth's embrace, deep into a velvety blackness and peace.

Gareth lay on his back, Jessica's sleeping form held snug against his side, and tried to think practically. It was hard—all his mind wanted to do was revel in what they had done and join his body in utterly relaxed abandon. But it had to be done. Cautiously he sat up, adjusting her against his shoulder, smiling at the complaining grumble before she burrowed in again and slept.

He loved her. If he had believed it before, he was certain now. He had lain with many women, but he had never felt that it was anything but a mutual exchange of pleasure. This, for him, had been an exchange of hearts. But would she feel the same? Even to think not was painful; then he looked down at her, confidingly wrapped around him, and smiled. No, Jessica would never have come to him like this if she did not feel for him what he felt for her, surely?

That just left the practical obstacles that stood between him and happiness. They had to marry—anything else was unthinkable. He knew nothing about her family, but she had obviously been raised as a gentlewoman. Noblemen married actresses and weathered the storm; he could marry his respectable governess with no more harm than a few raised eyebrows.

But. But society knew her not as modest, hardworking Miss Jessica Gifford, mistress of the harp and the Italian tongue. They knew her as brazen Mrs Carleton, adventuress. To admit who she really was would involve them all in scandal—Bel and Eva, their husbands, the Maubourg court and Maude. Goodness knows what it would do to Maude's reputation if it became known he would install a false mistress rather than marry her.

There was an answer, of course, he just had to think of it. Gareth slid down the bed again, reaching to pull more covers over the two of them. As his eyes closed, he wondered how he had ever managed to sleep before without the warm weight against his shoulder of the woman he loved. He imagined her response in the morning when he told her how he felt, drifting off with the image of her smile, of the wide green eyes gazing into his, of how she would tell him of her feelings for him.

Jessica woke, not slowly as she usually did, but all of a piece, knowing exactly where she was. Her back curved warm into the long male body holding her protectively. Yet even as she smiled at the safety Gareth's strength offered her, she caught her breath at the evidence of such blatant masculinity hard against her softness. He was asleep, she could tell from his breathing—was it normal for him to be so aroused?

Not sure whether to be alarmed or flattered, Jessica closed her eyes again and tried to drift off again into this perfect dream. The creak of a floorboard, the subdued rattle of fire irons, had her eyes snapping open again. There was a servant in the room making up the fire. In Gareth's room. She was in Gareth's bed, had slept there all night after they had made love. This was not a dream, this was not a fantasy. This was real life and now she had to pay the penalty of last night's indulgence.

The floorboard creaked again as she cringed under the covers, half-expecting a shriek of outrage. But, of course, in an earl's household no one would turn a hair if his lordship chose to spend the night with a troop of opera dancers and a performing bear in his bed.

Dare she get up? Better not, not until she had her mind clear, she was sure to wake him. Jessica wished she could move away from his heat, the warm sleepy scent of him; it made it so hard to concentrate on the right things.

I love him. I have lost my virginity to him and last night it seemed the world was well lost for love—but of course it isn't. The world would certainly have something to say about it if it knew—and I have to live in the world again now. This is not some romance. He likes me and desired me and now he has had me. He was very careful and considerate about it. Probably, like all males, he is going to feel awkward about last night's sins this morning, so I have to show him it is no great matter. I am not going to make demands, become hysterical.

Behind her Gareth shifted, nuzzling his mouth against her neck, his morning beard rasping with a pleasurable, almost painful, friction against the soft skin.

He is going to wake up in a minute. Think what you are going to say. Gareth sighed and turned over, his imprisoning arm lifting from around her waist. Jessica slid carefully out of bed and found that the servant had picked up her scattered clothing and laid it carefully over a chair back. Was it going to be possible to leave without seeing the staff? She would sink through the floor, she knew it.

Where were her garters? Jessica scrabbled on the floor and found them under the trailing hem of the coverlet. Shift, corset. She gritted her teeth as she struggled to tighten the laces by herself. Petticoat, gown, shoes. Decent, covered, shielded against temptation.

Gareth turned again, throwing back the covers until they tangled around his feet. What was temptation if it were not this? Jessica crept up to the bed, reached out her hand, palm down, hovering just above his heart, her eyes aching with unshed tears as she tried to imprint this image on her mind. No, she could not talk to him when he woke—she was too vulnerable to her own weakness here in his bedchamber. With sudden resolution she turned, scooped up her cloak and let herself out on to the landing.

As she crept down the stairs into the hall, Jordan stepped out of the shadows. 'Miss Gifford?'

'Call me a hackney, please, Jordan.'

'Is his lordship awake, Miss Gifford?'

'No. I do not wish to disturb him.'

'He would wish me to apprise him of your depar-
ture, ma'am.'

'In which case I will be out on to the street, trying to
call a hackney myself before you reached his bedchamber, Jordan,' she said steadily.

'I see. I will do as you request in that case.'

By the usual alchemy of butlers a cab materialised
within minutes of him stepping outside, despite the
empty streets. Jessica slipped down the steps and into
the vehicle unobserved except by a hod carrier deliver-
ing coals, two interested maids scrubbing area steps
and a porter with a basket of vegetables on his head.

'I have paid the cab.' Jordan closed the door, carefully
tucking in her trailing skirts. 'He knows where to take
you.' He hesitated, one hand on the ledge. 'What shall
I tell the earl, ma'am?'

'Why, that I have gone home and will await his instructions on which further events he wishes me to
attend.' She smiled with a brightness designed to hide
any distress. The butler bowed his head in acknowl-
edgement and signalled to the cabby to drive on.

Goodness knew what Jordan made of all that. He
must have known she had spent the night in Gareth's bed
and he would know, too, that under no circumstances
would Gareth have let her leave the house without his
escort, at least as far as the front door. His lordship was
not going to be pleased about any of this.

Not that she could be described as happy either,
although whenever she thought about last night Jessica's
mind seemed to become fuzzy and a treacherous warmth

spread through her. It had been magical. And, like all things magical, it must vanish in the harsh light of dawn.

The cabby set Jessica down at her own door step. It was still a wildly unfashionable hour for any lady to be about, which was why the presence at the kerb of a vehicle she recognised as the Pangbourne's town carriage had her frowning in indecision. It surely was not Maude, which meant Lord Pangbourne must have decided to deal with this personally. Walking round to the mews and sneaking in through the kitchen door was tempting.

Jessica took two rapid steps up the street, then turned and marched up the steps. She was not going to be brow-beaten. She would tell Lord Pangbourne what she thought of his tactics and his unpleasant messenger.

The door was ajar and she pushed it open as Hedges was saying, 'I am afraid that madam is not yet at home to visitors, Lady Maude.' His expression as he took in the sight of her would, under other circumstances, be amusing, but Jessica realised suddenly that she was still dressed in an opera gown and a velvet evening cloak and the ready tarradiddle of an early morning walk was completely unsustainable.

'Good morning, Hedges. Good morning, Maude. Will you take breakfast? In the dining room as soon as possible, please, Hedges—my apologies to Mrs Hedges.'

Leaving her cloak in the butler's hands Jessica ushered Maude through into the dining room. 'Yes, I have spent the night with Gareth before you ask,' she said flatly, sitting down at the head of the table. 'For the first and last time.'

Maude, who had been staring wide-eyed, found her voice. 'Was it nice?'

Her question so startled Jessica that her 'Wonderful!' was out before she could bite it back. 'I am not going to talk about it.'

'No. Of course not.' Maude tried to look prim and failed utterly. 'But why aren't you going to do it again?'

Because I do not wish to end like my mother, was one very honest answer. One that she was not prepared to give. *Because I love him and it would hurt too much to be just a mistress*, was another, just as unsayable. *Because being with me puts him at danger from your father's unsavoury minion*, was another. She shook her head firmly. 'No, Maude, I am not discussing anything to do with it. Why are you here? Look at the time.' To underline her point the clock struck eight with clear thin chimes.

'I wanted to warn you about Papa.' Maude was stripping off her gloves with nervous jerks at the thin kid. 'He has some sort of plan; I heard him muttering to Captain Grahame last night, just before the captain went to your box. What did he say to you?'

For a moment the idea of telling Maude everything was powerfully attractive. She would rush home and berate her parent, shame him into calling Grahame off. But it was not the money that was the issue. Jessica could, and would, ignore that. It was the threat and that, she was certain, was the captain's own embellishment, not Lord Pangbourne's idea at all.

'He offered me money to leave London and Gareth,' she said, calmly dismissing it. 'The obvious ploy and the usual solution in such matters, I believe.' Mama had received a very nice 'gift' on one occasion, shortly before they moved temporarily to Cheltenham and visits from a youthful sprig of the nobility ceased abruptly. She thought of explaining to Gareth just how they had survived in the years after her father had died and shuddered. Better heartbreak than humiliation and the sight of his face changing as he realised just who his respectable governess was. There were reasons enough why she could not continue an intimate relationship with him without needing to go into that.

'Oh.' Maude had obviously been expecting something far more Machiavellian. 'What did you say?'

'No, naturally. I am sure that will be the end of it. Maude, I would appreciate it if you would not tell anyone about this morning.' She stared down at her own reflection, hazy in the highly polished mahogany surface. 'I do not regret it, but I have no wish to confide in anyone upon the subject.'

'Cross my heart and hope to die,' Maude swore, her face solemn despite the silly schoolgirl oath. 'I will not tell a soul, and I won't ask you any questions now. But when I want to seduce Mr Hurst, may I ask your advice?'

'No!' Hedges, entering with a salver, almost dropped it at the vehemence of Jessica's reply. 'Thank you, Hedges. A very large pot of coffee, if you please.' She waited until the door shut behind the butler again. 'And for goodness' sake, do not try to flirt with Hurst—that man is dangerous, I am certain of it.'

It was probably the worst possible thing to say to Maude, whose interest was piqued enough, without Jessica idiotically portraying the theatre owner as some sort of Byronic hero. As it was, breakfast was enlivened sufficiently by hissed exchanges on the subject of choosing the man of one's dreams, the inadvisability of flouting one's parent's wishes and the hypocrisy of one unmarried lady lecturing the other on modest behaviour while still warm from a man's bed, for Jessica to be able to ignore the lump of lead that was establishing itself heavily just under her heart.

Chapter Twenty

~~~~~~~~~~

Jessica and Maude had bickered themselves back into friendship by the time the last of the toast and strawberry jam had been consumed. 'What are you going to do this morning?' Maude asked, cupping her pointed chin in her palm. 'Wait for Gareth?'

She ought to, of course—anything else was cowardly. They should have a civilised talk about what had happened. If only she felt civilised. 'No. I am going shopping, I need all kind of trivial things.' *All of which can wait*, she chided herself.

'I wish I could come with you,' Maude grumbled. 'But I hardly suppose we can be seen so much as smiling at each other. In fact, I think I must go before anyone sees me here.' When she had whisked out of the door, Jessica sat regarding the remains of breakfast, then got to her feet. She must get changed and prepare to deal with Gareth—once she had done her shopping. Dealing with him would be easier if she had some time to think about what to say about last night.

The sound of the knocker just as she was donning her

half-boots and picking up her pelisse had her starting in alarm. 'Are you all right, madam?'

'Mirabelle, please run down and tell Hedges that I am not at home if his lordship calls.'

The dresser was too well trained to allow her feelings to show on her face, but the very speed with which she scurried off showed she knew there was something afoot.

'It isn't his lordship, Mrs Carleton, it is another gentleman,' she reported back, panting slightly.

'Who?' Not Captain Grahame, surely?

'Oh, I'm sorry, ma'am, I didn't ask. Mr Hedges has shown him into the drawing room.' The dresser patted her hair into place, recovering her breath. 'Shall I run down again?'

'No, here is Hedges.'

The butler stood in the half-open door. 'Mr Wayman, ma'am, sent by his lordship.'

It was Gareth's man of business, with the house details. Jessica put down her pelisse. 'Excellent. Thank you, Hedges.'

His timing was a relief, she realised as she opened the drawing-room door. She could not sit here and brood, thinking of nothing but Gareth, and an inner core of self-knowledge warned her that wandering around the shops with nothing more to distract her than the exact shade of silk stocking to buy was likely to see her giving way to tears in the middle of Harding and Howell.

Mr Wayman was brisk, cheerful and businesslike. And, despite her fears, he did not appear to think he was dealing with a pensioned-off mistress or some other disreputable female beneath his touch. 'His lordship has given me a free hand to find exactly the property that best suits your requirements Mrs Carleton. Shall we start with the area where you would like to reside?'

'Winchester.' She had given it some thought and the cathedral town seemed perfect. She had visited it briefly to see the cathedral on her way to a new post eighteen months before and it was just the right size to provide comfortable society for a respectable single woman, just far enough from London that she need not worry about meeting anyone who might recognise her and with all the right contacts to identify suitable poor children who she might help with free schooling. That, she had decided, would be the most satisfying and useful way of spending her time.

'Excellent. I see you are a lady of decision, Mrs Carleton.' Mr Wayman produced a folder, a sheet of paper and a travelling ink well. 'Now, let us discuss the details of the accommodation and I will send a reliable man off tomorrow to establish what is available.'

Gareth woke slowly, knowing he was happy before his sleepy consciousness provided him with the reason why. Jessica. 'Mmm.' He stretched luxuriously, remembering the night before, the way she had turned to flame in his arms, the scent of her, roused and feminine, filling his nostrils, her innocent, instinctive reaction to his caresses, her passion. His love.

Eyes closed, he stretched out a hand, his imagination already shaping the warm, sensual curves it would find. Nothing. He froze—only his hand moved, fruitlessly searching the cold dent in the mattress where she should be. Then he dragged his eyes open. The bed was empty, the room was empty and all her clothes had gone.

'Jordan!' He was out of bed, the bell pull clenched in his fist as the butler appeared, far too soon. The man had known she had gone and had been lurking on the landing, awaiting this summons. In some rational part of his brain Gareth could only admire the butler's *sangfroid*, confronted by a naked, and incendiary, employer. 'Where the hell is she?'

'Mrs Carleton left at half past seven, my lord.'

'You just let her walk out of the house?' Gareth ground out between clenched teeth.

'I was not aware, my lord, that wrestling young ladies to the ground to prevent them leaving your lordship's establishments was amongst the requirements of my position, my lord.'

'Damn it, Jordan—' This was bad enough without being confronted with one's butler's manifest disapproval and frigid 'My lords'.

'I hailed a hackney carriage for Mrs Carleton and, acting upon her instructions, paid the man and directed him to take her to Half Moon Street.'

'Thank God.' He sat down on the bed. For a moment there he thought she had run away.

'Mrs Carleton said that I might tell you that she was awaiting your further instructions on which social events you wished her to attend, my lord.'

'Did she, indeed?' Jordan was not rash enough to answer that. 'I will take breakfast in half an hour and I will require my carriage immediately I am finished. Send Malvern to me. And water for a bath.'

Gareth sat on the edge of his bed, his hands braced

on his thighs, head bowed in thought. So Jessica had gone home. Why? Had he scared her? He did not think so. It must be modesty about facing him in the morning, or perhaps anxiety about the difference between their stations. Well, that was easily taken care of by a declaration of his feelings and his intentions. She would be anxious about that. He stood up and began to pace as his valet entered.

'The new-sage green coat and the cream pantaloons, Malvern.' The man bowed and began to open drawers as the footmen entered, lugging the hip bath. Gareth continued to pace, unselfconscious of his nakedness. He needed a tangible statement of his intent. Why the devil had he not thought to buy a ring when he was buying the other jewellery? *Because you didn't know you loved her then. It took you long enough to work it out*, his inner self supplied. So best to call at Thomas Grey's or Rundell and Bridge on his way to Half Moon Street.

'My lord?' His bath was ready. Absently Gareth climbed in and took the soap while footmen and valet effaced themselves. He was not a man who expected others to scrub his back for him, even if Jessica probably assumed he was. He was aware as he lathered the soap and began to rub it into his torso that he was washing the scent of her from his body. But it would soon be engrained again, he could not doubt that.

Clean, Gareth laid his head back on the rim of the bath and looked round the room, remembering it last night. How right Jessica had looked in it, the firelight catching the emerald flames in her eyes. *Emeralds!* 'Malvern!' The valet's head popped out from behind the dressing room door. 'Get that emerald parure out of the safe.' Time to make this serious with a serious gift. No woman confronted with that was going to doubt her suitor's intentions.

The morocco leather case was tucked under his arm as he ran up the steps and beat a tattoo on the knocker. 'Good morning, my lord.' Hedges stood squarely in the door opening.

'Good morning Hedges. Is Mrs Carleton up yet?'

'Madam is not At Home, my lord.' Behind the butler's arm, Gareth could see a tall hat and a pair of gloves on the side table.

'Yet she clearly has a visitor, so you appear to be mistaken, Hedges,' he said, aware from the sudden narrowing of Hedges's eyes that his smile had been nothing but a baring of teeth. He moved his left foot so that he was standing squarely on the threshold, breast to breast with the other man. *Grahame?* The wave of sheer territorial possessiveness that swept through him was almost shocking, it was so primitive.

'I am quite clear about madam's instructions, Lord Standon.'

She is not at home to me*? What the hell is going on?*

'Please do not make me get past you forcibly, Hedges.'

'I should like to see you try, my lord,' the butler said gamely, squaring his shoulders.

The encounter was brisk, short-lived and surprisingly satisfying. Leaving Hedges puffing on the floor, recovering from the effects of a neat cross-buttock throw, Gareth deposited his own hat next to the one on the table, took a firm grip on his cane and strode into the drawing room without knocking.

'My lord!' Wayman was on his feet instantly, bowing and smiling. Beside him Jessica rose more slowly.

'Good morning, my lord. Did you by any chance see Hedges on your way in?' Her tone was chill, her back ramrod straight; if he had not come to know her very well by now, he would have missed entirely the look of blank panic in her eyes.

'The poor man slipped on the marble,' Gareth said, placing his cane and the morocco jewellery case on a side table and stripping off his gloves. 'I believe he is recovered now, though.' Behind him the door opened.

'Madam—'

'Thank you, Hedges, that will be all for now.' So, whatever it was that was wrong, Jessica had enough self-control to preserve a calm face before Wayman and her staff. In fact, Gareth was coming to think, she had enough self-control to captain an artillery crew.

'I did not expect to see you here, Wayman.'

'No, my lord? I must have misunderstood your in-structions. However, we have had a most productive meeting and I am sure I will soon be able to meet Mrs Carleton's requirements.' Something about Gareth's steady regard must have penetrated his efficient good cheer, for he began to gather up his papers. 'I will be in touch, madam. No, please do not trouble to ring, I will see myself out. Good day. My lord.'

The silence as they each waited for the front door to close was almost tangible. Gareth had the illusion that if he put out a hand and touched the air between them there would be a twang like a harp string.

'You left,' he said curtly into the stillness.

'Yes. I thought it best.' She walked away from the

table and went to stand on the other side of the room, one hand resting on a chair back. 'After last night, I feel I should make it clear that I do not see that what occurred should affect our agreement in any way.'

'I took your virginity,' he said, trying to make sense of the way this conversation was veering wildly away from the way he had rehearsed it.

'I gave it to you,' she corrected gently. 'I was curious, and I was attracted and perhaps I should not have done it if I did not trust you as I do.' A faint smile played around the lips that last night he had kissed until they were swollen.

'So just what—' To his horror Gareth heard his voice begin to crack, cleared his throat and tried again. 'So just what are you expecting to happen now?'

'Why, nothing. We go on as we did before.' Jessica moved gracefully to sit down. 'Please, Gareth, do sit.'

Bemused, he did as she bade him, feeling like an awkward seventeen-year-old, not the experienced man he was. Obviously the panic he had seen in her eyes was an illusion.

'You will forgive me if I had other ideas, Jessica.'

'Other—' She broke off, biting her lip. 'Yes, of course. I realise that you might well expect that I would become your mistress after such a wanton display. But that is out of the question. I have every intention of completing this assignment as we agreed and then retiring to the country. Last night was just an…aberration.'

'Aberration?' He felt she had kicked him in the gut and the groin simultaneously. 'Jessica, I came to give you this.' He stood, lifted the morocco case and held it out to her.

She took it and sat with it unopened in her hands, a frown between her brows. 'This? Why?'

'To show you my intentions.'

There was a long silence after she opened it, while she stared down into the fitted interior and its contents. Gareth thought he could see the reflection of the emeralds in her eyes as she raised them to meet his. Then she shut the case gently, laid it on the table beside her and got to her feet. There was colour in her cheeks and for a moment her lower lip trembled. *Thank God, she realises at last...*

'It is all my fault, I realise that,' Jessica said, forcing herself to stand just in front of Gareth. 'I behaved very immodestly, led to you make assumptions. I did not think, though, that you would attempt to pay me for what happened last night. I am justly rewarded for my behaviour by that insult. I behaved like a...a loose woman and you recompense me as such.'

She felt her lip quivering and bit it savagely before she could disgrace herself. Mama had done this, but to live, so that her daughter could live. She, Jessica, had no excuse whatsoever other than her weakness for this man. Loving him was no justification.

'It was just lust, then?' he asked, his voice hard.

'What, did you think I had fallen in love with you?' she asked. The mocking laugh was a triumph of acting, she thought from somewhere inside the cold, hard shell that was growing around her like frost on a window pane. 'My lord, I am a professional, although not a professional whore. And now, if we have finished with this subject, perhaps you would be so good as to tell me which event we are attending tonight?'

'Is that it?' he demanded. The vein in his temple throbbed with suppressed emotion—anger, rigorously controlled. 'Jessica—'

'The hairdresser is coming this afternoon—it would be helpful if I know how I will be dressing this evening.'

'For the Eversheds' ball.' He picked up his cane and gloves. 'You will oblige me by wearing the emerald parure.'

'But—'

'That is an instruction from your employer, Miss Gifford. I will collect you at nine.'

The case seemed to burn her hands as she lifted it to carry it upstairs. She had thought he would understand that last night had been a single moment of recklessness, not the abandonment of everything she had worked so hard for in exchange for the gaudy insecurity and disgrace of a life as a kept woman. Had she been so very wrong in thinking he understood her, or was it all a delusion? Perhaps loving him was a delusion too.

'Madam?' Mirabelle eyed the morocco case with interest and Jessica realised she must have been standing in the middle of her bedchamber, unspeaking, for several minutes.

'His lordship has lent me this to wear to the ball tonight. What will be the best gown to complement the stones?'

The dresser gasped as she opened the box. 'Madam, these are heirloom-quality gems!' She hurried to the dressing table and picked up the goldsmith's loupe that she used when cleaning Jessica's jewellery. 'But they are new—this is not a family piece.'

No, of course not. You give your wife the family pieces,

for your mistress you buy new. 'Will the pale green silk and net go? Emerald is such a hard green to match.'

Mirabelle lifted down the large box and folded back the silver paper so Jessica could lay the necklace against the bodice of the gown. 'It is perfect. Exactly the right shade, just many tones lighter. With such a parure you will need nothing else—in fact, I think I will remove the lace trim.' She looked up for approval and Jessica nodded, remembering to smile.

How many days before we can end this? She would talk to Eva and Bel, explain that she was finding it increasingly difficult to sustain the role and asking them when they thought Lord Pangbourne would be sufficiently convinced of Gareth's unsuitability for Maude. But it would not be yet, not if he was trying to buy her off.

Another week? Another month? How was she going to bear to be with him, acting the part of his mistress, loving him and yet knowing he thought her at best a foolish, confused creature who did not know what she wanted, at worst a tease and a wanton?

Chapter Twenty-One

⟨∼⟩

Gareth arrived that evening not alone, but in company with Bel. 'Poor Ashe is laid low with a shocking head cold,' she apologised, as the footman helped Jessica into the carriage. 'So I sent Gareth a note to ask if he would pick me up too.' Mercifully she seemed inclined to chat. Jessica had been dreading the ride to the ball, being alone with Gareth.

'Which gown are you wearing?' she asked, hoping Bel could not sense the chill reserve that seemed to her to roll off Gareth like mist off a frozen lake.

'A new blue one with blonde lace and a French hem. What about you?'

'Pale green silk with a gauze overskirt in a slightly darker shade. There is plaited detail at the neckline and hem and the sleeves are puffed.' Jessica chattered on, her hand clasping the throat of the crushed silk evening cloak to keep the hood up over her elaborate hairstyle. 'I had my hair done again this afternoon; I believe I am growing used to the colour.'

'Will you wash it out again, once this is all over?'

Bel asked, glancing, for some reason, at Gareth's still profile against the lights outside.

'Oh, certainly. Beside anything else, it is so distinctive; I am sure that once it is gone no one will recognise me if they should see me.'

There was the usual crush of carriages in the straw-strewn street, the usual crowd jostling politely for their places on the wide red carpet laid between the flambeaux and the lines of footmen.

Both women vanished into the retiring room to remove their cloaks and repair the damage to coiffures their hoods had caused. 'My dear!' Bel stared wide-eyed at the emeralds that emerged from Jessica's swathing layers of taffeta. She drew her to one side and whispered, 'Wherever did you get those?'

'Gareth produced them and ordered me to wear them.' Jessica made a business of tweaking her hair into order to show off the emerald clips holding up all but one trailing curl. The earrings quivered against the whiteness of her neck, the necklace lay heavy on her breast and both wrists were clasped with emerald cuffs over the long white gloves.

'Ordered?' Bel was still staring. 'They are fabulous. What a statement of intent! He might as well pin a large *Private Property Keep Off* notice on your gown.'

'I imagine that was in his mind when he bought them. I am not…happy, wearing them.'

'Well, you may give them to me in that case,' Bel said, half-laughing, half still shocked by the magnificence of the gems. 'I have nothing so splendid.'

Jessica was smiling at the frank envy in Bel's voice

as they emerged into the hallway where Gareth was waiting to escort them up the stairs to the receiving line.

'I had better go up alone,' Bel said. 'Gareth? Did you hear what I said?'

'Yes,' he said vaguely. Bel rolled her eyes at Jessica, picked up her skirts and began to edge into the line, smiling and waving at acquaintances. 'Jessica?'

'My lord?'

'You look—' He shook his head. 'Words fail me.'

'It's these wretched stones,' she said in a whisper, walking to his side and taking his arm. 'Come on, we are holding up the line.'

'No. It is you. You look…' he tried again. 'Utterly ravishing.'

Jessica tried to tell herself that it was the effect of Mirabelle removing all the lace trim at the bodice, thus creating an almost indecent expanse of bosom on which to display the trembling stars of the necklace, but the heat in his eyes was producing too extreme a reaction inside her for common sense to have much effect.

She had not realised how it would feel to be so close to him again, to feel the heat of his arm under hers, sense the discreet fragrance of oriental spice and citrus over-lying warm, clean man, to glance up at the hard-cut line of his chin and the familiar, beloved crookedness of his broken nose.

This is so hard. I love you, she murmured under her breath. Gareth glanced down, but she merely smiled and, remembering to play her part, brushed an almost invisible fleck of lint from his lapel.

People moved aside slightly as she passed, skirts drawn back from the courtesan's contaminating touch.

Jessica felt the colour mounting in her cheeks and moved closer to Gareth. 'They are staring at me.'

'I'm not surprised. Jessica—' Something had changed. The anger that had gripped him that morning seemed to have evaporated, leaving the old Gareth behind. Imperceptibly she relaxed; she had hated being at odds with him.

'Shh! Someone might hear.' They had reached the head of the stairs. The Marchioness of Evershed stood, formidable and frosty, awaiting them. Jessica braced herself for the *cut direct*.

'Aunt Hermione, what a quite fabulous gown.'

His aunt? Jessica attempted to melt into the background as Gareth was kissed on both cheeks, then had his wrist slapped with a large lacquer fan.

'You are a very naughty young man—still, I don't blame you. That Maude Templeton is a flighty little thing.' She fixed Jessica with a hard stare. 'Is that a family set, Morant?'

'No. It is new,' Gareth said politely—Jessica could hear the mingled exasperation and amusement in his voice.

'Good. I congratulate you, young woman. Hold tight to your Maubourg protector, though, and remember, all men are bastards.'

Jessica was still gasping as they reached the end of the receiving line. 'Did she really say that?'

'Oh, yes. Aunt Hermione worked her way through two husbands and four lovers that I know of, before netting Evershed. Jessica—'

'Yes?' He was looking at her with a sort of rueful tenderness that made her heart twist painfully. 'I only want you to be happy, you know. You must do as you wish.'

It undermined her determination more than his expectation that she be his mistress had done. He would miss her, that look said. He wanted her, but he would let her go.

'Thank you,' she said firmly, with a hard-won smile. 'I believe you, Gareth. Now, we must not look so serious or people will think we are quarrelling. Look, there is Eva and Lord Sebastian. Who is that in the blue uniform?'

The tall, distinguished officer in pale blue and silver lace was standing, head cocked to one side, listening to Eva. 'That is the Maubourg uniform,' Gareth said. 'He didn't come over with Eva—he must have come with messages from the Regent.'

They stood for a moment, watching the magnificently dressed throng passing to and fro. Most of the men greeted Gareth, their eyes running over Jessica with carefully shielded assessment. The ladies nodded coolly to him and ignored her. It was strange to be treated as though she were invisible, or a curiosity, but she was becoming used to it; if she had Gareth by her side she did not care. It was not for much longer; she needed to hoard the memories for the long, lonely years.

Cross with herself, she gave her head a little shake, setting the earrings swinging. Not *lonely*, she corrected. *Independent*. It was what she had worked for, what Mama had sacrificed upbringing and morality for. She could not, must not, allow a man to make her weak. This, with Gareth, was for days. She had the rest of her life to be prudent for.

'Penny for them?' he asked, smiling, and her treacherous pulse beat hard.

'Do you think the world would be well lost for

love?' she asked lightly, expecting him to make a teasing response.

'Yes,' he said bleakly. 'I do. But you have to find it first, do you not?' Then, as quickly as the darkness had entered his eyes, he was smiling again and sweeping her on to the dance floor as a waltz struck up.

They danced until Jessica's feet in her glacé kid slippers were aching, dance after dance together, both of them smiling and talking and, to any onlooker, she was certain, enthralled in their own private world.

But she was hiding herself from him and he was guarding his inner thoughts from her, she could tell. Being in his arms, the rhythms of the music, the heat and the heady scent of flowers heightened her awareness of him as a male animal and an insidious pulse began to beat low down and inside, where he had filled her, she ached, missing him.

Gareth felt it too, she sensed. His eyes were hooded, his hands when they touched her were firm and possessive, and when those grey eyes lifted and met hers, the heat in them scorched her.

'I must go to the retiring room for a minute,' Jessica confided as they walked off the floor after a vigorous country dance. She stood on tiptoe and whispered, 'One of my garters is loose.'

'Come out on to the terrace and I will tie it for you,' Gareth suggested wickedly.

'Certainly not.' She hesitated as she turned, one hand spread on the breast of his coat as she smiled up at him. 'We know where that sort of thing leads.' It was a risk, alluding to last night so lightly, but his mouth quirked and he smiled as she had hoped he would. Thank goodness—perhaps they were finding their way back on to solid ground again.

'I will fetch champagne and wait for you here,' was all he said as Jessica began to weave her way towards the door leading to a withdrawing room. It would, she thought, give her a short cut to the corridor where the ladies' retiring room was situated.

It was empty. People were beginning to leave the dance floor for the supper room and it was a little too early for weary dancers to be wanting to rest their feet. It would only take a second to tie her garter and if she did it here she would not have to run the gauntlet of supercilious feminine stares in the retiring room .

Jessica put one foot on a low table and pulled up her skirt to her knee. The garter knot had pulled tight and she had to wrestle with it before she could free it and retie the ribbon to secure her stocking. As the door opened behind her, she tossed down her skirts and put both feet on the floor with more haste than grace.

'Tying your garter in public? Tut, tut, Mrs Carleton.' It was Captain Grahame in uniform, the formality of a dress sword by his side.

'An empty room is hardly public, Captain, and a gentleman would have taken himself out again the moment he saw a lady who obviously wanted privacy.' Jessica smoothed down her skirts with a steady hand, the baleful gleam of the emeralds at her wrist lending her courage.

'But then you are not a lady, are you, Mrs Carleton? You are a light heeled wench, one who prays on her back.'

'I have no intention of listening to your smutty talk, Captain. Kindly take yourself off.' She should turn and walk out of the door in the far corner of the room, but she was damned if she was going to give him the satisfaction of routing her.

He grinned, a feline smirk that made her want to slap him, and moved close, so close that she could give way to that temptation very easily. She should have walked away, she realized, as his hand came up and he gripped her right wrist, forcing the metal of the emerald cuff painfully against the narrow bones.

'No wonder you sneered at a paltry couple of thousand pounds,' he remarked, turning the cuff back and forth, twisting her arm with it. 'I must tell Lord Pangbourne to raise his offer.'

The pain brought tears to her eyes and she bit back a cry of distress. She would *not* give him the satisfaction. But she could box his ears. Jessica clenched her left fist and raised it, catching him sharply.

'You little slut!' Jessica found herself yanked hard against his chest, her ears filled with a stream of obscenities. He was furious, as big as Gareth and as strong and she was being shaken like a rat by a terrier. Then as she staggered, breathless, he took her mouth in a hard, wet kiss.

She bit his tongue and he pushed her away. She should scream, she knew it, scream the place down before he really hurt her. But if she did that Gareth would know and would challenge him and that was what Grahame wanted, the chance to wound, perhaps to kill.

'Whore!' He was following her across the room as she backed away from him, her eyes searching for something, anything to use as a weapon. Then the backs of her knees came up hard against an obstacle and she stumbled, threw out a hand to save herself, found something, gripped it and crashed to the ground in a great shattering of porcelain.

There was water everywhere, flowers, something hard and metallic hit her on the head and rolled away to crash against a table covered in bibelots.

'My God!' That was Eva, her voice carrying, and the room was suddenly full of noise. A man bent over her, brushing away the flowers.

'Are you hurt, *madame*?' His accent was foreign; she shook her dizzy head and tried to focus. Blue and silver: the officer from Maubourg.

'No, just shaken, thank you.' He helped her to her feet and she stared round the room in horror. In falling she had taken down a tripod with a vast flower arrangement perched on top; the results appeared to cover half the floor. Eva, a young couple she did not recognise, a distinguished elderly man with the ribbon of some order across his chest and Lady Evershed were all staring with horror at her. Captain Grahame, his face white, one ear scarlet, stood in the middle. The officer in blue kept his hand under her arm. The door into the ballroom was, thank God, shut.

'I tripped,' she explained, trying to sound as though the only thing on her mind was the demolition of her hostess's best Worcester. 'I am so sorry about the vase.'

'Madame did indeed trip,' the man beside her said. 'She was fleeing this…person.' He gestured at Grahame, who began to bluster.

'How dare you, I was attempting to assist Mrs Carleton—'

'Liar.' The officer added something in French, which Jessica did not understand, but Grahame obviously did.

'You will meet me for that,' he stormed.

'But certainly, *monsieur*. Name your—'

The door opened and Gareth walked in with a champagne bottle and two empty glasses dangling from the fingers of one hand. It was obvious he had heard nothing, but had simply come in search of her.

Eva made as though to put out a hand and then stopped, arrested as Jessica was by the expression on his face as he took in the scene.

'My darling, there is blood on your wrist. Who put it there?' He might have been discussing the weather, but there was rage in his eyes.

'Mrs Carleton fell—' Captain Grahame began.

'*Silence, cochon,*' the Maubourg officer snapped. 'My lord, this pig was assaulting the lady as I entered the room.'

'Then I thank you for your assistance, Colonel. You…' he stalked forward until he was almost nose to nose with Grahame '…will name your friends. Should you have any.'

'I regret, my lord,' the Colonel said, 'I am before you. This creature has challenged me. However, should you wish, I am more than willing to merely wound him so you may have your satisfaction in turn.'

'I would not put you to so much trouble,' Gareth said with an awful politeness, bunching one formidable fist and punching Grahame squarely under the chin. His fall completed the demolition of the bibelot table.

Gareth did not stop to look at what damage he had inflicted, nor did any of the onlookers move to help the captain. No one spoke as Gareth lifted Jessica's hand in his and stared down at the red marks that stained her white gloves. 'My love. Let me take you home.'

Home. My love. The room was spinning. Eva seemed to be coming towards them, very, very slowly. But someone else was moving. 'Gareth! Behind you!'

He spun round and Grahame's dress sword ripped through the fabric of his coat. She saw him wince, then he completed his turn with total control, seized the other man's sword hand and bent it back. There was a small disgusting noise like twigs snapping and the captain screamed.

'Her Serene Highness says this would be a good moment to faint,' the Colonel whispered in Jessica's ear. 'I will catch you.'

She did not need the suggestion. Jessica fought against it, but blackness was pressing in, her view of the room was getting smaller and smaller and she felt herself falling and being held. 'Gareth. My love…' But it was not his arms that supported her and it was not his voice that murmured reassurance as she slipped into blackness.

'Jessica?' That was not Gareth either. She dragged open her eyes to see Eva sitting by the bed she was stretched out upon. The room was totally unfamiliar.

'Gareth?' She sat up and the chamber spun. 'The sword—'

'He is alive,' Eva reassured her briskly. 'He has a nasty scratch all along his right side, that is all. Now lie down. You are in one of Lady Evershed's guest chambers. The Marchioness is explaining to the witnesses of that little scene that both she and I are relying upon their utmost discretion. Colonel de Arnheim is removing Captain Grahame to a surgeon while explaining to him that he, as a gentleman, has no intention of meeting someone who draws on an unarmed man and attempts to run him through from behind. The Colonel is pointing out to the Captain that the resignation of his commission, coupled with a speedy retreat to his country estate, would be the healthiest option open to him.'

There was a tap at the door and Bel peeped in. 'Oh, good, she is awake. Look, I have warm water and bandages, I think we should do something about that wrist.'

Bel was inclined to fuss, Eva to use the same technique that Jessica used with small children who had fallen over: speak firmly and calmly and they will conclude there is nothing to worry about. The only problem with that approach was that it only worked if the recipient was not aware of it.

Jessica submitted to having her glove cut off and her wrist bandaged by Bel. Over the top of her friend's bent head she met Eva's dark gaze squarely. 'How much of a mess are we in?'

'Less than one might expect.' Eva kicked off her shoes and put her feet up on the bed with a sign of relief. 'That's better. Goodness knows how one is excepted to stand about when the baby gets any bigger, my ankles are swelling already. This episode has brought forward my strategy to have you run away back to Maubourg by a few weeks, that is all.'

'But it is too soon. Maude—'

'Maude having got wind of what has occurred— naturally I told her—has informed her father that she is utterly humiliated by his attempts to buy you off so that Gareth would return to her and marry her. Pangbourne has finally grasped that the match would be a disaster and has promised her he will not pursue it.'

'Thank heavens for that,' Jessica said with feeling.

'Indeed. Now, unless you are enjoying playing, Mrs Carleton—no, I thought it was beginning to pall—I think you have been frightened and disgusted by the demonstration of masculine violence you have just been the focus of. Colonel de Arnheim, who was not the officer I had in mind, but who will do very nicely, will take advantage of your feelings and bear you off to Maubourg tonight. Gareth will be left broken hearted and will, no doubt, retreat to his estates to lick his wounds.'

'How very neat,' Jessica said faintly. 'But I cannot go to Maubourg.'

'You are very welcome, but I understand Gareth's man of business is busy finding you a nice house in Winchester, so you can go and stay with Bel's second cousin who lives just outside the city. She is elderly and almost blind, but I dare say you will not mind that for a week or two until your house is ready.'

'No, it is so kind of you, if the lady does not mind,' Jessica said faintly. It was very strange being organised like this.

'Cousin Mildred will be delighted,' Bel said. 'If you do not mind reading to her and walking her lap dog, it would be appreciated, I am certain. It will help establish your credentials in the city, for she knows everyone and can introduce you all around.'

'Excellent, thank you so much.' Jessica smiled, finding to her horror that the thought appalled her. Respectable society in a cathedral city, chatting politely to well-bred and staid ladies. She could get herself a pet dog. She would certainly need to hire a lady companion. There would be useful charitable work to be done. Only a few weeks ago she would have seen that as the height of her ambitions, the fulfilment of her dream of independence—now she rather thought she would rather run away to the Grand Duchy with Colonel de Arnheim.

Life without Gareth was insupportable, she realised that now. And she was probably never going to see him again.

There was a knock at the door. 'May I come in?' It was Gareth.

Chapter Twenty-Two

'We are just going.' Eva and Bel were on their feet and out of the door before Jessica could protest.

Gareth stood aside for them, then closed the door and stood with his back to it, watching her. He looked paler than usual. He was without his coat and waistcoat and his shirt, presumably borrowed, was open at the neck. He seemed to need the silence and the stillness, so she did not speak, only wished she could smooth back the hair that was falling across his forehead and massage away the line between his brows.

'How badly hurt are you?' he asked abruptly. If she had not known him so well, she would have thought him curt; now she knew he was controlling himself with some difficulty.

'I have a graze on my wrist,' she said temperately, ignoring the fact that it was raw and burning like fire. 'And I expect I will have bruises in unmentionable places after landing on the floor like that. I have no need to be lying upon this bed, other than to stop Bel fussing; it is you who should be lying down.'

'My ribs are sore, that is all. You fainted. I should have killed him.'

'And would have had to flee abroad,' Jessica snapped, relief making her irritable. 'A very sensible reaction, my lord.'

'Let us be sensible at all costs.' Gareth smiled faintly and came to sit on the end of the bed. 'And I have to admit, it was very satisfying, hitting him on the spot rather than having to hang around for a meeting.'

'Good. I wish I had punched him myself, but he is rather large. I did box his ear, though.'

'You should not have needed to, I should not have left you.'

Oh dear, he is going to be very male *about this*, she thought, trying to steady her nerves with some inner humour. But it was not working. It was touching that he cared and his anger and his response when he had hit Grahame were shamefully arousing. And his words when he had seen her…

'You could hardly escort me to the ladies' retiring room,' she pointed out prosaically. *We are not going to make a drama out of this.* 'Eva has been telling me about her clever plan for me to appear to run off with the colonel. I am afraid it will make you appear to have been—what is the word for losing your mistress to another man?'

'Outbid?' Gareth chuckled. 'My pride and my dignity will stand it. Eva thinks I should retreat to my estates and brood, but I think I will walk around town looking brave and broken hearted for a week or so.'

'All the young ladies will try and comfort you.' It was hard to produce the little laugh and the smile to accompany her teasing.

'I will not need comforting.' He lifted her uninjured hand and looked down at it, playing with her fingers. 'Jessica, I realised something last night, something I should have seen days before. I love you. I want to marry you.'

For a moment she thought she was going to faint again, she who had never fainted in her life before this evening. The emotion that swept through her was so complex that she did not know what she was feeling. Joy? Love? Despair? Yes, all of those, because, of course, it could never be.

'Gareth.' His fingers closed tight around hers and she made herself look at him, at the strong face and the deep eyes and the freckle on his cheekbone and the dark sweep of his lashes. 'It is impossible.'

'It is if you do not love me,' he agreed. 'Tell me the truth.'

'I love you.' To deny it would be to deny herself. His eyes closed and against her fingers his pulse thudded, hard. 'But it cannot be.'

He did not answer her with words, simply pulled her into his arms and lowered his mouth to hers, parting her lips, thrusting slowly, possessively, into the heat of her mouth, stroking the softness into desire. When he lifted his head, his eyes were dark. 'It can be. You are worried that society knows you are Francesca Carleton and that will be a challenge to overcome, but we will overcome it somehow, I just have to think of some stratagem.'

'No. That is not why.' She had hoped never to tell him, but whatever else happened this evening she was not going to lie to him. 'I am not a suitable wife for you.

It has nothing to do with this masquerade we have been acting out.'

'You are a gentlewoman, a lady of accomplishment and grace. You have obviously been gently reared. There is no disgrace in your profession,' Gareth said fiercely. 'If anyone thinks to slight you—' He would have gone on, but she put up a hand and pressed her fingertips to his lips, silencing him.

'My mother was the daughter of a banker, a prosperous, respectable man. My father was the younger son of the Buckinghamshire Giffords, an ancient family. They do not seem to go about much in society, but I believe they have connections to many of the great families.'

'That is perfectly eligible, Jessica. I do not see—'

'You will if you let me finish,' she said quietly. 'Papa was a captain in the infantry. He was handsome, charming, wonderful fun and completely feckless in his private life, although I understand he was an excellent officer. He and Mama eloped, for her father would never countenance such a match. Then he sold out and lived on his wits—he was a gambler. I suspect, a sharp.

'Sometimes we had money to burn, sometimes we found ourselves sneaking out of lodgings in the early hours because of the rent. It was feast or famine.' She smiled, reminiscent, and Gareth did not try to speak. 'They were so much in love, so happy. It was always fun. And then he died.'

'And there was no more money?' Gareth lifted her hand and kissed the knuckles, lingeringly. Jessica rubbed her cheek against the back of his hand.

'No. Mama's family would not help, she had been cast off. Nor would the Giffords. If I had been a boy, perhaps, but I was just a girl. So Mama used what she had, her looks and her charm and her wits. She found a protector—a string of them, in fact. She never spoke of why they gave her money, only that Mr this and Lord that were so kind, so generous. She knew, as I got older, that I knew, but we never spoke of it.

'What happened?' Gareth asked. He was still holding her hand, he had not recoiled in disgust yet. But he would know, now, that this was impossible. Earls might marry bankers' granddaughters, but they do not marry the daughters of barques of frailty, or whatever nice little euphemism you used to indicate that a woman sold her body.

'She died of a summer fever when I was seventeen. The protector of the moment made me an offer which I refused, politely. I sold everything, buried her decently, and resolved to never have to be ashamed of how I earned my living.'

Gareth put down her hand and got up from the bed. Jessica tried to read his face, but he looked merely thoughtful as he wandered round the room, fiddling with the books that lay on a side table, adjusting the lamp slightly. When he spoke she realised that he had been giving himself time to control his voice. 'And are you ashamed of last night?'

'No! I wanted you and I love you and I needed that night to give me a memory for the rest of my life. I would never feel shame for that.'

'Nor should you feel shame for what your mother did. If anyone should it was your grandparents, all of them, for their lack of charity and their intolerance. Jessica, I love *you*. I do not care if your father was a card sharp or a bishop, I do not care if your mother was a duchess or a courtesan.'

'But society will care, and someone will remember and will talk. As a governess no one noticed me—even if an employer had once been royally rooked by James Gifford, why should he connect him with me? And if he once shared Miranda Gifford's favours, he would not connect her with the governess. But the marriage of an earl is news and the eyes of all society will be on your bride. What will you do—call out every man who mentions my mother?'

'If that is what it takes,' Gareth said steadily. 'I love you, Jessica. Marry me.'

'I love you too.' She got up and went to stand in front of him, her hands flat on his chest, his warmth and the beat of his heart under her palms. 'And I will not marry you.'

'I can make you.' His voice was rough as he took her in his arms, pushed her back so she sprawled on the bed. 'I will make love to you until you say yes, until you have no will left to resist me.' His weight on her was heaven, his mouth on hers, bliss. Her body knew his now, knew how to arch into his, knew what the heat and hardness stroking against her belly meant. She wanted him. If he lay with her again, she would go up like dry leaves at the touch of his flame and if he asked her to be his mistress she knew, to her shame, she would say yes. But she could never marry him. Never.

'I cannot resist you, you know that perfectly well.' He had lifted his head to watch her face as he moved against her and she saw his triumph at her capitulation. Her breathing was all over the place, but she managed to say the words. 'I will be your mistress, Gareth.'

'No!'

Oh, but it was cold and lonely without him, even though he was only feet away where his instinctive recoil at her words had taken him. Jessica sat up, clutching her knees for want of anything else to hang on to. 'Yes. Or nothing. There is no other way for us to be together without disgracing your name and you know it. I would have no shame in being your mistress, because I love you.'

'Take it or leave it?' he asked harshly. She nodded. 'Then I leave it. Wayman will be in touch; our former agreement stands.'

She bit down hard on her lip, determined that she would not cry until the door closed behind him. But when it did, they would not come. There was no relief to be had that way, only a future where her consolation had to be that she had done the right thing.

'Thank you, Lucy. Will you go and make some tea now please?' Jessica sank down on a packing case and watched the May sunlight streaming through the window making the dust motes dance. There was plenty of dust and a lot of sun streaming through the uncurtained windows.

One housemaid, one footman, a cook and a tweeny made up her new household and all of them seemed to have spent the last week covered in dust. But the little house was coming together now, the curtains and the carpets would be delivered soon and she almost had enough parlour furniture in place to invite old Mrs Chivers, Bel's cousin, and her equally elderly friends to tea.

In the weeks since she had left London, Jessica had

felt she was watching a play in which a character representing her had moved upon a stage, smiling, talking, organising. She, the real Jessica, had sat in her box, her cold, dark and empty box, and watched the fictitious Jessica acting out her life.

People had been so kind. Winchester was everything she had hoped it would be. The house was a gem, the garden a delight. She rinsed the dye out of her hair and braided it up neatly. She had bought a puppy, all feet and tail and lolling tongue and its soft warmth gave her something to hold against her breast and a reason to put on her bonnet and take exercise, greeting her new neighbours, just as though she was a real person and not a ghost.

Mr Wayman had sent a young man to make sure everything was just as it should be, to help hire servants and to escort her to the furniture warehouses and the upholsterers. Her elderly friends all adopted him and made a great fuss of that nice young Mr Peters, and he showed no sign of having to rush back to London, but ran errands for them and was fattened up on cakes and scones. He mentioned Mr Wayman frequently, but never Gareth, and Jessica assumed he knew nothing of her background.

She looked around the dining room, absently wiping one grubby hand across her damp forehead. The mouldings around the ceiling were charming, but a perfect dust trap, and she and Lucy had spent the morning taking it in turns to steady the stepladder while the other wielded the feather duster. She should have waited until the tweeny, twelve-year-old Gertrude, had finished helping Cook to scrub the scullery, but hard physical work seemed the only thing these days that made her feel real.

The knock at the front door was unexpected. Her small circle of new friends knew she was not receiving yet, so it must be a delivery. She waited a moment, but there was no patter of feet along the hallway; Lucy was obviously still in the kitchen.

There was a second knock. Jessica twitched her apron into place and pushed back her hair as she went to answer it. Pansy the puppy skittered out of the drawing room as she passed, claws clicking on the polished boards, tail flailing. Jessica reached down for her collar as she pulled open the door. The last time Pansy had managed to escape it had taken three of them to catch her again, much to the amusement of most of the inhabitants of the square.

'Sit!' Jessica ordered, squinting upwards from her doubled-up position at a pair of well-muscled thighs in buckskin breeches, a broad chest and a very familiar chin.

'I will sit if you order me to so firmly, but these steps are likely to be cold,' Gareth said, managing to sound pained while grinning at her.

'I didn't mean you!' Jessica scooped up the puppy and stood upright, hanging on to it until it squeaked in protest. 'Gareth, what are you doing here?'

'Collecting my bride,' he said, ignoring her gasp of shock. 'Peters, come and deal with the household—my orders are clear, I hope?'

'My lord.' It was Mr Peters, nice helpful Mr Peters who wasn't supposed to know anything about her, tipping his hat as he slid past her and into the hallway.

'Gareth, you cannot walk in here and take control like this!'

'It is my house,' he pointed out reasonably. 'And

you, my love, are about to become my wife now I have worked out how to do it without causing a scandal to distress you. Come along.' There was a travelling carriage at the kerb, there were trunks strapped on behind and a greatcoat-clad driver up on the box.

'Come along? I can't just *come along*, for goodness' sake! I told you I cannot marry you and why—Gareth! No!' He bent and picked her up, puppy and all, with as little effort as she had picked up Pansy. The puppy, with her usual promiscuous affection, licked him on the nose.

'I hope she's a good traveller. I made no allowance for puppies in my abduction plan.' Gareth strode down the steps and bundled Jessica and Pansy into the carriage, following them in before Jessica could reach the far door handle. The carriage moved off and he sat back, smiling at her.

'I had no idea you were such a messy housewife,' he observed.

'What?' Jessica put the squirming puppy on the floor where she promptly started to lick Gareth's boots. 'Oh, for goodness' sake, look at me!' She was swathed in a vast apron that had begun the day white and was now streaked with dirt, her front hair was in her eyes and her hands were filthy. No doubt her face was too.

'I am looking, my love,' he said, leaning forward and removing a cobweb from her hair. 'I rather like my prim and proper governess like this, all hot and bothered. It brings on an urge to make you even more flustered.'

'I am as flustered as I need to be,' Jessica said, striving for control. But this was Gareth; he was here, and suddenly she was real again. 'Gareth, what are we *doing*?'

'Driving to my estate near Romsey—you see how

very convenient it was of you to choose Winchester? We will be there easily by dinner time. Tomorrow we will be married in the parish church by special licence and the day after that, my love, the Earl and Countess of Standon will depart secretly for the Continent on my yacht from Southampton.'

'But—'

'Which is where everyone thinks I am at this moment.'

'But—'

'In the course of my travels—nursing my wounded pride and broken heart over Mrs Carleton—I shall meet the charming Miss Gifford, educationalist, who is making a study of French art. She is somewhat like Mrs Carleton in looks, as people will notice when we return to London after our prolonged honeymoon. Miss Gifford is a lady of elegant restraint, of course—not at all like the other lady everyone will be too polite to mention—and society will be too kind to remark upon Lord Standon's obvious partiality for blonde ladies with green eyes.'

It was inspired. It would work, of course it would. People saw exactly what they expected and she had hardly exchanged a word with anyone except Gareth's cousins. But… 'Gareth—my parents.'

'No one will remember,' he said gently. 'And if some gentleman saw something of your mama in you, would he want to hurt the daughter of such a sweet lady? I do not think so.'

He was right. It was going to be all right. She was going to marry Gareth. Tears were welling up; the only way to fight them was with briskness. 'I have been here *weeks*. Where were you?'

'It has taken me weeks to work this out, make all the arrangements, be seen brooding darkly around town. I sent Peters to keep an eye on you—some days I have had to make do with reports that simply said *Miss Gifford is undecided upon the colour of the drawing-room curtains. It rained today, so she has purchased an umbrella.*'

'I thought my heart was broken,' she managed and then she was in his arms, her hands tangling in his hair and she was kissing him as she had dreamt of kissing him through the long, lonely nights. 'But now you have mended it.'

'Then let us go home, my love, because I have a very pressing need to carry you over my threshold, up the stairs and into my bedroom.'

'Not before we are married,' Jessica said firmly. 'We will shock the servants.'

'Very well.' He reached for the blinds, jerking them down. 'Let us shock one impressionable puppy then, because, my love, I need, very badly, to show you how much I love you and have missed you.'

An hour later Jessica became vaguely aware of the sound of muffled chewing as she lay, bare and hot and slicked with perspiration in Gareth's arms on the cramped seat. She slid up his chest, provoking a sleepy male grumble, and peered down over his shoulder. Pansy, blissfully happy, was chewing the tan top of one of Gareth's beautiful boots. It had all been rather too much excitement for one barely housetrained puppy: Gareth's breeches were not going to be wearable and his valet was going to be very unhappy indeed.

'Gareth,' she murmured into his ear. He grunted,

nuzzling his face into her neck. 'I'm afraid Pansy has demolished your clothes. We are going to end up shocking the servants after all.'

He opened his eyes and regarded her severely. 'Then, madam, I suggest you ensure I am in a very good mood by the time we get to Standon Hall.' His pocket watch was hanging by its chain from a hook on the squabs. 'I think you have about three-quarters of an hour.'

'Oh.' Jessica contemplated some of the things she had dreamt about doing to the long hard body stretched beneath her. 'Very well, my lord.' She began to slide down his body again. 'Would this put you in a good mood, my love?'

'It puts me in Heaven,' he murmured huskily, reaching out to play with her hair as it flowed over his chest. She stretched out a hand to link her fingers through his, feeling the strength and the tenderness, and knowing, with all the years ahead, that it was only going to get better.

* * * * *

The much-anticipated finale to the Moreland quartet!

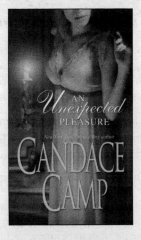

London, 1879

Had Theo Moreland, the Marquess of Raine, killed her brother? American journalist Megan Mulcahey had to know. But to find out, she needed to infiltrate the marquess's household.

The new American governess intrigued Theo. Miss Mulcahey had come to Broughton House to teach his young siblings. Now the strange pull of their immediate desire both troubled and excited him. But why was this delicious vision snooping around his mansion like a common thief?

Available 19th September 2008

Celebrate 100 years of pure reading pleasure with Mills & Boon®

To mark our centenary, each month we're publishing a special 100th Birthday Edition. These celebratory editions are packed with extra features and include a FREE bonus story.

Plus, you have the chance to enter a fabulous monthly prize draw. See 100th Birthday Edition books for details.

Now that's worth celebrating!

September 2008

Crazy about her Spanish Boss by Rebecca Winters
Includes FREE bonus story
Rafael's Convenient Proposal

November 2008

**The Rancher's Christmas Baby
by Cathy Gillen Thacker**
Includes FREE bonus story *Baby's First Christmas*

December 2008

One Magical Christmas by Carol Marinelli
Includes FREE bonus story *Emergency at Bayside*

Look for Mills & Boon® 100th Birthday Editions at your favourite bookseller or visit
www.millsandboon.co.uk

FREE!

2 Books
and a surprise gift!

We would like to take this opportunity to thank you for reading this Mills & Boon® book by offering you the chance to take TWO more specially selected titles from the Historical series absolutely FREE! We're also making this offer to introduce you to the benefits of the Mills & Boon® Book Club—

- ★ **FREE home delivery**
- ★ **FREE gifts and competitions**
- ★ **FREE monthly Newsletter**
- ★ **Exclusive Mills & Boon Book Club offers**
- ★ **Books available before they're in the shops**

Accepting these FREE books and gift places you under no obligation to buy, you may cancel at any time, even after receiving your free shipment. Simply complete your details below and return the entire page to the address below. You don't even need a stamp!

YES! Please send me 2 free Historical books and a surprise gift. I understand that unless you hear from me, I will receive 4 superb new titles every month for just £3.69 each, postage and packing free. I am under no obligation to purchase any books and may cancel my subscription at any time. The free books and gift will be mine to keep in any case.

H8ZEF

Ms/Mrs/Miss/Mr ....Initials ....

Surname ....

Address ....**BLOCK CAPITALS PLEASE**

....

....Postcode ....

Send this whole page to:
UK: FREEPOST CN81, Croydon, CR9 3WZ